PRAISE FOR OSGOOD AS SHE GETS

This book freaked me the fuck out!

— CHRISTOPHER PIKE, AUTHOR OF
WHISPER OF DEATH, MONSTER, AND
SCAVENGER HUNT

Jam-packed with ghosts, mayhem, murder most foul, ancient evil, and a kickass, flawed queer hero; Beckett has really hit it out of the park with Osgood As She Gets!

— JESSICA DRAKE-THOMAS, AUTHOR OF
BURIALS, BAD OMENS, AND HOLLOW GIRLS

Prudence Osgood, the bad habit you didn't know you needed, is back! Beckett treats us to an anti-hero made entirely of disasters and sass, plunging her and her paranormal investigator team into another of the deadly urban legends we love so much.

— BP GREGORY, AUTHOR OF *FLORA & JIM*

Creepy, sexy, and addictive, *Osgood As She Gets* grabs you from the first shocking chapter and never lets go, bringing us what we desire most; a sexy and scary book that's a whole lot of fun!

— MEG HAFDAHL, CO-AUTHOR OF *THE SCIENCE OF WOMEN IN HORROR*

A trippy, cosmical joyride grappling with terror, pain, guilt, and bad decisions.

— KATHERINE SILVA, AUTHOR OF *THE WILD DARK*

An immersive and engaging read with a compelling protagonist, an extremely eerie mystery, and some truly chilling scenes. Couldn't have asked for more!

— EMMA MEDRANO, AUTHOR OF *NOTHING SERIOUS*

The specter of the past haunts us all, but the spirits here steal the show. Beckett meticulously crafts a cosmic tapestry that dares us to look away, and we simply can't.

— AQUINO LOAYZA, AUTHOR OF *DEEP*

Although this was my first Osgood/Spectral Inspectors book, it won't be my last. Beckett's portrayal of disability and chronic pain, queerness, and trauma made me feel seen, and I loved how flawed and realistic the characters were. I like psychological suspense in my dark fiction, and *Osgood as She Gets* has no shortage of that. An engrossing, evocative read.

— BRIANA MORGAN, AUTHOR OF *THE REYES INCIDENT*

Cooper S. Beckett writes with such charm, wit, and verve, his stories both poignant and utterly chilling. I look forward to reading more from him.

— ERIC LaROCCA, AUTHOR OF *THINGS HAVE GOTTEN WORSE SINCE WE LAST SPOKE*

In Cooper S. Beckett's latest chapter, Osgood remains as much a lovable disaster as ever, delightful in her status as a human train wreck the reader simply cannot look away from. Beckett's writing is sharp, taut, suspenseful and will keep readers fixed and ready for the next entry!

— ZACHARY ROSENBERG, AUTHOR OF *HUNGERS AS OLD AS THIS LAND*

Highly imaginative, richly detailed, and satisfying in its graphic intensity.

— ALEX VORKOV, AUTHOR OF *ALL THE COLORS OF THE DEAD*

An engaging and grisly caper, Osgood as She Gets is the kind of horror story that shows how closely our most outrageous nightmares can walk hand-in-hand with our most intimate of fears...and lays bare the existential truth that there's more than one way to be haunted. Beckett presents something that's deeply chilling, yet profoundly human.

— MICHAEL VARRATI, *THE MIDNIGHT MASS PODCAST*

Prudence Osgood is a protagonist for the ages: bold, brash and absolutely captivating. The spookiest aspect of *Osgood as She Gets* is Cooper S. Beckett's supernatural ability to summon a sense of vulnerability and pathos and manifest it upon the page.

— CLAY MCLEOD CHAPMAN, AUTHOR OF *WHAT KIND OF MOTHER* AND *GHOST EATERS*

A haunting, dream-like urban fantasy that stings and satisfies like a bitter-sweet shot of whiskey.

— ANGELA SYLVAINE, AUTHOR OF *FROST BITE* AND *THE DEAD SPOT*

Beckett writes with the accessibility and charm of Stephen King, but with the queer knowledge and language to appeal to an often-ignored audience. *Osgood As She Gets* is the paranormal page-turner with literary backbone queers and bookworms alike have been craving. Absolutely mesmerizing.

— BLAYNE WATERLOO, CONTRIBUTING EDITOR AT *FANGORIA*

OSGOOD AS SHE GETS

THE SPECTRAL INSPECTOR

BOOK THREE

COOPER S. BECKETT

HORROR & CARNAGE PRESS

*for all those
who've had those
darkest of
moments*

;

Interior Illustrations by Kym Slade

Cover & Book Design by Cooper S. Beckett

Published Internationally by Horror & Carnage Press

1 3 2 8 4 5 6 7 9 0

ISBN: 978-1-946876-30-0

BISAC: Fiction / Horror

Horror & Carnage Press

Chicago, Illinois

CooperSBeckett.com

OSGOOD AS SHE GETS

THE SPECTRAL INSPECTOR
BOOK III

COOPER S. BECKETT

THE SOUNDTRACK

If you'd like to get just a little more fun out of your reading of *Osgood as She Gets*, head over to

OsgoodAsSheGets.com

Click the soundtrack link to get the playlist, and listen as you read!

PROLOGUE

igh school be damned, thought Beth. *Sophie and Anna wanna hang out again!*

She tried to remember the last time the three of them had been together but could barely pinpoint it. It hadn't been August, possibly not even July. No, it must've been the last week in June because they'd made plans to bike down to Navy Pier for the fireworks on the 3rd of July. But they hadn't biked down, had they? No, only Beth had, after all. She'd waited and waited and waited some more at the bike racks just out in front of the dock turned mall turned tourist mecca. When the fireworks began to rain down reds, oranges, and blues, she'd gotten off her bike to watch from behind the entrance to the pier. That heaviness in her stomach had returned as she stood there—Elizabeth Garcia, age 13, separated from the fun by seemingly the most inconsequential of walls: a school year.

Now, though, she joyfully followed Sophie and Anna up the embankment crammed with bushes; thorns tugged at her coat, which was much too warm for September but was the only one that fit her. As her father kept mentioning, she'd hit a growth spurt that year and was ... Beth cringed even thinking of the word ... developing. Sure, she was happy to *be* developing, especially here with the older girls (further along in their own development), but that didn't mean she wanted Dad to point it out, especially at dinner, something she'd mentioned to Sophie and Anna as they walked down Bryn Mawr Avenue. The older girls giggled and nodded, perhaps empathizing, though she'd wondered if they were laughing at or with her.

But no, Sophie Moreau wouldn't laugh. Not at something like that. She had been Beth's best friend since Beth was in first grade and Sophie was in second. She'd only lived a block down and around the corner, in the apartments on Ravenswood. Back when they were little, with dishwater blond hair that their mothers would still put into pigtails with ribbons, they'd even looked so similar. Only seven months separated them, after all; it was just seven in the wrong way—Sophie (and Anna) were early in the months cut off, April and June respectively, while Beth's September 1st birthday was late enough that she'd been forced into classes a year behind.

That was another thing, too, that she wanted to mention to them. She understood that they might be too busy for her. Freshmen at St. Gregory's High School and all. But they could've sent her a text on her birthday. Or at least a TikTok video. She'd watched both their feeds in case they might take a moment to recognize their long-time friend. But neither had. Only lip-synced to T-Swift and played games, both Graveyard and Elevator. Beth didn't understand high schoolers yet. She hoped things would start to make sense as she got closer, but that felt so far away. Just under a year of junior high left, just under a year of those friends.

"Shit," said Anna. "Hide!"

The three dropped to their knees in the bushes, a thorn scratching Beth's leg deep enough that it tore a small rift in the side of her thermal leggings. *Shit is right,* she thought. She looked up from her calf, where, thankfully, the thorn had only made a thin pink line through the baby-fine blond hairs that her mother had said she was too young to shave. Thank god they were blond. Unless you were looking or, like Beth, knew they were there, you couldn't even see them. The other girls in her grade had yet to notice as they stripped down for gym, their locker room full of the puberty spectrum. So far, though, she'd been able to keep her head low.

Finally, she saw why they were hiding in the bushes. A homeless man pushed a shopping cart stacked high with clear garbage bags full of crushed aluminum cans. His face was clean, his features sad. At once, the pit in her stomach made Beth wish she could offer her winter jacket to him, but he was too big, and she too little. When the homeless man pushed past, Anna popped back up, her sea-green eyes wild with excitement. Something far back in her mind reminded Beth of that weird old British show her father had insisted they watch together. Something about "How Not To Be Seen." The answer, she remembered, was not to stand up. Thankfully, Anna hadn't exploded when she stood.

At the top of the embankment ran an oft-used Metra train track. Beth hadn't always noticed, but when playing in her backyard down on Gregory Street, she could hear the train dimly rumble past multiple times an hour. With that in mind, Beth looked first north and then south. In the evening's dimming light, she could see a hazy headlight far down the track, still faint due to layers of low-hanging air pollution. That train wouldn't be here for ten minutes or more. The other way, toward Rogers Park and then Evanston, showed no such light. The time to walk along the tracks was now.

So, the three girls walked. Beth was in the lead, with Anna and Sophie bringing up the rear a few yards behind. Beth wanted to ask if they'd walk *with* her instead of following. It made it seem like they were part of an entirely different group.

Of course, that was the truth, wasn't it? A reality that couldn't be denied or helped. No matter how much Beth wanted it to be otherwise, the gap between them was more than just a grade now. While it hadn't mattered much going from grade school to junior high, the gulf between junior high and high school seemed nearly insurmountable. But she *had* surmounted it, hadn't she? By getting them here at all. They hadn't spoken for the month since school started, which seemed to be happening earlier and earlier as the years went by. But that had changed when their WhatsApp text chain reawakened this morning with a simple **hey**, from Anna, followed by a **Hay, Miss u**, from Sophie.

Beth, still in bed because Mom and Dad were out and there'd been no one to chide her for wasting the day away, had been elated. Some light back-and-forth texts followed. All surface, no substance. They agreed, though, that there should be a hang and that hang should be soon. That evening? Glory of glories, all were free. What should they do? **Hang,** said Beth because she knew someplace cool. She didn't have an actual plan, but Sophie and Anna didn't know that. Beth only knew that her older brother had spoken about this route to a parent-less wonderland. She could see it ahead, in fact, the path created by mountain bike tires and jeans-clad ankles leading down the other side of the elevated tracks. As Glen had fore-told, that path downward was on the other side of some chain link fence with razor wire up top, behind several squat yellow brick buildings with sizeable white garage doors.

"What did you find back there?" she'd asked him.

"Porn," he said.

She'd scrunched her nose in disgust at the idea of her older brother, a senior now, finding dirty pictures behind that build-ing. She certainly didn't like that it made her think momen-tarily about his thing getting hard. She'd shoved that image from her mind before it could cause any lasting damage.

Beth may not have liked porn, but something felt so adult about it, and going somewhere that had it felt like the kind of rite of passage the older girls would appreciate, hopefully as much as the box of Marlboros in her pocket. Sure, the crushed box only held six cigarettes, and some sawdust was bouncing around in the package, since she'd taken it off the shelf from Dad's workroom in the garage. But she doubted anyone could feel she wasn't cool enough or advanced enough when she lit up a smoke on the edge of a truck delivery bay.

"This is it," she told them, pointing at the beaten trail.

"Good," said Sophie with a shiver.

The wind blew cold up here, colder than in the trench of the streets because it had a straight path nearly from the Chicago Loop up to their neighborhood. She wondered why the older girls hadn't worn thicker coats. Sophie wore a thin blue windbreaker, and Anna wore a purple and black plaid flannel. Both appropriate for this time of year, sure, but neither could defend against a blast of Chicago's wind. Beth, though, felt a bit of sweat at the small of her back. Whether from her heavy coat or from other things on her mind, she couldn't be sure. Because she barely knew those other things.

Leaning back at an almost comical angle to keep their balance, they descended the embankment on the far side of Ravenswood onto the cracked and faded pavement of this liminal space. Here, four buildings surrounded them in a C-shape, butting up against the tracks, forming a communal area large enough for trucks to move in and out, to back into berths in the buildings and unload their miscellaneous goods and services to the various companies that used these yellow warehouses as their storage and supply. One cargo trailer sat fallow, its cab having abandoned it maybe a foot away from a closed garage door. Beyond that, this area was empty. Exactly as Glen had promised.

"If you tell mom I told you about it," he'd warned, "I'm

taking your Switch to college." An idle threat, perhaps. Beth wasn't sure Glen was going to college. At least not in a way that taking her Nintendo Switch meant anything other than removing it from her room to his. Also, he wouldn't dare. She knew what he got up to with Alisha Torres in his room at night when the door was supposed to remain open. Even a cracked door didn't prevent them from making out, as the sound of anyone coming upstairs would give them plenty of time to wipe lipstick from their mouths, fix their hair, reseat that bra. Across the hall, though, it gave Beth a clear view, and that was how she'd seen her first nipple on an entire teenage breast. It was brown, which surprised her. She'd only ever seen pink. She'd stopped watching when she saw Alisha fumbling with her brother's strained zipper. There were definitely things that Beth Garcia didn't want to see.

"Oh my god," giggled Sophie. She slapped her right hand to her mouth, her left occupied with a short maple branch she was using to poke at *something* behind a cinderblock cove. Anna's exultation when she walked up was similar. All that was left was for Beth to see what had surprised them. Even toward the end of last school year, when they all still were in junior high, Sophie and Anna had started to make jokes about "tits" and "bush" and "pussies" that made Beth uncomfortable in a strange way. Down deep in her stomach came an ache, and her cheeks got hot. Thankfully, she didn't flush red when she felt this, so no one but her knew. She'd hoped that she'd grow out of it but hadn't yet, and as she walked over to Sophie's discovery, the flush she felt was hot and the ache deep.

Sure enough, Sophie had found porn. And while Beth had seen the centerfold in her father's Playboy once, thanks to a sleepover dare that had involved bringing it to the circle of giggly girls in the basement, she'd never seen porn of this ... what? Level. *Intensity*, thought Beth. She looked, though, because while Beth Garcia may not have been comfortable, she was no prude. She'd seen illustrations of "the act" because her mother kept a copy of *The Joy of Sex* in the nightstand next to her parent's bed, beside to that round thing that vibrated. Beth only had the faintest notion of what that was for, but she knew that seeing it gave her that uncomfy feeling. This, though, made her feel sick to her stomach. The man was behind the woman, and his thing bent upward into her butt. Objectively, Beth knew that this was something people did, she'd heard the term "buttfucking" thrown around school amidst the requisite giggles. But this was different. His ... dick ...was red and covered in thick veins. The wrinkly set of balls beneath were clothed in fine brown hair. But the most distressing bit was above, not the butthole, but her vagina, which seemed to all be coming ... out? Bright reddish-pink and gleaming with a sheen that Beth didn't quite understand but was sure she didn't want to see any longer.

She stepped back.

Anna laughed. "Jesus, who just dumps all these magazines." She crouched and flipped one, then another. "*Hustler. Barely Legal.*" Beth couldn't believe the older girl was touching them. The heat in her face spread, carrying the feeling of shame with it. Once she'd gotten caught stealing quarters from the mug on her mother's dresser. She'd felt that same shame when her mother had pointedly asked, "Did you steal from me, Lizzie?" Beth was sure she'd lied before that moment, but she couldn't remember any before as vividly as that lie – "No," eyes wide and glistening with tears at the very thought of such an offense.

"Oh, holy shit," said Anna. "Gimme your stick."

Sophie complied, laughingly asking, "What?" as she did. Anna poked the stick down, and when it came back up, it had a yellowed ... bag on the end? No, not a bag, too small for...

Anna swung it around, a wide grin on her face, her freckled cheeks scrunching. The thing on the stick passed within six inches of Beth's face, and she smelled something rank.

"What *is* that? Beth cried.

"Anna, don't," said Sophie, putting her hand on Anna's arm.

"You really don't know what this is?" Anna chuckled.

Now Beth was sure the older girls would see the embarrassed flush of her cheeks. She looked at the thing on the stick, thankfully further from her now, and tried to figure it out.

"It's okay," said Sophie. She took Beth's arm and walked away from giggling Anna.

Beth wondered if she should share the cigarettes now. She reached into her pocket and felt her keys, the metal, and the crinkly packet.

"Dude," called Anna.

"I told you not to call me 'dude,'" said Sophie.

"I just wanted Beth to see," Anna said. They watched as she pursed her lips and flung the thing away from them. It arced over the dumpsters to the bushes on the embankment.

Beth was thankful that it didn't land where she planned to climb back up. She pulled out the cigarette pack, a Bic lighter tucked inside. "Smoke?" she asked the girls and saw a pleasing wave of esteem pass through their eyes. She'd impressed them.

"Since when have you smoked?" asked Sophie.

Beth shrugged, hoping that'd be the end of it. She certainly didn't want to tell the truth, that this was the first time she'd put a cigarette in her mouth. She flicked the lighter once, twice, *C'mon...* then she got it, a flame. She held it to her lips and sucked, getting a lungful of acrid smoke. She coughed hard, doubling over, gagging before she came back up, cigarette pinched between her outstretched pointer and middle fingers and blew the remaining smoke in her lungs in Anna's face. Anna coughed but blocked her mouth so they couldn't see. Then she reached out and snapped her fingers for the lighter. Beth obliged. Her second puff of the cigarette went better; she didn't draw the smoke all the way in, but just held it in her mouth. It tasted horrible. Why did grownups do this? She knew it had something to do with addiction, and Dad said "the influence of big tobacco" was responsible. Mom had told him that was just an excuse.

Both Sophie and Anna's puffs seemed effortless. Here again, Beth felt behind. Her friends had clearly smoked before. Seen porn before. They knew what that thing had been, that thing that Beth now suspected had been a used condom. She wanted to ask them, to ask why that woman's ... pussy ... seemed so red and angry. But she didn't want them to laugh. Sophie might not, but Anna would. She wanted to ask why they hadn't hung out with her. Did they think she was a baby now? She wasn't *that* much younger. No more than she'd ever been. She wanted to ask what had happened when they'd played the Graveyard Game. What had they seen?

She knew what *she'd* seen.

"Now what?" asked Anna.

The older girls looked at Beth with expectation in their eyes. She didn't know what they wanted. She'd taken them someplace cool. She'd given them cigarettes. She noticed that Sophie had already crushed hers out after only taking, what? Two, three puffs? But Anna, Anna was sucking on that thing, "Like a dick," said Beth.

"What?" asked Sophie.

Beth pointed at Anna. "You're sucking on that thing like a dick."

Anna's eyebrows went up in surprise, but then she laughed. Then Beth and Sophie did, too. As the three stood laughing, Beth felt things were as they should be. This trio, friends for years, through sleepovers, and runs to the McDonald's up the street that they went to even when they weren't supposed to cross Ashland Avenue, and the 7-11 across Clark

Street where they'd steal lip balm and Bubble Yum while one of them would distract the clerk at the weird hotdog roller station. This moment of shared laughter brought a joy to Beth that she hadn't felt in weeks. A pleasure that suggested things would be alright, what she'd seen hadn't been real, and nothing needed to happen here beyond friends enjoying each other's company.

But then Anna's laugh turned mean. Beth couldn't quite explain the shift, but she knew it when she heard it.

"You only say that because you suck clits," said Anna. Sophie told her to stop, first with her eyes, then her words.

"I don't!" said Beth defensively. But she stopped before saying, "I don't suck anything," knowing it would put her back in that uncomfortable spot. The little girl. Instead, she stopped Anna's laughter another way.

The knife in Beth's pocket had been purloined (this week's hardest vocabulary word in Miss Belzer's class) at the same time as the Marlboros. Same place, too. Her father's toolbox. She'd been looking for one when she found the other. That it worked out that way had helped her come to grips with what she was about to do. What her plan was. After all, she'd seen it. She'd seen the crossing of the tracks, the discovery of porn behind the dumpsters. She'd seen it, despite never having been there. Another bit of the mystery of the Graveyard Game, perhaps. Beth hadn't posted hers on TikTok when she'd done it. Hadn't even brought her phone. She'd just gone and looked. Had seen what she saw. Felt what she felt.

Then, around a week later, she arrived at the most critical bit. The knife was thin and razor-sharp, which Beth learned when she almost immediately cut her finger "testing" it. It had something to do with fishing. At least, she thought so; it smelled like the Chicago River in late summer. The seven-inch blade easily unfolded from its silvery blue handle. Getting it open was easy, Beth knew, but closing it back up was when one was apt to lose a fingertip. Once opened, Beth knew that she didn't have time to waste; too much time would mean both getting caught and inflicting more pain than necessary, and Beth absolutely didn't want Sophie to suffer. She would've started with Sophie, were it not for Anna's laughter. *That* needed to end.

End it did when Beth pushed the blade up through Anna's chin. She had expected a lot more resistance because if it went to the hilt through her chin, didn't that also mean it had pushed through her mouth into her sinuses? Beth flicked her wrist to the right, slicing the knife through the inside of Anna's head, again amazed by how smoothly it happened. With her fist around the knife handle and pressed firmly under Anna's chin, blood hadn't yet begun to flow, but it would, and when it did, Sophie would see and scream and be afraid, and Beth did *not* want that. She didn't want any of this. But she had to. She knew she had to. It was them or her, and *the thing* was watching.

Sure enough, Sophie told her, "Don't hit her," clearly thinking the stab had been a punch or hit. That was good.

Beth pulled the knife down and out, and while the blade was red now, the wound in the girl's chin seemed to be just a sideways slit, like a giant paper cut. Beth hoped it felt like the worst paper cut ever. Anna could be so mean to her. Especially lately. And she infused that meanness into Sophie. Sophie, her friend. Sophie, her best friend. Sophie, with whom she'd hoped to sit up late in their future dorm room, talking about their first loves, first heartaches, and first explorations. But none of that could happen. Not if Beth wanted those things for herself. Her swing was true, thankfully, and the knife split Sophie's throat so effortlessly that Beth wasn't at first sure she'd done anything. Had she missed? No, Sophie staggered backward, bringing her hands to her throat, and then the blood sprayed in an arc as she fell backward and to the ground.

Beth turned her attention back to Anna. A *thock* sound came from the girl's mouth, or maybe her throat. Her eyes seemed unfocused, and Beth wondered if she'd actually lobotomized her. She'd read about how psychiatrists used to do that with an icepick. Well, she'd read about it until her mother had read the book jacket and took it away. No more unsupervised trips to the library for Beth Garcia.

Lobotomized or not, Anna was still standing, so Beth moved behind her, careful to not stand close enough for Anna to grab in one of her involuntary hand spasms. Beth slid the knife deftly across Anna's throat. *Just cutting a chicken breast,* she told herself. *Almost done, almost done.* After the slice, Beth put the toe of her pink flowered galosh against Anna's butt and shoved. The older girl went first to her knees, then her upper half hit the ground with a decisive crunch. A bloom of red spread beneath her.

Back to Sophie. Beth felt tears on her cheeks and whispered, "I'm sorry." She'd hoped Sophie's slit throat would be a decisive ending, but soft sounds, like hiccups, were still coming from her friend's mouth. Was Sophie trying to breathe but couldn't? Beth thought so, seeing bubbles in the blood at her throat. She whispered another apology, one she meant with all her heart, as she slid the knife's thin blade between Sophie's beautiful blue right eye and the bridge of her nose. She felt it grind just a bit and realized it was sliding along Sophie's skull, so she pointed it up toward the crown of her friend's head and, with her wrist, flicked it back and forth and up and down. The hiccup sound stopped. Just as the *thocking* sound from Anna had.

Beth pulled off her winter coat, shivering as the wind tried to winnow its way through the stitches of her sweater. She turned the coat inside out so the blood (*surprisingly minimal,* thought Beth) was on the inside. She climbed up to look into the first dumpster. Mostly paper and boxes. Beth frowned, wondering if this place had ever heard of recycling. Despite the horrible stench that grew as she climbed up the side, the second dumpster was what she'd wanted—an appalling stew of decaying groceries, bags and boxes, and other miscellaneous waste. She was pretty sure she saw a poop floating by. Beth lowered her coat into the dumpster, submerging it in the stagnant water, and nervously slid her leg down atop it, using her galosh to push it entirely under. When it stayed below the water line, Beth swung her leg up and around, landing next to the dumpster in a dismount that would've made Miss Stephanie, her gymnastics coach, proud.

One more thing, and then we're done, she thought. But then she stopped and wondered, had she actually thought that? The sentence had felt so alien, so external.

The roar of the northbound Metra train snapped her back to the moment. It had about a mile between her and its next stop at Ridge, so it'd be going full speed when it reached her. Quickly, Beth scrambled up the side of the embankment, her hands digging into the mud and dirt on the path. They were nearly black when she reached the top, as was the knife she still held. She looked at it for a moment, mesmerized by what it had done, what *she* had done. The train whistle, still probably half a mile out, brought her back again. She carefully laid the knife on the track and looked toward the train. She couldn't see the conductor, not even with her vision, which the eye doctor had said was better than perfect. She hadn't been sure how that was possible, but it assured her of one crucial thing: if she couldn't see him, he couldn't see her as anything more than a shape or shadow near the tracks. She crouched down in the bushes. Thorns grabbed her, but her adrenaline was pumping so intensely she couldn't feel them. Her eyes stayed fixed on the knife on the track, set so close that it surprised her when the commuter train entered her field of vision. She heard a *clank,* then a whistle over her head that she assumed was the knife, and in another moment, the train had passed on its way to the station.

While a commuter or two could have seen the bodies, they wouldn't have had a chance to get a good look and certainly wouldn't have seen her in the bushes in her navy sweater. She looked over her shoulder down the embankment and saw, thankfully, the shimmer of the knife. She scrambled back down, and when she reached it, she felt pretty pleased. The blade had been flattened out in several places, so that it resembled a hunk of scrap metal. The handle was also nearly flat and gnarled to indistinguishability. Beth pressed the toe of her galosh, which had done so many things already, down upon the blade and lifted the handle, snapping it off. She tossed the handle into the murky sludge with her coat, and, after looking around for other options, took a deep breath and flung the blade. When she heard it clunk atop the semi-trailer, she let her breath out slowly.

That was it, right?

The thing near their bodies nodded.

After climbing back across the tracks, she rinsed her galoshes and hands at the hose spigot sticking out next to the sign designating the Ravenswood Community Flower Bed. She heard the bells of St. Gregory's, letting her know it was six o'clock. Time to get home for dinner. She walked the couple of blocks cautiously, wondering if someone would leap from the shadows at any moment to shout, "I know what you did!"

But they didn't.

She snuck past her mother on the phone in the kitchen and made it upstairs without being seen. In the hallway, she ran into Glen. "Were you rolling in mud, you weirdo?" he asked.

"I fell, dick." Then, for good measure, Beth stuck out her tongue.

Glen laughed and raised his hands. "I surrender." He pushed past her and went downstairs.

As Beth Garcia showered, washing her hair and rinsing her body, the entire afternoon felt like a strange, hazy dream. By the time she sat down for dinner, all she remembered was that she'd seen her friends. When her mother asked Glen and her what they'd done that day, she listened to him talk about his girlfriend, ready to say she'd gone out with Sophie and Anna. She knew her mother would be happy. Shannon Garcia had been concerned enough about the relationship between the three girls that she'd been prodding recently. Beth knew she'd tried to keep her inquiries relaxed and casual, but her mother was incapable of either.

When her brother finished and Beth's turn was up, she said, "I..." and stopped.

She had no idea how she'd spent her afternoon.

ONE

Prudence Osgood spat a sharp exhalation and glanced at the time on her phone. 1:11. "Make a wish," she grumbled.

From one end of the subway platform to the other, there wasn't another soul about. Unsurprising after one in the morning, especially here in the Loop, the central hub of downtown Chicago. The L train's service was always sporadic at this time of night, but even so, one could usually be counted on every twenty-ish minutes. She sat on the blue plastic-coated steel mesh bench and watched as the clock on her phone's lock screen clicked over. An even forty minutes since she'd descended from State Street, also relatively barren but not entirely bereft of life. Flicking her eyes from the large Helvetica 1:12, she scowled at the red "battery saver mode" icon in the upper right corner. Less than ten percent of battery life remaining. "Of course."

"Please keep this with you," Zack had said when he'd handed her the small black brick no bigger than a pack of playing cards. "It'll quick-charge your battery fully twice over ... and you won't just drop out of sight."

She'd taken it, of course, and promised her friend, the gadget maestro, that she would always keep it and know where it was. She did, in fact, know exactly where it was at this very moment, 1:13 a.m. on September 17th. Zack's gift of a backup battery was sitting under a cashed Monster Energy can on the desk, in her office in Andersonville, that had once belonged to her grandfather. "So very helpful," she told herself.

Feeling droplets of sweat run down the shorn side of her head, she sighed. "Why is it so fucking hot down here? It's September!" She couldn't decide which side of her head felt worse—the right side, surrounded by billowy magenta curls longer than she'd allowed for ages, almost to her shoulder like a blanket, blocking any air or breeze, or the left, bald save a few day's growth, and covered in a sheen of sweat trying desperately to keep her brain cool, but unable to evaporate in the stagnant humidity of subterranean Chicago. This was nothing new, of course. In a city with such extremes on either end of the temperature spectrum, those nether months in between always make for a desperate attempt to predict what the weather will do and account for it. Clearly, somebody had thought it'd be much colder than the 50 degrees topside and girded the loins of the subway to obliterate frigid temps, even though it'd been a balmy 85 just last week. To Osgood, it felt like standing under a heat lamp.

She moved to the platform's edge, her Chucks sliding more than stepping over the bumpy blue line, and leaned, eyeing carefully the fabled third rail that would flash-fry her if she fell. She let her breath out slowly and looked down the rails to the tunnel to the south. Its gape was dark, save for a green traffic light deep within. Not even the barest glimmers of the L headlights.

"Seriously, what the fuck?" she asked the platform, hearing her words echo off the white tile ceiling back to her.

She could probably text Zack and ask for a ride. Or Audrey. However, after the endless complaints about her staying connected and planning ahead and blah blah blah, that conversation would be intolerable. Or a few taps on her phone could draw forth some weird stranger in a car scented with artificial pine or new-car-smell, belying the smoke scent beneath that made even her, a once and likely future smoker, gag. Who knew if they would be up to date on vaccinations or the type to cough incessantly into the windshield as they drove, spreading whatever germs and viruses they incubated at the moment? That'd been her last rideshare. She supposed he could also be the North Side Ripper. Though she always suspected she'd be able to see through a serial killer's "quiet and kept to themselves" exterior to the evil nougat inside. *No, she thought, I shall continue to wait for this train.*

Her eyes squeezed shut as the sweat reached them. She yanked off her glasses and rubbed with the back of her hand, seeing the flashes of light in her personal darkness. She wiped the sweat from her upper lip as well. Able to open her eyes again, she waved at her face, desperate to cool it even a little bit, but alas, all that did was push the heavy and hot air at her. Glancing up and down once more to ensure she was truly alone, Osgood grabbed her shirt at the waist and yanked it over her head. The slight movement of air against her bare stomach and the tops of her tits managed to cool her for only a moment. She wiped her head and face and arms and pits and tits and belly with the shirt, then paused for a moment before defiantly throwing it over her shoulder. "If anyone's on the Red Line this time of night, they'll get to see my bra," she said, then added, "assuming a train ever comes." Initially, the sound that replied to her was quiet enough that she didn't even notice. When it repeated, though—a dull muttering, loud enough to echo in the distance but not loud enough to reach her coherently—she perked up.

A woman stood down at the other end of the station, maybe fifty yards away. She, too, faced the tracks, looking down, maybe also willing the train to come. Perhaps if they both sent psychic pleas at once, it would happen.

"Hello?" Osgood asked, then regretted it. Who down in this pit would want to speak to anyone else at this time of night? Apparently not the woman, who continued to look at the tracks and mutter softly. Osgood again rubbed her eyes to clear them and squinted at her. The woman's hair was dyed black, the inky color of raven's feathers. She wore black shorts and a black T-shirt as well. Osgood couldn't quite tell at this distance, but she'd be willing to lay money on those black shoes with the bit of white being Chuck Taylor All-Stars. Osgood was wearing her own battered pair just now as well, but she'd long since given up the bleakness of goth dress in favor of a "come fuck with me, I dare you" style of queer, gaudy, mismatched color.

Getting no response from the woman at the other end of the platform, Osgood shook her head and returned her gaze forward, seeing a half-ripped-down poster for another *Hunger Games* movie. She couldn't remember when the last one had been released but thought that series was long over. The muttering grew louder, and Osgood bit her lower lip, attempting to ignore it. *C'mon, Pru, you don't want any part of that,* she told herself, unsure why her inner voice was so forceful. But she didn't listen. She turned her head and jumped, not at the woman but at her absence. Maybe she'd never been there. This late at night, it was not surprising she was seeing things.

Hearing things, too, her mother's voice reminded her in a prim and mocking tone, Cynthia Osgood's specialty. Though at the moment, the muttering had stopped. Still, she waited, until, like a signal in the noise, she picked it back up in a different place. Osgood stretched her neck, swinging her head to the left, then right, finding both ends of the platform still empty. She felt the muttering switch ears as she did so, which pretty much meant that it was coming from the other side of the tracks. She crouched, finding the sound somewhat easier to hear at this level. Below her, near the third rail, a pair of exceedingly well-fed rats led a tiny rat in a procession around and over and under the rails, then through a space in the wall. With her eyes focused on that space, her brain felt like it had triangulated the murmuring, which began to resolve. A female voice, maybe? A child? She didn't know but felt closer. With all her energy, she pushed her focus through the haze of shots she'd done earlier this evening with that girl. What had her name been? She'd tasted like red rope licorice.

"Way out."

The clarity of the words startled her backward, and she fell on her ass, banging her coccyx against the pavement floor of the platform. She knew instantly that she'd feel that tomorrow morning, never mind the simple crouch she'd been in. Her body, damaged both in factory and aftermarket, just couldn't do shit like that anymore. She had put a hand behind her to lift herself back up and perhaps figure out what had said those words when she felt the briefest suction in the room as the northbound Red Line arrived at the station, slowing to a stop in front of her. She blinked at it, wondering how on Earth she could've missed it coming.

An artificial chime, *bing-bong!*, rang out. The pre-recorded voice of Chicago's public transport proclaimed, "This is the Red Line train, service north to Howard." She looked into the empty car before her and slowly stood. After a pregnant moment, the car announced, "Doors closing." Why wasn't she getting on? She'd waited forty … (she glanced at her phone) … four minutes for this train, and now...

She heard a *chunk* as a window near the front of the two-car train slid down. An older woman with a tired face stuck her head out and turned to look at Osgood. "You getting on or what, honey?"

Yes, right? Of course, I'm getting on. But Osgood felt herself shake her head.

"Heh," the woman proclaimed. "One of them nights, eh? You sure? Not going to be another for an hour. Running slow tonight."

Why on Earth wouldn't she get on? This was foolishness. A bit of muttering in the L station late at night, when she was tipsy and exhausted? *Get on the train, asshole,* she told herself, then did.

Bing-Bong! "Doors closing." This time, the L's voice sounded irritated.

A scream echoed through the station, and the doors reopened. The tired L driver rushed through the first car and onto the platform. Osgood sat for a moment, desperate to absorb the coolness of the air conditioning. *Just until I stop fucking sweating!* But the sound of sobbing rose up, and Osgood couldn't let that lie. She gingerly approached the open doors of the train car and looked left, nothing, then right toward the front of the train. The driver knelt at the very edge of the platform atop the blue caution line. She reached down toward the tracks. Her bulk shifted in a way that made Osgood sure she would fall in, so she rushed to the kneeling woman's shoulders and put her hands on them.

Osgood managed to get out half of "What happened?" before she smelled it. There is nothing like the scent of burning hair. She'd only experienced it once or twice, but it's the kind of smell that doesn't leave when you're out of range. It sorta climbs into your nose and sticks around. When the smell hit her, she knew what'd happened.

The driver heaved, spilling her latest meal into the well,

where it splattered. She wiped at her face and mumbled an apology. Osgood just squeezed her shoulders and stood back up. The driver stood as if moving in slow motion, reached through the window into her driver's cabin, and grabbed a radio mic. "I... I... We had..." She turned to Osgood, her dark eyes wild and her hand shaking. "I don't know what to do," she implored.

Taking a deep breath, Osgood nodded and took the microphone from her. "Dispatch?"

"What's happening?"

"We had a jumper fry herself on the tracks in front of a train car... Um. Red line car 5242. I'm a passenger. Your driver is having a hard time." Osgood looked from the body on the rail to the driver who, while standing, was still bent over, hands on her knees. Osgood couldn't tell if she had finished hurling or planned to loose more. "Jackson stop. Please send someone. For both of them."

"Immediately."

Osgood put down the microphone, gave the bent-over driver a quick, comforting pat, and walked to the edge of the platform herself. She peered down at the blackened tracks where, sure enough, she saw a black All-Star, its sole melted, the white bits covered with blackened soot. The shoe was by itself, but she found the rest just a few feet further. The muttering woman with the black hair, smoldering now, lay back bent over the third rail. The electric rail. The rail that one touch would get you singing, *Toot toot tootsie, Goodbye!* Looking at the woman's purple face, Osgood realized she'd overestimated her age. This was a girl. High school, maybe a sophomore. Her shirt had shredded enough that Osgood could see the faintest color change from pale white stomach to the pink of areola. Only then did Osgood remember she, herself, wasn't wearing a shirt. She hastily looked around for— *What? Someone else down here? Just you and the driver and—*

(Toot toot tootsie, don't cry.)

She pulled her tee over her head. On backward, she realized, not seeing the slice of cherry pie and coffee cup with *Damn fine coffee.* printed above it. *Oh well.*

Osgood looked back to the girl on the rail. Her lips were blackened and blistered, and her eyes ran like egg whites down her cheeks. Os knew *that* would stick with her for a while. She wanted to leave, but the L would go no further for hours, she knew. She thought she should at least stay for the driver. Stay until the cavalry?

A spark in the northern tunnel drew her attention. Sprays of blue and orange sparks weren't uncommon on the L line. Perhaps an unlucky rat had pulled a fork across and regretted it. Like fireflies, though, the sparks lingered, and serenity came over Osgood. For a moment, this all fell away—the sobbing driver, the dead goth girl, the unbearable heat of this tunnel under Chicago— and she was back in her yard as the sky went from pale to deeper shades of azure and the streetlights came on. She and Audrey had caught lightning bugs, as they'd called them then, and put them in mason jars with some holes in the lid and a sprig pulled from their magnolia tree. The sparks, the lightning bugs, seemed to drift up from the tracks, making a lazy loop before flickering out one by one.

The spell was broken when a pod of EMTs shuffled down the stairs from State Street above. Not wanting to answer any questions (she hadn't seen it happen, after all), Osgood snuck into the shadows until the men were occupied by the driver and the corpse, then she fled up the steps, her Chucks slapping as she went. The rush of cool September air hit hard, and her sweat-damp body immediately began shivering. The cold hurt. And it reminded her what she'd seen. A woman, a very young woman in exaggerated goth clothes, the way she'd used to dress when she felt edgy, had just taken her own life. But she was also reminded of something else. Something she hadn't registered when she saw it, something that winnowed its way into her brain as she stood on the corner of State and Jackson, watching the traffic light click from red to green, with no cars to beckon.

The image began to swarm, like the fireflies, going from something she hadn't seen to maybe a trick of the light to a weird surety. In the darkness, beyond the fireflies, had been a set of narrow stone steps up to a metal door. She knew from long-ago research that this door led to a maintenance tunnel parallel to the tracks. But neither the door nor the stairs concerned her. It was what had peeked out from behind the stairs. Out far enough that she'd seen its eye and nose. Trying to hide but also seeming indifferent. How was she just now remembering it? A pale wraith, no more than twenty feet away. Something told her to rush back into the tunnels and look for it, but her body rejected that impulse, staying firmly in place. Because, though she hadn't seen more, she knew it was more than just eyes and a nose. Pale printless fingers, long and flattened, pulled it around the stone steps in a perverse game of peek-a-boo. Leaning out to show her its milky eyes and purple-lined slit of a mouth. It had been *smiling*.

Osgood shook her head and asked herself, "What the fuck?" As much as she loathed her mother's voice as her inner critical monologue, there were times when Cynthia Osgood's simulacrum was right. *You saw a dead body and some sparks. No need to invent horrors, Pru; you've seen plenty tonight.* Yes. That made sense. That was logical. She knew that voice could've come from her mother or from Audrey, probably at home asleep. Both would say the same. She'd seen something horrible for real and then made something horrible up. Logical. She should forget that thing, whatever it was

(*long, and pale, and completely mad*)

and go home.

(*smiling at her*)

But forget she couldn't. She lifted her head to the sky, nearly starless thanks to the orange glow of Chicago's streets, and birthed a scream that cracked her voice. Then she, and the city, fell quiet again.

Osgood began to walk.

Two

Below the proclamation that **Jesu Sav**, the church marquee's oversized clock showed the time was nearly four when Osgood made it to her building. On the lower floor, deep within Mary's Diner & Bar, a dim light illuminated a lone soul sweeping. Whether the last vestige of the late-night staff or first in for the morning shift, Osgood didn't know, but she stepped past the plate glass windows of the diner to the nondescript doorway between it and the building next door. She shuffled in the pockets of her jeans for keys and came up with an ID, an expired MasterCard, a tube of cherry lip balm, and a joint, long-since rendered useless by the sweat from her very long walk. The arched front windows of her apartment above showed darkness and a vague blue glow from the window all the way to the right, she'd left her computer monitor on.

"I'll be using the cane tomorrow," she said, stepping back from the building. *The cane?* asked her mother's voice with a chortle. *Pru, you'll be lucky to get out of bed.* That sounded right. She wondered if Zack had procured that wheelchair he'd promised. She wouldn't need it often, but those times had become somewhat more frequent of late. Twenty-year-old spine and leg injuries, check. Enormous drinking problem and opioid addiction, check. Long COVID trails scrambling her brain… Well, at least she could use that one as an excuse for forgetting her keys. And her phone charger. After a deep breath, she tried the knob, knowing that, despite Zack and Audrey's carping, there was almost always a greater-than-fifty-percent chance she'd forgotten to lock the outside door. When she'd gone out the night before, she could have forgotten, but standing here, barely on her feet after her seven-mile walk—

"Seven *plus!*"

—she was shit out of luck, and the knob didn't budge.

Her finger hesitated, hovering above the button labeled Osgood/Frost, backlit by a flickering yellowed LED. Surely, her arrival would net several lectures at once, starting with, "You walked home drunk?" and continuing with, "Why on Earth didn't you call?" before arriving at, "Jesus, you're irresponsible, Pru." and "You know, there's a serial killer out there?" But what other option did she have? Her right knee buckled as if answering that question, and Osgood reached out to steady herself on the carved stone ornamentation around the door. Concerned she might collapse altogether, she pressed the buzzer, holding it well past the polite duration.

"*I'm gonna guess Pru or cops,*" came Audrey's voice from the speaker. Osgood couldn't tell if she sounded tired or annoyed.

¿Por qué no los dos? "It's Os," she croaked. The wind had been harsh on her throat on that walk, hadn't it? Why *had* she walked again?

Audrey didn't respond, but an almost imperceptible click unlocked the front door, and Osgood stepped inside. The long wooden staircase, likely unchanged since the building was erected at the dawn of the 20th century, mocked her as she climbed. She realized that the adrenaline on which she'd relied to carry her home, rather than spending one more moment in that subway station, had decided she was close enough that it could ebb away. She quietly asked that it just help her all the way to bed, or if not, at least to her medicine cabinet and the sweet relief that any number of pain relievers, both prescription and otherwise, could provide.

The look on Audrey's face was that of a mother about to say, "I'm not mad, just disappointed." Like Osgood's mother, in fact. Though Cynthia was usually mad as well as disappointed. Audrey, her normally rail-straight dirty blond hair bunched and nearly curly, squinted from the entryway as Osgood kicked off a shoe.

"It's my apartment," said Osgood.

"It's *our* apartment, Pru," said Audrey.

"When you call me *Pru* like that, you sound like Cynthia."

At the mention of the C-word, Audrey's face softened, but not entirely. "It's very late, Os..."

"Very early," corrected Osgood, slumping to the floor to deal with an exceptionally tight Chuck that wouldn't slip off and had to be untied.

Audrey stepped back and squinted further, seeming to get a good look at Osgood for the first time. After a moment, she flipped on the ceiling light above them. Osgood recoiled at the light, holding up her hand.

"What happened to you?" The anger was gone from Audrey's voice, replaced with a feisty concern that blared, *Who do I hafta fight?*

"I walked home."

"You walked—"

"Home," Osgood nodded. "Yes."

"From the Loop?"

Osgood didn't answer, just reached out to her friend. When Audrey stared at her hand, Osgood waved it around.

Audrey reached out and pulled her to a standing position, the totality of pain receptors in Osgood's body seeming to all come online at once.

"Why?"

"That can wait." Osgood pushed past Audrey, feeling her reserve energy fading fast.

"Do you know how dangerous that is? A woman walking—"

"I have my rape whistle," said Osgood. What she had was far more than a rape whistle; it was a small hex. Some arcane words without modern meaning, to be said when eye-to-eye and touching or being touched by someone who deserved ... absolute awfulness. Her Aunt Eliza had relished teaching it to her, even though it had taken four separate Zoom calls for Osgood to remember the words. In that sense, the lockdown had been very helpful. Osgood had *not* managed to get any of Eliza's other hexes down.

"That's not the *point,* Os!"

Osgood moved past one door, Audrey's bedroom, to a second, the bathroom. She shoved her way in and made it to the sink, to the medicine cabinet. She held up her hand to grab, well, really, anything, but her muscle memory knew what it wanted, what it needed more than anything else, and the last of that was on the top shelf, all the way at the end. Her fingers found the brown tincture bottle with the eyedropper and the flecked silver "O" drawn on its side.

"Os," said Audrey in the doorway, the concern in her voice growing.

"Yeah," said Osgood, meeting her friend's eye in the mirror, then looking at her own. "Jesus." Her makeup had eroded in near-Joker proportions: eyeliner streaks, sweat lines cutting through the foundation. She blinked at the specter before her, then shrugged. She unscrewed the stopper from the bottle and squeezed it, hearing air rush in. Again, more air.

Again, and a slight gurgle told her that she'd found the last of her bootleg OxyContin. Out of the corner of her eye, she saw Audrey's hand reach out to her as she dropped a single paltry droplet under her tongue.

"You've been without—"

"Yeah," repeated Osgood. She upended the brown bottle over her mouth, extending her tongue for anything, one more drop of relief. Please. But nothing came. She threw the bottle toward the trashcan next to the toilet but missed entirely, and it shattered into several brown pieces against the tile.

"Will you please tell me what happened?" Audrey's face betrayed the tears she seemed not to want to show.

"I'll tell both of you tomorrow," Osgood said, banging into the door frame as she shoved past Audrey, back into the hallway.

"But you—"

"I'm so exhausted from that walk," Osgood said, holding her index finger in front of Audrey's face to ask her to *wait a moment,* "that I may actually sleep tonight."

"That would be good," agreed Audrey, "But..."

"Quit the buts, Aud." Osgood grabbed Audrey's hands and fixed her friend's concerned deep brown eyes with her own. "I am alright."

"You—"

"I did what I needed to do to push the pain away. But there is nothing I can tell you tonight that cannot wait until I've found at least an hour or two of surely restless and night-terror-filled sleep." She waited for a beat, and when it was clear Audrey didn't intend to interrupt her again, Osgood calmly confirmed, "Okay?"

Audrey nodded.

"Thank you," said Osgood. She leaned forward and kissed the corner of Audrey's mouth. "I love you. Goodnight."

"Love you, too."

Osgood closed the door to her bedroom, and darkness enveloped her like the warm embrace of a long distant lover. The triple-layered black fabric she'd hung to block out the omnipresent orange glow of Chicago night made her room almost black enough she could barely distinguish shapes. Having lived in this darkness for so very long, like the stereotypical emo gal she reasoned she very well might be, she only rarely got tripped up by a pile of clothes or a mislaid sex toy. Tonight, she stepped on her vape pen and heard it crunch. A prodding tactile examination told her it wasn't leaking but was unlikely to emit any cannabis again. She threw it where she thought the garbage can would be and heard the aluminum *tink* as it hit home.

After allowing herself to fall onto her bed, Osgood removed her glasses and dropped them on her night table. She fumbled with the cord but managed to get her phone plugged in. Briefly, it assaulted her senses with the bootup screen; the battery had long since given up the ghost. She set it face-down on her night table and was in darkness again. It was in this darkness that she stripped and flopped, her head hitting the coolness of her pillowcase. Her white noise was the monotonous drone of the ancient window air conditioner unit, whose LEDs were taped over with electrical tape.

She heard the toilet flush through the wall and a single rap on that wall from Audrey. A last goodnight. A wordless, *I love you.* Osgood threw a giant stuffed plushie of the coronavirus, a macabre "get well" gift, at the wall to *thunk* her response. Then she smiled and closed her eyes.

As her body sank into the linens, for a moment, she thought she might actually sleep. The tugging disconnection of the oxy dulled the world and softened the focus as it always had but seemed reluctant to turn off her brain. And it was here in the darkness, in the safety of her bed, that her phantom returned. Not the one from the subway, thankfully, but the one who'd joined her so many times since he'd passed on. His eye rolled in its socket, almost disappearing into his head. The white was nearly blood red, but the iris was clear. It was him. At the end of their fight with the (no better way to put it, was there?) monsters from the margins between worlds, after their extraction that may as well have been an amateur exorcism, Sam Goddard, a man she'd once loved enough to fantasize about marrying, had died. There hadn't been blame in his eye as he went; Osgood had added that herself in the weeks and months since. *If only you hadn't—* Well, she could take her pick. *Hadn't started investigating the rest stop papers? Hadn't vanished into someplace other? Hadn't birthed a creature that consumed Goddard? Hadn't been unable to complete the bloody T on your* other *wrist? Hadn't survived your fucking car accident?*

"Hadn't been me," she told herself finally in the darkness where his single eye, the other concealed by swollen cheek and forehead, gazed upon her, conjured by her mind. And here she broke down, as she often did when he visited. He never said anything, and she acknowledged that meant he was probably nothing more than a manifestation of guilt within her mind, not a full-fledged spirit, but it didn't really matter, did it? She was here and alive because she wouldn't complete the tasks given to her, and Sam (sometimes Sampson) Goddard was dead.

Like an unwanted nanny, Goddard stayed by Osgood's side until just before noon, when Audrey rapped lightly to offer coffee.

Sleep never came.

THREE

"Zack up yet?"

"He's at Sandy's," said Audrey.

"Again?" asked Osgood.

"Again." Audrey shrugged. She set a mug on the kitchen table in front of Osgood and was about to pour when Osgood snatched the cup away and replaced it with one three times the size, a *Ghostbusters* logo on the side.

"It's like that, is it?" asked Audrey.

"Very much so," said Osgood.

"So..." Audrey dawdled, looking intently at her thumbnail.

Osgood waited an ever-lengthening time. Audrey's gaze was shifty, her cheeks slightly flushed. She twirled a strand of hair so tightly around her index finger that Osgood thought it might pop. "Out with it."

"What?"

"Clearly you're going to tell me something I don't like, so you may as well just tell me."

Audrey's eyes shot to Osgood, who nodded again to emphasize her point. "Kent..." said Audrey, trailing off again.

"...Kent," sighed Osgood, emphasizing the hell out of that T.

"Yes," came the response, Audrey seeming annoyed. "*Kent.*"

"What about your boyfriend?" asked Osgood.

"*Boy*friend..." dismissed Audrey with a theatrical roll of her eyes.

"Lover?" offered Osgood.

Audrey shook her head.

"Person that you fuck when he doesn't have his kids." The scowl appeared so quickly that Osgood knew she'd hit a nerve and withdrew. "Alright," she said calmly, then repeated the name, "...Kent."

"Yes, Kent. Kent is coming over tonight."

"Oh," said Osgood, feeling the *h* leak out of her mouth until it became nothing but breath.

"And you asked me to let you know in advance when he's—"

"I did," regretted Osgood. It had seemed like a good strategy after the night she'd been stood up and arrived home four or five hours early to find Audrey naked on the couch with *Kent*'s tongue in her cooch. "So, I'll be elsewhere."

"No, no," said Audrey.

"Yeah..." Osgood trailed again. "I'll be elsewhere."

"I'm really *not* trying to kick you out of our apartment."

Osgood nodded, her jaw cocked. She thought about the awkward conversation over coffee later that night when Kent, all blond hair and manicured scruff, had told her he'd heard a lot about her.

"I've ... also," Osgood had returned.

They'd sat silently until Audrey finished "making herself decent."

"He's just," said Osgood to Audrey now, "so monogamous."

Audrey raised her eyebrows and let out an exasperated sigh. "*You* said we shouldn't try to date again."

Osgood had.

"*You* said we'd just wind up splitting and hating each other again."

Osgood had also said that.

"*You* said you supported me going out and finding a new partner."

As much as she bristled at Audrey's use of that word, Osgood had to concede she'd also said that.

"And you agreed with me that, despite my bisexuality, I could still have a monogamous relationship with a man."

"I didn't think you *would!*" Osgood folded her arms across her chest, feeling every bit the petulant child she was sure she appeared to be.

"I don't want a fuck buddy, Os," said Audrey, reaching over.

Osgood tucked her fingers in so Audrey couldn't reach them.

"I know that *you* find it fulfilling when you—"

Osgood arched her eyebrow so high it knocked a curl into her eye. She blew it away.

"And there's nothing wrong with that," assured Audrey.

"It's just not you," finished Osgood. She'd heard this one before.

"It's just not me," confirmed Audrey.

Osgood threw out a dramatic sigh. "I wish everybody was sexually liberated."

Audrey rolled her eyes. "I'm plenty liberated, Os. I was going to tell you I pegged him, but I didn't know if you'd be proud or annoyed."

"I'm annoyed that I'm proud."

"I don't know what to do with that."

They both sat, looking into their coffee. The small swirl of creamer and dusting of sugar floating atop spiraled around Osgood's mug, spinning slowly, growing darker, and her brain saw the unexplainable, the

(great eye in the sky)

quasar that saw her right back, saw her deep. Deeper than any human, deeper than any being on Earth ever had or maybe ever could.

"Meeting with *The Chicago Reader* at two, remember. I've scheduled a Driver."

"You still use them?"

"Who else am I supposed to use?" Audrey snapped back. "Are you planning to come?"

"I'd very much like to come." Osgood sipped her coffee. "Didn't get to last night."

"To the meeting." Audrey's voice was flat but firm, refusing to give Osgood even a hint of a smirk.

"Oh, right." Osgood blinked, then blinked again, noticing the sensation of her eyelids sliding over her eyeballs, noting the swimming migraine tadpoles dying to become mindstorms. "I'm gonna ... sit this one out."

"Figured."

Audrey stood and dumped the last of her coffee in the sink, rinsed and wiped her mug, and put it in the drying rack. "Can you also take care of this before tonight?"

Osgood followed her finger to the rainbow dildo, standing at attention in the silverware bin of the drying rack. She blinked at it and tried to remember when she'd used it. When had anyone been over? "Yeah," she said finally.

"We're good?" asked Audrey.

"About?" asked Osgood, genuinely uncertain.

"Kent."

"...Kent," repeated Osgood.

"Yes."

"We're fine," she dismissed the concern. "You'd better tell Zack, though."

"He tends to enter through his own space..." Audrey trailed off, then added as a bit of afterthought. "And we have sex in my bedroom now."

"As the good lord intended," said Osgood.

"You're in rare form."

Osgood stuck up her index finger. "Insomnia." Then, her middle. "Pain." Then, her ring. "Manic depression." Then, her pinky. "The revenant of my former lover."

Audrey moved back to the table, standing behind her chair. She leaned down toward Osgood. "Sam Goddard wasn't your fault."

Unmoved, Osgood shrugged. "I've got so many reasons to believe otherwise."

"Well, you shouldn't." Audrey stared at her for a while, but Osgood just looked into her coffee. After a few moments, Audrey laid a kiss on top of Osgood's head. "I'll text you from the car, and you can tell me what the fuck happened to you last night."

"Dealio."

After she'd left the room, Osgood did gaze after Audrey, her friend, her beloved, her regret. The kiss had made her tingle in a way Audrey would never entirely understand.

"What the fuck happened to me last night," Osgood repeated under her breath, downing the final third of her coffee. Its burn down her throat piqued her alertness, at the very least. "Saw a suicide, and

(a wraith)

"something under the subway." Something, yes. "An eye and a bit of a face." *Like your eye in the sky?* asked the Audrey in her head. *And are you sure you want to gloss over that suicide so quickly?*

"No, like a ghost's eye."

We are *ghost hunters,* Zack's voice suggested.

"We are," said Osgood to herself. She could see the eye so vividly, the eye and part of a face, part of a face with a mad fucking grin. Her phone buzzed on the table.

Spill.

Holding a deep breath as she typed, Osgood laid out the two significant events from the night before. The girl who'd died on the tracks and the thing she'd seen in the dark. Thought she'd seen, anyway.

Audrey's ellipsis lasted a while.

i know what yur gonna say, texted Osgood.

Enlighten me.

That the trauma of the suicide knocked this super-natural idea into my head and it's nothing more than a manifestation of that trauma and sleeplessness.

Wow, said Audrey. **That's shockingly close.**

And Id agree with you if that phantom didn't feel so real.

I think that's the third person this year to jump on the tracks.

Seems like a lot.

Is **a lot.**

Osgood nodded. **MayB ask @ Reader?**

WD. Will do. Their old shorthand. Still gave Osgood flutters to see it. She closed out the text app and stood on wobbly legs, tossing the mug in the sink and snatching the dildo from the drying rack. Perhaps it could offer a distraction.

Instead, Osgood decided to have a whiskey in the shower.

She made it a double.

FOUR

*B*ang
Bang!
BANG!

The sound of wrenched wood creaking and cracking. Straining. Then another, much louder *BANG!* and the door to the bathroom slammed open hard enough that Osgood could hear the wall tile behind the doorknob shatter and tinkle to the ground. She opened her eyes at that.

"Jesus!"

The shower curtain was yanked aside, and there, above her, stood Audrey and Zack, eyes full of panic.

"What the fuck, guys?" Osgood looked past them to the now-open bathroom door and the shattered tile.

Zack averted his eyes, always shy around her nakedness.

Well, he shouldn't have come in here!

"You didn't answer," he told her.

"I didn't—"

"I called you," said Audrey. "Like a dozen times."

"I didn't." This time, Osgood just let the two words form

their own sentence. She hadn't answered, no, but that's because, "I didn't hear you calling!"

"How about pounding?" asked Zack.

No, thought Osgood with a shiver. Why was she so cold? "Fuck!" She grabbed the handle and turned off the shower, quenching its flow of icy water onto her body. Now, feeling the hairs standing up on her arms and neck, she could tell that the water she'd been soaking in was also ice cold. "Need a robe!" she coughed.

Zack, again without looking, grabbed her brown waffle-knit bathrobe from a hook next to the tub and held it out to her.

After Osgood failed two attempts to stand independently, using the shower spigot and the tub's rim, Audrey reached down and grasped her hands, pulling her to a standing position. "I m-m-must've f-f-fallen—"

"Asleep," finished Audrey.

"That's really dangerous," said Zack, with a level of judgment that nearly rivaled her parents'.

"Y-y-yeah," Osgood dismissed it, pulling her robe over her shoulders.

Audrey ran her palms up and down Osgood's arms, trying to dry them through the robe. "Better?"

"Better," said Osgood.

"Well, the sun's out, and it's over 80 today if you want to zap yourself with heat." Zack pointed at the battered doorway. "I'll, uh, see if I have anything downstairs to fix the frame." He disappeared into the hall, heading for the back of the apartment and the stairs leading to his own space, grumbling about her irresponsibility.

"He's in a mood," said Osgood.

"You worry us," said Audrey.

"Still?"

"Always." Audrey took Osgood's hand and examined it. "How long have you been in there?"

Osgood yanked back her pruned fingers. "Since just after you left."

"That was hours ago, Os."

Osgood nodded and looked away. Yep, she'd fallen asleep in the shower and laid there for hours. She noticed the empty rocks glass on the floor and kicked it behind the clothes hamper. Didn't need to hear that lecture today.

"C'mon," said Audrey, "Let's go stand on the porch."

Osgood closed her robe, knotting the tie around her waist, and followed Audrey through the kitchen to their back porch. This eight-by-four stretch of unstained and unrefined wood sometimes looked like it would fall right off the building, but every attempt to get their landlord to shore it up was met with, at best, a two-by-four and a couple nails. They never really let more than three people out here at a time. In the late afternoon sun and the heat of a schizophrenic Chicago fall, Osgood felt the water on her evaporating until the robe became smothering. She dropped it to the deck, and Audrey snickered.

"What?"

"As always," her friend said regarding Osgood's nakedness, "happy it's your name on the lease."

"Why? 'Cuz someone might complain?" Osgood waved her hands at the array of back porches that lined the other side of the alley parallel to Clark Street.

"For Chrissakes, Os!"

She turned to see Zack climb the stairs from his place and head back into the apartment, shaking his head.

"Better put something on," said Audrey.

"It's funny, though," said Osgood.

"It's ... kinda assault, though," said Audrey.

"Fine..." said Osgood, who gathered her robe back around her waist and headed to her room, only emerging once her dangerous bits had been fully clothed in sweatpants and, to make Zack smile, a shirt with the Spectral Inspector logo, their logo, a cartoon ghost in a hot pink circle, on the chest. With the frigid temperature wearing off, Osgood could feel every muscle in her legs screaming, and she remembered that she'd fucking walked home the night before. She yanked down her cane from the back of her bedroom door and let it help her into the living room, attempting to hide the extent of her need as much as possible when she arrived.

In the apartment's front room, Osgood found the other two Spectral Inspectors already in their battle stations. Zack eternally had several pieces of equipment with him, so his spot was the table in the front window nook. Audrey, ever the egalitarian, took the center of the couch in implicit invitation to anyone who'd want to join her. Osgood, seeing this, took her own regular spot, a battered BarcaLounger, acquired from the Brown Elephant thrift store to replace a slightly more battered La-Z-Boy which had gone to chair heaven a few months prior. She shuffled her butt to find the groove and kicked open the leg rest. She winced as it shoved her screaming legs up.

"Well," she said finally.

They both stared at her.

After a moment, Zack looked from Osgood to Audrey and back. "Do..." He stopped and seemed to rethink his tactic. "Would you like to tell us why you walked home last night?"

"I told Audrey."

"Would you like to tell *me*?" asked Zack.

Osgood sighed and gave Zack a slightly abridged version of the night before.

"That still doesn't explain why you walked home," he said.

Osgood attempted a pout. "I was traumatized."

He opened his mouth as though he would say something further, probably preparing to chide her for her irresponsibility. When he did that, he always got a deep crease between his eyes, and Osgood thought he looked just like his father, based on her limited interaction with Mr. Nguyen.

She refocused on Audrey. "How'd the *Reader* interview go?"

"Great," said Audrey, her eyes widened. "Oh, right, per our conversation..." She tapped through her phone. "Got this," she said and pressed play. "The other voice is Sushmita Das from *The Reader.*"

> **Sushmita:** -sfine.
> **Audrey:** You were saying about the suicides?
> **Sushmita:** Yes, well, suicides in the City of
>   Chicago were in decline right up through
>   2017. Then there was a shift.
> **Audrey:** Due to political circumstances?
> **Sushmita:** I'm inclined to think so. After
>   COVID hit as well. Had a lot of people
>   with long COVID who just couldn't take
>   it anymore.

Osgood noticed Zack's eyes momentarily flash to her, then back to Audrey's phone on the coffee table.

> **Audrey:** And this year?
> **Sushmita:** Spiking. Like, a lot. I hesitate to
>   call it an epidemic, but...
> **Audrey:** But it's an epidemic.

Audrey tapped her phone to stop the recording. "So..."

"Suicide epidemic," Osgood grumbled. "Can't they wait to get killed by the North Side Ripper like everybody else?"

Neither of them seemed to find that funny.

"*The Reader*'s doing the profile, by the way," said Audrey.

"Excellent," said Zack. When his face lit up, his youth was more obvious.

"Awesome," said Osgood through a grimace. Ever since fame had blown up in her face when

(you lied)

the truth came out about their faked hotel footage, Osgood had been fine with being a minor niche celebrity. Actually, even that often freaked her out. She'd felt far more comfortable talking to a hundred listeners on *The Spectral Inspector* podcast than she was now that it'd ballooned to almost twenty-five thousand per episode.

Zack broke the quiet. "I still can't believe you walked home." He shook his head.

"No L," said Osgood with a shrug.

"You could've ordered a—"

"Phone was dead," said Osgood, the thing she hadn't wanted to mention because—

"And lemme guess, you didn't have your charger." He may as well have been wearing an ugly Christmas sweater with *I Told You So* knit into it.

"I ... did not."

"Just careless," he mumbled.

"Not true," said Osgood. "I care very much about many things, just not that."

He shook his head again.

"Anyway," said Audrey. "Do you want to investigate your wraith?"

"Do we have anything else pressing?"

"You've been telling Nora you'll investigate her ghost," said Audrey with a slight smirk.

Osgood felt her whole body sigh. Nora was just one more person disappointed that Osgood didn't have time for her. "She's waited this long; she can wait more."

"Fair enough."

Zack scrolled through his tablet. "The only thing I have for this month is the thing with Sandy the last weekend."

"With Sandy," repeated Osgood.

"Yes." Zack didn't look up. "Other people are allowed to date too, Osgood."

"What thing with Sandy?"

"Oh," he did look up now. "That was just her and me investigating. *We...*" he spun his finger in a circle to indicate the Spectral Inspectors. "Don't have anything pressing."

"Just her and you," said Osgood.

"Let it go, Os," said Zack.

She found it challenging but ultimately did.

FIVE

"Just so we're clear..." began Zack.

"Crystal," interrupted Osgood, a strong dose of zest on the word.

"You don't have to be like that," said Zack.

The three of them stood at the Bryn Mawr station for the Red Line L. What would eventually become Chicago's subway as it neared downtown was here the elevated track that gave it its nickname, the "El." The southbound train's doors opened, and the trio climbed aboard.

"I'm not being like anything," said Osgood as they sat in the back corner, nearest the front of the train.

Zack set his black duffel bag on the floor and glanced around the train car. Only a handful of others were on board, likely owing to the earliness of the evening, still before rush hour, and the earliness in the route. The Red Line L train began at the tip-top of Chicago, running south from there. Bryn Mawr station was quite near the top.

"You are being *a little* like..." Audrey said with a shrug.

Osgood fixed her eyes on her friend. "I don't care that you both have dates."

"Dates," said Audrey with disgust. "We're adults, we don't—"

"No," corrected Zack. "Mine is a date. Osgood is right. Sandy and I are going on a date."

"Are you going steady?" groused Osgood. "Gonna give her your pin?"

Zack scowled and handed her a small box with a needle on it. "Just because you can't find a—"

"Can't find—"

"That!" Zack hit the word hard to cut off Osgood's train of thought, "is a new EMF detector. We can dial the squelch knob there," he tapped a clearly aftermarket knob, "to reduce the standard EMF being produced by the trains. It will be hard within an aluminum box, but this is just recon."

"I can find a date, Zack," insisted Osgood.

He ignored her and handed Audrey a digital meter. "This one is *uber* sensitive and records the numbers based on time. You're going to hit the button on the side as we hit the subway portion of the Red Line, again as we near Jackson stop, and then again when we pass it."

"Had a date last night, in fact," Osgood continued as Zack continued to ignore her.

"Because of ... plans tonight," Audrey began, clearly choosing the words carefully, "We're only going to be taking a trip down and back. I thought we'd jump off at Roosevelt and get back on going north."

Osgood frowned. "Not at Jackson?"

"We don't have the time to do a full investigation into—"

"The spot where I actually saw the thing."

"He's right, you know," said Audrey.

"What is he right about?" asked Osgood.

Audrey sighed for effect. "You've become a pain in the ass since we started dating."

"*We're* not dating," said Osgood.

"You know what I mean," said Audrey.

Osgood sat back in her seat, feeling the disoriented rush of facing backward as the train moved forward, shuddering from side to side as it went. She looked between them, seeing the challenge on both faces. Frustration. Probably anger, too. She looked away. Outside, the north side of the city rushed by. Rows and rows of two-flats and three-flats. Larger courtyarded apartment buildings. She sighed. *You know exactly what she means, Pru,* she told herself, irritated that the voice was that of her mother once more. As the L train shook and chugged its way downtown, Osgood closed herself in.

The conversation between Zack and Audrey, the chatter of the dozen or so others in the train car, faded away until she was alone with her thoughts. She *was* a pain in the ass. In general, sure, but especially now, especially when both of her friends, her partners, had partners. The better kind of partners. Leaving her here, to be herself. There really were two distinct Osgoods, weren't there? One distracted, be it by investigation, projects, vices, or genitals attached to mildly exciting people, and one bored and aimless. That second Osgood, she knew, was a cunt. Even though she'd been on an ostensible date last night, had it really been anything? Or has it just been rather impossible to do anything resembling "date" since

("You're the one who said we shouldn't date.")

she and Audrey had ended their sort-of coupling as the COVID lockdown lingered. Riding the L toward the city's heart, she could chill her attitude and turn her attention to investigation. To the thing she'd seen in the depths of the subway. She took a long breath and held it, refusing to look away from the window. Held. Held until the pressure came, held until her lungs ached, held until tears leaked from her eyes. Then released.

"I'm sorry," she said, flat and without looking in their eyes.

She refused their attempts to accept her apology with a raised hand. "What else do we have? Equipment-wise."

Zack flicked his eyes to Audrey, and Osgood allowed for the momentary ache that accompanied the knowledge she'd been replaced as de facto leader of this team. It was nobody's fault, to be sure. What else do you do when someone disappears for more than a year? Audrey had always been a better leader anyway. Less likely to fuck everything up for fame or profit or pussy.

Zack reached deep into his duffle and retrieved three small cubes with suction cups. Cameras. He leaned in to direct them further, then paused and sat back in his seat, flicking his eyebrows toward the other side of the train. Osgood followed the unsubtle gesture and found a member of the Chicago PD standing at the opposite end of the car. The cop's thumbs were in his pockets, and his belt barely managed to hold back his ample gut. The cop's eyes moved around the car but seemed to only register surface details. Failing to find a person of color to harass, perhaps, he departed when the doors opened at Belmont.

"Since we're doing a quickie," whispered Zack, "we want to get as much data as possible."

"I always try to get as much as possible from my quickies," said Osgood.

Zack just blinked at her. She sighed.

"We're going to do a camera stuck to each side, bottom of the windows should give us the best field of view. And, if we can..." he trailed off, looking toward the front of the car.

Osgood followed his eyes to the small enclosure at the front, where two men in suits sipped beers they hid awkwardly inside their jackets. In front of them was the goal, a nearly floor-to-ceiling window that looked directly out the front of the car.

"I got it," said Osgood, grabbing a camera from his hand.

She stood and grasped the pole as the L shuddered down the track. She rotated and shifted the small camera cube in her left hand behind her back until her index finger found the button with the slight bump. *That's record,* she told herself. She turned it again so the suction cup, and thus the recording lens, faced out.

"Hey there," she said as she sidled up to the men, leading with her tits in that way that made her back ache. The suits turned to her, instinctively tugging their coats shut to hide the beers. Neither said anything, and both stood very much in her way between the car and the window. She smiled. They smiled back. Osgood wondered if she wasn't thrusting enough. As the car shook again, she grabbed the bicep of the sandy-haired guy. "Oh, I'm sorry! I almost fell over," she giggled.

"It's fine," he said, his eyes darting back to his friend.

She leaned into the dark-haired one, who stank of alcohol. "Have any extras? I could really use a drink."

"These are our last ones," he said. "But we're headed back to my place..."

"Your place," repeated Osgood with a sly smile, sliding past the men until she stood between them and the large window. She glanced over her shoulder quickly and saw the train being swallowed by the ground as the elevated track became a subway.

"We have drinks. Other things."

"Other things," repeated Osgood, fumbling in the temporary darkness until she managed to stick the camera on the window's bottom corner and press the button. With her hands free, she rubbed the shoulders of both men. "As enticing as that sounds, I'll have to take a rain check, gentlemen."

"Your loss," said the sandy-haired one.

"I'm sure," said Osgood with a smile. She began to move away, to force her way past them again and return to her seat when she felt the oddest sensation of ... déjà vu. Not quite that she remembered this, but that this was significant. She looked out the front window and saw a cluster of sparks shooting upward. After a moment, she gave the men another smile and returned to Audrey and Zack, hearing, "The fuck was that?" and, "Uptight bitch," as she went. The final volley, "Old and ugly," nearly got to her, but she shoved it aside.

"Seems about right." Osgood nodded to her friends at the assessment from the suits, who watched her a moment longer and then resumed their conversation. "You both get yours up?"

Zack indicated the window behind him with his head, and Audrey nodded, flicking her thumb. "You should dial down the squelch," Zack said, pointing to Osgood.

Osgood looked at him. His words didn't make sense to her. "I should dial down..." *Right!* She reached into her bag and pulled out the EMF detector he'd given her. Right now, traveling on an electric rail in an aluminum box through a tunnel lined with electric cables, the needle was jumping. She turned the dial, and it calmed. She turned it further, and the needle hopped around zero. The numbers wouldn't be accurate, but the adjustment would make a sudden spike more obvious.

After a while of the shaky train making its way through underground tunnels and stations, Audrey sat up straight. "We're coming up on it." She clicked the button on her detector.

The voice of the L confirmed Audrey's assertion. *"Jackson is next. Doors open on the left at Jackson."*

The Spectral Inspectors watched as the doors opened at Jackson (*bing-bong!*), the station she'd spent nearly an hour in last night. The L train paused as folks further down the train climbed on and off, then descended into the tunnel between stops. Osgood's needle didn't even bounce.

"Get anything?" Osgood asked Audrey.

"A tiny jump, probably just from sparks." Audrey turned to Zack. "You?"

Zack shook his head.

"Well," sighed Osgood. "How often do investigations turn something up immediately?"

Zack sighed and yanked his camera off the window with a sharp pop. Osgood saw that the enthusiasm of the mission had definitely faded and quietly went to get the camera from the front of the train, no longer bothered by the suits, who'd exited at the Lake Street station.

"So, dates tonight," Osgood said as they waited for the northbound Red Line train.

Audrey sighed.

"I am happy for you both," she finished.

Zack cocked an eyebrow at her.

"Really," said Osgood.

Zack and Audrey looked at each other again, taking a moment to share whatever sixth sense sharing they did these days. Osgood took a breath as they thanked her.

Six

Osgood felt the itch, the itch to get right down into it. Dig in. Go balls deep.

But, of course, she wouldn't. Not right now, because Zack had the equipment in his space. Could she go in there and get it? Sure. She knew all the codes, and she even had her own login on his computer command center. But she wouldn't. Because there were lines in partnerships. While the bathroom incident had left some … gray area when it came to those lines now, she still needed to respect Zack's line.

Instead, she sat on her back deck as the last deep blues faded in the sky behind her apartment and Chicago turned on the dark. Tonight was cooler, and Osgood thanked whatever gods might be responsible for that. Inside the apartment was a different story. They had little control over when the landlord fired up the steam-heated radiators, and their settings were pretty much on or off. In the times between distinct seasons, their apartment was always Too Hot or Too Cold. Very rarely had she experienced Just Right.

Osgood snickered. *Such is life!*

She took another deep drag on her joint and followed it

with a slug of bourbon. Why not? There was no one here to look askance at her choices. And when the others did return—Audrey to the apartment behind her, and Zack down those stairs to the converted warehouse space he (though not the city of Chicago) considered an apartment—they'd both have other things on their mind than old drunken druggie Prudence Osgood. "Pussy and dick are powerful distractions," she said to the night and took another drag and slug, enjoying two of her three viciest vices, even if they were both legal these days. The other, her OxyContin, was the illicit substance. Sure, drug companies were still beating down doors to hock it. But as the truth had come out about the addiction potential, many doctors had started asking people in real pain to grin and bear it. THC and CBD helped, especially at medicinal levels, but nothing had ever compared to the big O for her over the years, more than twenty on from her accident now, the one that had killed her...

"Not literally," people would say.

She'd give them a weary nod and intone, "Literally," right back. "It just didn't stick."

For most people, to be sure, death did stick. But for Prudence Osgood, eight minutes in the void had been enough to get her to slough off that pesky wrist-cutting habit for good.

But Osgood, once the *only* Spectral Inspector, would not continue the current investigation alone. Mainly because she didn't know how. Things used to be so simple. A Nagra recorder, a Polaroid camera, and an analog EMF detector. But now everything needed fucking USB cables and the right programs, and, well, Zack was just *better* at that. Osgood sighed, knowing that being *better* in this instance simply took basic competence. Zack was so much more than better. He was essential. And that's why this whole *thing* was better now, right? That the Spectral Inspector was plural. That it was the three of them. The varied and diverse skills that, when they weren't making Osgood feel irrelevant, complimented each other tremendously and allowed them to do some spectacular things. Even if those spectacular things occasionally brought them face-to-face with mortality. Or, in the case of Sam Goddard, caused said mortality.

Another slug of the bourbon, and she refilled the glass, not bothering with rocks this time. What better time to podcast?

Osgood reached for the microphone and her Specterinos. Well, *their* Specterinos. Because now, when she pressed that "podcasting for dummies" Go Live button Zack had put on her computer's desktop and sent the spectral birds to notify listeners in their apps, or whatever, that she was going to monologue on her platform, those listeners numbered in the thousands and tens of thousands. She'd stopped looking at the number months ago, instead imagining herself back in the once upon a time when she believed no one was listening and she was speaking into the void. An affordable alternative to a therapist. Though, Osgood supposed, when one treats their podcast as therapy, they probably ought to lose listeners, oughtn't they?

"Interesting day," she said, pulling the microphone bolted to the top of her grandfather's old desk close until the pop filter almost touched her lips. She warned them all that the investigation was only beginning, knowing she'd jumped the gun too many times to count, leading the Specterinos to believe her in the middle of a battle between heaven and hell when she was only pontificating existence.

"An empty subway station at night. With darkness encroaching. Those tunnels below the city almost spill darkness into the light, right? Darkness marks the edges of our understanding. We don't know beyond. We knew this when we were children. We knew then, as modern children also know, that there could be horror in the spaces closest to us. The darkness beneath our beds, behind our doors. Inside our closets. We train our 'rational' adult minds to believe fear of the dark is simply a manifestation of fear of the unknown. To understand the closet, and that no monster is within it, all we need to do is shine a light and see nothing but clothes, shoes, and discarded toys.

"When our species was young, avoiding that scary darkness was how we survived. Those who craved the darkness, like myself and many of you, Specterinos, didn't survive. Because they were not fittest, and we were right to fear. The cave bears were ready to maul us when we wandered into their den without torches. Those who had the sense to avoid the darkness built communities because more people could tend to the fire, could expand its reach. As humanity aged and became citizens of the world beyond our tribes, we wrote the dark areas into our maps. In the unknown waters beyond our explored world were serpents. There be tygers in the deepest, darkest jungles and monsters off the edges of the map. Of course, this darkness was really the internal darkness of so many of our original sins. The sin of racism, the othering of human beings. Our prejudices were the darkness within, made manifest in the dark without. And they cannot be wiped away with a swipe of the flashlight.

"But what was I talking about?" she puffed on her vape pen. "I know you'll say, 'Osgood, I like it better when you don't get political.' But I'll say 'Fuck you,' to that.

"Ahh, right. The differences in the darkness. Prejudicial darkness is a lack of willingness to gain knowledge. Because understanding the dark is paramount. That's why we investigate it. What is monster and what is human. And sadly, our society has tended to investigate only to the point of their satisfaction, not to a universal truth. One never knows what dwells in the dark, and one must always arm oneself with a flashlight, a search for knowledge. In the light of day, it's easy for the world to rationalize. We hide behind simple truths. There's nothing under the bed, behind the closet door, down the yawning chasm of the basement staircase. Those sounds are the furnace knocking, the house settling, the scraping of branches blown by the wind outside our bedroom window. And these rationalizations are likely true, aren't they? When your son bursts through your bedroom door at 4 a.m., tears streaming down his face, informing you that there is a bogeyman under his bed, you patiently smile and inform him of The Truth, that there is no bogeyman, and you'd be happy to show him, with that flashlight that you keep beside your own bed. You both kneel at the edge, your son further away because he still knows what our ancestors did, that you don't have to be the *furthest* from the monster; you just can't be the *closest* to it when it makes its presence known.

"Your breath catches as you light your torch, put your hand on his mattress, and begin to crouch. That's the moment, isn't it? You're committed now. The same as that moment when you watched the last episode of *The Haunting of Hill House* for the night and flipped off the TV and the lamp next to the couch, but you forgot you'd left the hallway light off, didn't you? And then you did that little shuffle, moving faster than you would in the light. To get to the," Osgood slashed air quotes in front of her, "'safety' of your bed.

"So, here you are, crouched and ready. And the feeling remains, doesn't it? Even to us, as ghost hunters, people who desperately *want* there to be something under the bed or in the closet, in that moment before the unknown becomes known, we experience the truest form of fear. As we tilt our heads and lean down, anything could be there, when the expanse beneath the bed is still in darkness. Our light offers us protection. It offers us knowledge. Truth. And darkness? Well, darkness offers us fear, and violence, and desperation. But there's nothing there, under the bed. The fact, the truth you demonstrate. 'See?' you say. 'Nothing.' And you smile and hug, and now he can sleep because you've proved safety through knowledge and understanding, as your ancestors did long ago. Stay near the fire, my son, and you will be safe from the darkness. Pursue knowledge, and you will be safe. For in ignorance be dragons."

Osgood stared out the window, looking at the distant buildings of downtown Chicago over the rooftops of Andersonville. "So, why would I tell this story that seems to uphold the conventional 'wisdom' that there's nothing in the darkness to fear, except the occasional brown recluse?" She was asking herself as much as her listeners. "I tell it to remind us all that the conventional wisdom is usually right! It's incredibly unlikely that there is, or ever will be, anything of concern under your child's bed. Or in his closet. Or in your attic, or basement, or crawlspace. In fact, it's almost a foregone conclusion that the average person will never encounter anything paranormal at all. As those of us who hunt them are well aware, apparitions are extraordinarily rare. Real entities, beyond those orbs we all know are just the light of the flash reflected off motes of dust and showing up out-of-focus in our pictures. I am privileged and cursed to have seen them, after all.

"But that privilege makes me immediately think that thing I saw in the subway is a phantom. And I cannot believe that. Because the truth is I saw a woman dead. A real woman. Nothing hazy or questionable about that part, a woman threw herself on the subway tracks to ride the third rail. And then I saw something in the darkness. But I need to be skeptical, with eyes wide open. To recognize the absolute horror and trauma that's everywhere around us. This suicide is real, like the deaths that the Sun-Times loves attributing to the North Side

Ripper. The people are real. Ghosts, spirits, monsters—they usually aren't.

"As ghost hunters, our first priority, our default, should always be to disprove a potential haunting. We must remain skeptical. So we don't show pictures of those out-of-focus orbs to non-believers and say, 'See! Ghosts!' Instead, we look at every angle, every possibility. Everything it could be that *isn't* paranormal. The more vigilant we are about this, the more likely our methods will be respected when we find something. And we will be less likely to present something fake to the world. And I know a little something about presenting fakery to the world. Never again." She pressed the button and stopped the recording, sitting with it a moment longer.

"Never again," Osgood repeated, returning to her porch in the dark. Her investigations would be methodical, and the evidence would drive them. The act of investigating was a pure act. So, tomorrow, when they read the evidence and explored what they did today, they'd determine the next steps. And tonight, Osgood would drink, get more stoned, and find another distraction.

And, seemingly on cue, a distraction presented.

I have thoughts on today's podcast, said the text from an unknown number to the app on her phone for Spectral Inspector messages. **And I'd love to buy you a drink.**

tonite? Osgood thumbed back.

Unless you have a better offer?

Osgood glanced at her empty glass and nearly-spent joint. **I like to know who I'm drinking with.**

Yes, right. Ramona Yeagher. Maybe you know my radio show?

The name sounded familiar, but Osgood couldn't place it. She began to type just that, then instead jumped to a browser to search for the name:

Ramona Yeagher is a self-help guru and host of Chicago's late-night radio show *Feel's Good*.

Self-help guru? thumbed Osgood, hoping the skepticism came across.

You googled me! said Ramona.

I did, said Osgood.

Well, I've never in my life called myself that, said Ramona, **and I imagine you know a little something about being called things you'd rather not be.**

Osgood did indeed and said so.

I can come to you, offered the self-help guru.

After another glance at her empty glass and a rumble in her stomach that reminded her she'd not eaten anything today, Osgood asked: **Do you know Mary's?**

Ramona did.

SEVEN

"Before we go to drink," said Ramona Yeagher through the open window of her cherry Trans Am, "I'd like to take you somewhere."

"My father told me never to get in the car with a stranger," Osgood said, leaning down. She was being obstinate, but the truth was she desperately wanted to get in that car. Ramona's blond hair hung in curls cropped above her jaw-line. She wore minimal makeup, just a bit of shadow over her eyes and a brownish red tint on her lips. The sprinkle of freckles across the bridge of her nose entranced Osgood. Most people she knew with freckles seemed desperate to cover them up, maybe to be taken more seriously, but Ramona apparently had no such concerns. Osgood's brief research had turned up Ramona's age (52) and height (6'3"!). *Built like an Amazon*, thought Osgood.

"That's a good tip, but you've read my bio, you know my podcast, and surely you have a tracker on your phone there."

"A rape whistle, too," said Osgood, neglecting to mention the mace and far less legal taser in her satchel.

"See, you'll be fine."

Although a killer might be on the loose, Osgood knew she would. She could roll the dice on Ramona. With the help of her cane, Osgood climbed into the Trans Am. "Where are we going?"

"Not far," said Ramona. The muscle car roared as it pulled away. "I'm sure you're asking yourself what this woman could possibly want, especially considering we've not met before. But I've listened to your podcast long enough to—"

"You're a Specterino," slurred Osgood. She realized that she was, in fact, still quite deep in the thrall of liquor.

"Yes." Ramona laughed. "I can't help but feel affinity with you, Osgood. Can I call you Osgood?"

"Osgood is fine." She shrugged. "Os is better."

"You can call me Remy," she said, almost as a throwaway.

"Not Ramona?" asked Osgood. "Reminds me of—"

"Quimby?" suggested Remy, referring to exactly the young heroine of Beverly Cleary's series Osgood had in mind. "While Ramona is a wonderful name, and my professional name, I prefer to not be reminded of a little girl when with friends."

"Understood," said Osgood

"So," Remy began again. "You think a certain way. And, well, I think a certain way." A pause either belied an attempt at dramatic effect or nervousness. Even looking closely at her driver, Osgood couldn't tell which. "I have also died," Remy said.

Osgood's eyebrows went up. Of all the things Specterinos had told her to demonstrate, "We're the same, you and I," she'd never had someone else talk about their own dance with death. "To be clear, you don't think you're dead *now*, right?"

"No, I'm very much alive, but..." Remy brought her lithe fingers to the buttons on her blouse, nails painted the kind of deep red that could be mistaken for black in the right lighting. The first and second buttons of the flowy button-down were already unbuttoned, but she quickly unfastened two more and spread the gap. Thinking this a very unusual seduction technique but approving, Osgood leaned over to see what was to be seen. Remy Yeagher's pale skin was bisected by an angry pink scar running vertically between small, still-obscured breasts. The scar was old, whitened on the edges.

"Heart surgery?" asked Osgood.

"Transplant, in fact," said Remy. "My body didn't like it at first. I died for two minutes."

"Eight," said Osgood with a short laugh. She glanced at the scar again and shuddered, reminded of what had clawed its way out of her own chest once.

"Having died, I look at life quite differently. And try to be open to seeing what's beneath life. Behind it."

"The great existential question: Why are we here?" agreed Osgood.

"What *else* is?" corrected Remy.

Osgood stared, and Remy was silent for a moment. She didn't know why this woman had contacted her, but she was plenty intrigued.

The Trans Am slowed to a stop in front of a brick building, about three stories tall, sitting alone. The name etched above the door was St. Gregory's Gymnasium. Osgood looked at it and then back, "Remy... This is not what I expected."

"I know. Trust me, you will leave this building understanding why I brought you here."

"You're not going to try to convert me to Catholicism, right?"

"Don't you have to believe in something to convert?"

"I believe in plenty," laughed Osgood, "Just not the big Judeo-Christian sky bully."

"Fair enough." Remy climbed from the car, hustled around to the passenger side, and opened Osgood's door. The woman's legs were defined beneath her chinos and so incredibly *long!* She offered her hand, and Osgood took it. Like

Osgood's, Remy's fingers were cold, but something about her touch comforted Os. More than she'd felt comforted in quite a while. *That* was interesting.

They descended steps into the building's basement. Dingy mint and maroon linoleum lined the floor in a checkerboard pattern. The ceilings felt low, pocked with recessed light. When they turned the corner into the room that seemed to fill this entire lower floor, Osgood saw lines of cafeteria tables and chairs and fifty or sixty people milling about. Their average ages seemed to be around 13, maybe, and adults in their 30s. One of those adults, a woman with dark hair and dark circles beneath red and watery eyes, approached Remy, holding a tissue.

"Thank you so much, Dr. Yeagher," said the woman.

"I'm here for anything you need," assured Remy. She hugged the woman, and after a moment, the teary woman seemed lighter, upbeat enough to introduce Ramona Yeagher to the room. Many knew her, it seemed, and more knew *of* her. Osgood wondered if her date was a big *get* for this event, whatever it was.

As Remy made small talk with a small cluster of adults at various levels of tearfulness, Osgood roamed until she found a table adorned by two school photos of young girls. Teenagers, maybe, but just barely. One blond, one redheaded. Both wore strained smiles that betrayed their disdain for these non-selfies. The girls were dressed identically, in powder blue polo shirts with a monogrammed left breast. Osgood couldn't quite make out the initials. SGG, maybe? Printed on the photos in a calligraphic typeface were the names Sophie below the blond and Anna below the redhead. Looking at the table, Osgood saw a memorial guest book and more scattered photos of the girls, both together and separate. Next to the printed photos, a framed digital slideshow flickered through images, nondescript instrumental music quietly playing, as though someone had wanted to turn it off but could only manage to bring the volume way down. A 4x6 print caught Osgood's eye. Three young girls. The two from the portraits, but younger, one with the telltale line of a retainer crossing her teeth, the other with full-fledged braces, and a third, another blonde, with a mouthful of teeth that would need intervention. The trio was bunched together, squeezing each other tightly and putting on the largest grins their little faces could manage. Osgood felt a melancholy nostalgia for growing up with Audrey. Their early days. The excitement of friendship, of exploration, of those little inklings of love.

"Aren't they adorable?" asked a woman in her early forties, pointing at the photo in Osgood's hand.

Osgood gave her a smile and a nod; of course, they're adorable, two of them are dead, they're the cutest children ever. *Prudence! I raised you better than that.* "Sophie and Anna?" Osgood asked, holding the photo in the direction of the portraits. "And..."

The woman took the prompt. "Elizabeth. My daughter."

Must be hard for the girl, thought Osgood. A quick glance around the room found Elizabeth standing in a cluster of kids her age.

"You are?"

Osgood turned back to the woman. "Osgood."

"Just Osgood?"

"Just Osgood." After confirming, Osgood scanned the room again to find her driver. Remy, standing amid a group, gave her a wink that set Osgood's tummy aflutter. *Let's try to be a grownup here, Pru.* "And you?"

"Shannon," she said. "Garcia," she added after a moment.

After a bit of silence, Osgood said, "Please give my condolences to your daughter and the families." Then she moved away, making for the cluster of adults speaking to Remy.

"—happy to schedule it at St. Gregory's. Why don't you

have someone call my office on Monday?" Remy took an opportunity to step back from the group, now murmuring about her suggested plan.

Osgood flicked her head toward the door, and Remy nodded but held up a single long finger. Then she went to a few of the adults, took their hands, spoke comforting words, and returned to Osgood. "You're much better at that than I am," whispered Osgood.

"Twenty-five years as a grief counselor makes one emotionally bullet-proof," she whispered back.

As they left the building and returned to the Trans Am, Osgood watched Remy. The interactions had seemed to do some good for not only the adults in the room, but also Remy. A flush had reached her pale face. "So," said Osgood. "Not just a self-help guru."

"I like to think I'm much more than that," Remy replied, pulling away from the gymnasium. "What are your impressions?"

"My impressions," repeated Osgood.

"Those two young girls were killed a year ago today."

Osgood waited, still uncertain what she was being asked. "How ... did they die?"

"Knife," said Remy flatly. "The details have been withheld by CPD, but one was stabbed through the lower chin upward, and the other in the eye socket. Both had their throats cut."

"Seems extreme," said Osgood. She looked down at her hands and wondered what emotion she was expected to present. Grief? Would that be the standard? She hadn't known the kids, after all. Shock, surely. Yes, the idea of dead children should always elicit a shock response.

"You don't need to show any emotion or reaction," said Remy, without looking away from the traffic on Ashland Avenue.

Osgood squinted at her. *You read my mind*, she thought, waiting to see if Remy might confirm that. She didn't.

"I brought you there because I wanted you to get a feel for them before I dumped something on you."

Holding back a scatological joke, Osgood nodded and said, "Hit me."

"Drinks for that," said Remy.

"You read my mind," said Osgood.

EIGHT

Like so many other restaurants, Mary's Diner and Bar had closed during the highest-risk times of the COVID crisis. The purple and pink haven for drag brunches and enormous cheeseburgers, and Osgood's favorite bar (mostly because it filled the first floor of her apartment building), nearly didn't reopen when Chicago's restrictions had started to ease. The expanded outdoor seating on the street between Clark and Ashland had to be returned to the motorists, and ultimately, Mary's had to forfeit the other half of the restaurant to an expansion of the Brown Elephant thrift store. The bar, though, remained.

"I'm guessing you come here often," observed Remy when Esteban (a delicious androgynous twink who Osgood had been disappointed to find out was really-for-real gold-star gay) set a Scotch, no rocks, in front of Osgood and handed Remy a drink list.

"Where everybody knows my name," said Osgood, making quick work of half the Scotch. "At least they did, at one point."

After Remy ordered a glass of Barbera, she folded her hands on the table and smiled at Osgood.

Osgood gave her a light smile back. Nothing toothy, of course, because that dying tooth on the back right wouldn't do to be shown. *And when do you plan to take care of that, young lady?* Someday. Surely, it'll stop hurting. *When?* Osgood remembered the words of C.J. Cregg. "When I die." But they hadn't come here at her behest. Didn't Remy have something *she* wanted to share?

"Tell me about your inner monologue." Remy sipped her wine.

Osgood's brow narrowed. "My..."

"Don't say you don't have one; I can almost see the ongoing conversation happening in your head. Is it your voice or someone else's? Mine is usually mine, occasionally my sister's. She's the more critical voice. I'm rather nice to myself."

A laugh escaped Osgood's lips. Damn, this woman was straightforward. "While I am most critical of myself, the voice is usually my mother."

"Is she still alive?"

"Pretty sure she's going to outlive me. Who else will stand by my graveside as my coffin is lowered and say, 'See, that's why you shouldn't drink so much.'"

Remy swirled the red in her glass. "Is that what's going to kill you?"

"At this point, I'd be surprised."

"Why?"

Again, Osgood searched for something in Remy's face. An angle, a motive, a deep-down desire. She found only interest. Interest emitted from a beautiful face. Her eyes, which Osgood had initially thought very pale blue, seemed not gray but radiant silver. Osgood stared into them, noting the slight smile wrinkles on either side. She was looking at Remy's lips when the woman said her name.

"Am I making you uncomfortable, Os?" asked Remy Yeagher.

Yes, you are, thought Osgood, *but in some rather confusing ways.* The throb between her legs felt so powerful that surely Remy could hear it, but at the same time, there was the other discomfort on top. Osgood didn't like to talk about herself or her past. She preferred to focus on things external. Outside. Facts. Finally, she asked Remy to "Please tell me why we're here."

"Very well," said Remy. "You witnessed a suicide last night."

"I was there when a suicide happened, but I didn't see it happen," said Osgood. A minor distinction, surely, considering what else she'd seen, but *that* could be omitted. Especially when speaking to one of the "straights."

"My radio show is the money maker, but my practice is grief counseling," said Remy. "I suspect you have a burden, and if I can help you relieve it, I would be most happy."

Osgood cocked her head to the side. A grief counselor. Randomly showing up for her. Was it Zack or Audrey trying to relieve some guilt they were feeling for not being around as much? Had her mother and father finally gone insane and decided to force their adult daughter into some sort of therapy, or—

"You don't like therapy, do you?"

"It's never helped me," growled Osgood.

"Me neither," admitted Remy. The woman leaned back in her chair, crossed an arm over her chest, and drank down the rest of her glass. "That isn't why I'm here, anyway."

"To counsel me?"

"Do you need counseling?"

"No."

"Would you like counseling?"

"No."

"It's a fool's errand for a therapist to try to counsel those who don't wish to participate in the process." Remy got Esteban's attention at the bar, then pointed at her empty glass and Osgood's, also nearly gone. He nodded and began preparing the next round. "Then what do I want?"

"Yes, Remy, what *do* you want?" Osgood said. "You're not some starfucker who wants to fuck the lauded Spectral Inspector, are you?"

"Would it be so awful if I was?" Remy's smile was devilish but mirrored Osgood's own.

"No," said Osgood. "You're fucking hot. I love tall women. I bet you could destroy me with a strap-on."

Remy just smiled as Esteban set down their drinks and scurried away with their empties. "I'll admit, I had two reasons to want to meet you. First, I read a galley of your book that your publisher sent over. The first supernatural book I've ever read that felt as much like a meditation on death as a treatise on the supernatural."

Osgood nodded. "Her" book, titled *Shadows of Reason*, had been chiefly written by Audrey, but some of the longer and more meditative passages had come from Os's rambling monologues on the podcast, edited and organized by Audrey. It had been a team effort.

"Well done there," continued Remy. "The second reason is that Chicago is experiencing a strange spike in deaths."

"The North Side Ripper?" asked Osgood. A table nearby got quiet, the women there seeming to want to hear more. Mention of the ripper was enough to draw everybody in the neighborhoods of Andersonville, Edgewater, and Rogers Park into a communal sense of morbid curiosity laced with fear.

"Partially," said Remy. "Did you know that the school hosting tonight's memorial has had four students murdered, and two commit suicide, in the past year?"

"I..." Osgood stopped. How had she not heard this? "That seems like an absurd statistical anomaly; that's a grade school, right?"

"It's K through six, middle school, and then high school. One of the suicides was in middle school, the other a junior at the high school. One of the murders was an 8-year-old girl, Ashley Morales. Her father is in the Cook County system, waiting to be tried. He insists he had nothing to do with it. A freshman boy, Rodney Karras, the two girls from tonight, Sally Benson and Anna Kolciech. Those three have been attributed to the 'North Side Ripper,'" Remy said it in such a way to make the scare quotes known. "Across the north side of Chicago, there are six more murders. The youngest is 6, and the oldest is 23. In this collection I'm identifying, I mean; there are far more deaths than that in general. The more disturbing thing, though—"

"More disturbing than a 6-year-old being murdered?"

"As the crow flies," offered Remy. When Osgood didn't understand, she added, "Big picture, I mean. 30,000 feet."

Osgood nodded.

"Eleven suicides. The youngest 9, oldest 22, all in unusual ways." Remy finished another glass of wine. "You know the usual: wrist cutting—"

Osgood held up her left wrist, the faded white T scar still visible, a semicolon tattoo beside it. Remy gave that a moment's reverence before displaying her own semicolon tattoo on her right wrist. Osgood nodded. Respect.

"Wrist, uh, cutting," continued Remy. "Garage asphyxiation, you know the drill."

Only too well, thought Osgood.

"But these thirteen suicides are different. Your Red Line jumper, by the way, was 16-year-old Callie York from Ravenswood."

Osgood knew that the mid-teen years were when many teenagers became suicidal. Some actually tried, but most didn't. Most were brooders. Her own first attempt had been at 15, but a curling iron in the bath attached to an outlet with a safety shut-off didn't do much of anything. *But 16.* The woman from last night. The goth woman with the black Chucks had indeed been just a girl. Osgood looked down, noticing a pearl droplet of Scotch on the lacquered tabletop. She poked at it with her finger, and it burst.

Remy rolled the stem of her wineglass between her fingers, looking at it thoughtfully. "I hope I don't seem callous, not bringing the emotion to this discussion."

This startled Osgood back to attention. "What? No. It's fine. I just—"

"Have feels," suggested Remy.

"Feels," said Osgood. "Yes."

"Then I'll cut to the chase. Suffice it to say, these suicides fall into the statistical anomaly camp. And the murders? Well, while they share some common themes—most are blade killings, a couple are gunshots—there's nothing really tying them together except that the CPD would rather look for one person than ten."

"You don't think it's the North Side Ripper?"

"I don't think there *is* a North Side Ripper."

Osgood finished her Scotch. At the bar, Esteban cocked a black pencil-darkened eyebrow. She shook her head. "You're building to something."

Remy nodded.

"But as a professional woman in psychology," suggested Osgood, "you're hesitant to wade into the paranormal?"

"Not exactly," said Remy. "But you're not the first person I've explained this to."

"No one bit?" asked Osgood.

Remy shook her head.

"What makes you think I will?"

"Truthfully?" asked Remy. It was a rhetorical question, but Osgood nodded anyway. "No one understands broken people like broken people."

Osgood chortled. Had her reputation preceded her?

"Not only you, Os," said Remy. "Me. This is why I can see it."

"See what?"

"Have you ever heard of the Graveyard Game?"

Osgood shook her head.

"It's a TikTok thing."

"I don't do social media," said Osgood. Then she laughed and rolled her eyes. At Remy's expression, she explained, "I always hated people who'd say, 'I don't *have* a television,' yunno? Like that makes them somehow superior to those of us who center our rooms around them."

Remy waited.

"Well, I don't mean to sound like that. I *did* do social media, but after Twitter crashed, I didn't see a point in finding anything new," Osgood dropped her voice a bit. As she leaned forward, she felt the slosh of the Scotch. "And I don't understand TikTok. Looking at that app made me feel ... *ooooooolllll-llldddddd*."

Remy laughed and nodded. "Don't worry, I didn't take it negatively."

"So, the Graveyard Game."

"Yes. The Graveyard Game. You go to a cemetery. First, you find a stone with your birthday on it. The year is irrelevant. Then one with your parents' birthdays. *Now*, you look for the year you were born. If you can only find a death year for your birth, you move on to finding your first name. If you can—"

"Kids are doing this?" interrupted Osgood.

"And filming themselves all the while."

Osgood laughed. "In my day, we used to just go smoke and fuck in cemeteries."

"I'll skip a bit," said Remy. She flagged down Esteban, this time asking for port.

"Two," said Osgood.

"I love port," said Remy.

"So do I," said Osgood.

"So, if you do the steps in the right order, it's said you'll begin to be drawn to the next step, and not have to look hard."

"How much time are they spending in cemeteries at this point?"

"Shush," said Remy.

Osgood smiled. There was something so familiar about the way she shushed. Not as though they'd known each other or had done this before, but there was a comfort level that would befit a longer relationship. *Don't attribute to fate what you ought to attribute to booze, Os.* That one was Audrey.

"You get to the end, and it's a statue. Usually hooded. Sometimes it's an angel, other times it's Death in a shroud, you know the kind. And if you climb up and look inside, you'll see your death."

Leaning back in her chair, Osgood frowned. She thought about it a moment. "Huh. And the deaths?"

"Every suicide had TikTok on their phone. I've confirmed that five of them completed the Graveyard Game."

"Not just played," said Osgood.

"Completed," said Remy. "And all of those did it a few blocks from here."

"At Rosehill Cemetery." said Osgood. One of Chicago's largest and oldest. The final resting place of Aaron Montgomery Ward, his business rival Richard Warren Sears, and John G. Shedd, president of Marshall Fields and benefactor of the Shedd Aquarium.

Remy nodded and pulled something up on her phone. She

slid it across to Osgood, who knew it immediately. The monument stood nearly at the direct center of Rosehill Cemetery, eight feet tall, dark metal, a shroud of a figure. No face, just a hood.

"The Guardian," said Osgood.

"The Guardian," repeated Remy.

NINE

Osgood made a point to lock the door behind her after stepping into her apartment. After all, she was sober-ish, at least by Prudence Osgood standards, and wasn't trailing a woman or man in some state of undress as they stampeded toward her bedroom. Not to say she hadn't tried.

Remy had been rather sweet about it. "I don't believe in mincing words when it comes to things like this," she'd said as they stood outside Mary's, closer than acquaintances typically stand, listening to the Clark Street traffic.

"Okay," Osgood had replied with a grin.

"You are lovely."

"So are you."

"But." A self-conscious smile had crossed Remy's face, and she looked away. The demure look only made Osgood want her more. "I get a real sense of 'stuff going on' from you. I can't be the balm."

Osgood had crinkled her forehead. She'd been about to ask, "Stuff?" But she knew what stuff. The same old stuff, after all. The stuff that kept her from a successful long-term relationship. The stuff that made her drink. The stuff that caused her to push away everyone, especially those she liked. Osgood had considered making a Hail Mary pitch, but instead she thanked the tall, gorgeous, brilliant woman, then watched her climb into her Trans Am and drive north on Clark.

"My stuff," she told the empty room with a sigh. The living room lights were low. On the table sat a single rocks glass with pale, watered-down whiskey at the bottom. "Curious," observed Osgood. She perked her ears up and heard only the sounds of Chicago: a distant siren, a souped-up coupe with a glass-pack muffler, the random shout of someone calling for their dog ... or wife, maybe?

Osgood turned to the hall and saw a line of warm light. Audrey's door. Open a crack. She walked to it and stood. Just because there didn't seem to be any fucking currently happening in that room didn't mean Osgood should be shoving her way into the evening her friend had planned with ...Kent. He'd always been ...Kent to Osgood, not because there was anything wrong with him, nor was he objectively annoying. He just had a face she wanted to punch, and the name went with that. Osgood saw the ellipsis, her brief pause, as that punch, though she'd never tell Audrey that. Still, she probably was foolish to think that Audrey didn't know precisely how Osgood felt about ...Kent. After all, this wasn't that different from how Osgood had felt about the other guy Audrey had dated. Or that woman, for a couple weeks. Though the woman had hurt more, hadn't it? Boys were stupid. Boys were boys. But Osgood was Audrey's girl, wasn't she? Traditionally, anyway. Historically.

"You're not as stealthy as you think," came Audrey's voice from the room. "I mean, for fuck's sake, you use a cane."

Lifting the cane from the floor, Osgood looked at it momentarily, then prodded the door open. Audrey lay in her bed, holding her arm straight up, Kindle in hand.

"You know that position is as like as not to give you a black eye in the morning."

"New Kindle's lighter," said Audrey without looking over. Her friend, her once-lover, her favorite human, Audrey, continued to read her book, making a showy tap of changing the page.

"Are we disgruntled with me?" asked Osgood. She chose to lean against the turquoise wall just inside the room. She glanced around Audrey's space, always so neat, clean. *Spartan* thought Osgood. *This is how a living area ought to look, Prudence. If your things are out, you either need more storage or you have too many things.* But Osgood knew the answer to that riddle from her mother. She had too many things and no intention of having fewer.

"Not disgruntled, no."

"That's good," said Osgood, affecting a tone that suggested she might not care. She waited.

"You came up," said Audrey, turning the page again.

Osgood's eyebrow lifted slightly, but she worked her ass off to keep it imperceptible.

"I may not have previously told him that we dated."

A chortle escaped Osgood. "Oh, really?"

"Not everyone is cool," defended Audrey. Now she set her Kindle on her bedside table, also spartan, with only a charging stand, a box of Breathe Right strips, and an oversized green water bottle.

"Very few are, I'd argue," said Osgood. "Are you saying I came up because he disliked that you'd dated a woman?"

"No. Well..." Audrey looked conflicted. "He seemed fine ... that I'd dated a woman."

"Such rousing support. Should we get him the cover spread for Allies magazine?"

"He doesn't like that we work together," finished Audrey, "and live together."

"Does he think I'll seduce you back with my magic vulva?"

Audrey fixed her with a look, and Osgood raised her hands. Yes, she was making fun, because this guy was a joke, right? Audrey had to see that, right? But her wide blue eyes suggested that *she* didn't think he was a joke or find it funny.

"You kept it from him because you feared he would react poorly," said Osgood. It wasn't a question.

A nod from Audrey.

"And now that he knows, he's reacted poorly." Osgood shrugged. "Take comfort that your instincts are correct, even if you're too thick-headed to follow them."

Audrey's eyes narrowed at her. "Try not to enjoy this too much, Os."

"I'm not enjoying it," she replied. "Boys are stupid. Case in point."

"Oh, like you don't ever date boys," said Audrey. "What about Sam—" Audrey stopped herself, her eyes widening. The silence had a presence of its own. Sampson Goddard. Yes, he was the prime example of a man Osgood had dated. Dated long enough and seriously enough that Cynthia had been thrilled her daughter might have gotten over that pesky lesbian phase. She'd refused to even acknowledge the concept of bisexuality.

Had Osgood wanted to hurt Audrey, she would've retorted "You mean the man I killed?" But she didn't. She knew Audrey was hurt just now, and hurt people hurt people.

"I'm sorry," said Audrey.

Osgood forgave, but she wasn't willing to cede the hurt, so she just nodded.

"Really," continued Audrey. "I didn't mean to suggest that..."

Shaking her head, Osgood smiled weakly and repeated the thesis, "Boys are stupid."

This time Audrey nodded.

TEN

It was in the wee hours that Zack Nguyen joined the women upstairs. Audrey and Osgood were deep into their White Widow vape by then, acquired via a bootlegging trip to Michigan, where pot was *also* legal, but the restrictions and taxes weren't nearly as high as in The Land of Lincoln. Osgood was about to tell him about their new shared mantra, "Boys Are Stupid," and invite him to be an honorary girl, when she noticed his trail. Behind him stood Sandy Hedges, of the South Side Ghosthunters. The first woman Zack had dated in the ... *jeez, almost a decade?* they'd been working together. Best not emasculate him now. Instead, she coughed out a "Hi," and offered the vape to them. Zack passed, Sandy puffed.

"Mind if we join you?" asked Zack.

Osgood laughed. In that near-decade, Zack had made a point to make whatever space he was in his own. In fairness, that had mostly been due to Osgood's inability to manage it herself. He was the one who locked doors, set up their systems, and organized the "smart home" installation, whatever that meant. All Osgood knew was that if she asked Jarvis to turn on the living room TV, he would, which delighted her. Realizing that Zack was still awaiting a response, standing next to his girlfriend, Osgood said, "Please do." She saw the relief in his eyes. For a moment, Osgood wondered how difficult it was to live with her, then recognized that was a thread she likely ought not pull.

"I showed Sandy the footage from the subway," he said. Was there a tinge of guilt there? "We also looked at the readings."

"Nothing?" asked Osgood. Her eyes were on Sandy: blue hair, eyeliner, and a pierced lip. Her own type. Osgood shoved the thought out of her mind as quickly as it had appeared.

"Mostly nothing," said Sandy. "Weird spike just before Jackson, though."

"Where I—" began Osgood.

Zack nodded. "Where you saw..."

"The thing."

"Zack couldn't explain what you saw to me," said Sandy.

"Because Osgood couldn't explain what she saw to *me,*" said Zack, an air of defensiveness in his voice.

"Weird spike," repeated Osgood, blowing off the idea that she needed to describe the thing she'd seen in the subway. The long thing, the smiling thing.

"Weird, in that the EMF spiked exponentially, but I'm talking only momentarily, microseconds."

"So short we didn't see it?" asked Audrey.

Zack nodded. He flipped on the TV above the fireplace. Taking his tablet from his satchel (Osgood wondered if he'd worn it on their date, and momentarily pictured his scrawny naked body on top of Sandy, satchel hanging from his shoulder, then shook it off), he tapped some apps until the screen showed a graph. "The subway itself registered anywhere from 65 to 85 milligauss. Its fluctuations were pretty consistent, though." He tapped, and the screen showed a rolling red line, muted hills and dips. "Occasional spikes up to 110 mG I attribute to the sparking of the third rail."

"Speaking of sparking the third rail," said Audrey. She snapped her fingers at Osgood and giggled. Os handed her the vape, stifling her own giggle with her hand. They looked over at remarkably sober Zack and tried to contain themselves at his baffled, or perhaps annoyed, expression.

"Proceed," said Osgood, twirling her wrist in a flowery fashion.

"Y'all aren't going to remember any of this tomorrow," said Zack. "Maybe we should—"

"Now, now," Osgood said. "We're all present. Right?" she asked Audrey, who bobbed her head in a wild nod. "Sandy?"

Sandy laughed. "Oh, I'm fine." Then she reached out for the vape.

Audrey, exhaling her own, passed it.

"I'm going to get a contact high," said Zack.

"It's not sexually transmitted," said Osgood. He fixed his eyes on her, and she shrank into the couch. "So, the gausses spiked?" She could tell that it took everything in Zack's power not to correct her, which amused her to no end.

"Here," he said, zooming in on the graph. Closer and closer until a red vertical line appeared, closer and closer until it became an inverted V spike. "1.5 Tesla."

"Wait, what?" asked Audrey, coughing, but not on vapor.

"It's the briefest of spikes, again, milliseconds, but that's 1500 mG."

"That's dangerous levels, isn't it?" asked Audrey.

"Sustained exposure, yeah," said Zack. "I mean, technically sustained exposure to the L train's base levels is dangerous, though."

"Great," said Osgood. "What does this tell us?"

The four of them looked at each other for a moment.

"Well," said Zack. "You know that EMF fluctuations can cause hallucinations."

"How did I know you would go there?" asked Osgood.

"Because I have a rational scientific mind?" asked Zack, with an edge in his voice.

"I didn't hallucinate," returned Osgood, with a matching edge.

"How do you know?"

"Because I've hallucinated before."

"That doesn't *help* your case."

"Guys, c'mon." Audrey held up both of her hands. "Zack, I'd like you to assume Osgood *didn't* hallucinate. What's next, then?"

Zack took a contemplative breath. "Well, I'd want to survey that route again with higher sensitivity equipment. Maybe compare it to other routes?"

"That sounds good."

Osgood looked between them and frowned. "I've got something else," she said. She knew she was bringing it up so she could once more be the center of the conversation, but she also recognized it was worth bringing to them. "The North Side Ripper doesn't exist."

Audrey cocked her head. "How do you mean?"

Zack nodded. "I agree with that."

Osgood looked at him. "You do?"

"Yeah," said Zack. "The MO differs so much from crime to crime that it's difficult to even categorize some murders as *potential* victims of the Ripper. Far more likely he doesn't exist, and it's just coincidence."

"I agree," said Sandy Hedges.

Osgood wondered if she was simply siding with Zack or if she truly agreed with his thesis.

"Six murders. Most of them college age or younger," said

Audrey. "People get killed all the time, especially in this city. But usually it's stray gunshots. Or deliberate gunshots."

"Didn't someone with a machete attack a tourist in Grant Park last week?" asked Sandy.

"Oh, you suburbanites," said Osgood dismissively.

Sandy laughed in surprise. Osgood couldn't quite tell if she was offended.

"Believe it or not," said Osgood, wrenching back control of the conversation, "I had a point. It's not just a wild, random theory. Anywhere from six to thirteen murders are attributed to the North Side Ripper, but ten seem to fit the pattern of random killings whose only connection is violent deaths north of Lincoln Park. But add to that an epidemic of suicides. Eleven, in fact. Same area, same schools, same ages. Something doesn't feel right."

"Where did this come from?" asked Audrey, skepticism in her voice.

"I met a woman tonight who—"

"So you *did* have a date," accused Audrey.

"What?" asked Osgood. "No. She wanted to share a theory she had with me. She's a grief counselor. Ramona Yeagher."

"Dr. Remy?" asked Sandy. The rest looked at her. "She had a sex questions radio show when I was in college."

"And how long ago was that?" Osgood asked, more venomous than she'd intended.

Sandy ignored it. "Seven years."

Osgood tried to do the math. How old was Zack, again? Younger than Osgood, but how old—

"Doesn't she do that self-help show now?"

"Yes," said Osgood, impatiently. "But she's *also* a grief counselor and said *this is all strange*." Osgood made sure to hit those last four words hard. Hard enough to make the three listening, two of them fellow Spectral Inspectors, one of them girlfriend (why did she feel the need to delineate like that, especially when here she was bringing someone else's theory to their group), understand and maybe focus. "What do you know about the Graveyard Game?"

"We did it on our podcast," said Sandy. "At Bachelor's Grove."

Knowing what she knew about the Graveyard Game, Osgood found the idea of doing it at Bachelor's Grove, one of the most haunted cemeteries in the country, abjectly terrifying.

Sandy shrugged. "Nothing happened."

Zack nodded, turning to his girlfriend. "That's when you did the thing with the tombstone dates, right?"

Sandy nodded back. "The statue didn't manifest."

"Okay," said Audrey. "What is this?"

They explained it to her. Sandy knew much more about it than Osgood.

"It's hot right now because it's on TikTok, so all the kids are doing it," she said. "But there've been variants of it for decades. In the '40s and '50s, it was a dare to test your mettle, and far less complicated. As the years passed, it was an urban myth that if you did these things at the exact right time of the year in the correct order, you'd find the statue and learn your destiny. It became a 4chan and Reddit thread, then a creepypasta story, something the kids did when they weren't too busy eating Tide PODS or ice bucket challenging each other. TikTok refined it, though. The rules always seemed arbitrary in earlier variations. You still had to look for dates and names, but they were often connected to numerology or moon phases. Once it shows up on TikTok, you can almost watch the rules solidify. But as they did, the results produced far more no-show statues."

Osgood nodded at Sandy, impressed. Maybe dismissing her as just "girlfriend" was a bad idea. "Zack, do you know the Guardian statue at Rosehill?"

He nodded and tapped his tablet. Within a few seconds, the ominous cloaked figure appeared on the screen.

"I know that statue," said Audrey. "Ambrose Ballard's wife is buried beneath it."

"So what does all this mean?" asked Zack. "It's really easy to work ourselves up with superstition and coincidence, but some real people are dead here."

"Kids," added Osgood.

"Exactly," he replied. "So, it'd behoove us to be cautious and compassionate."

Osgood smiled at that. He really was essential, wasn't he?

Audrey cocked her head. "Could we go through the TikToks of the people who've died, to see if—"

"Well, a weird part of the Graveyard Game is you're supposed to delete your video of it within the week. It's meant to be ephemeral, not permanent," said Zack.

"Well, without the ability to see how they did it," said Osgood, "I for one would like to try The Graveyard Game."

"I have this awful feeling you're going to say you'd like to do it tonight." asked Zack.

Osgood nodded.

"Os, we're really stoned," said Audrey.

"All the more reason," said Osgood. "Why? Don't you think this is a good plan?"

"Um," said Audrey. "For starters, again, really high, so probably not making great decisions in general."

Osgood chose not to concede that.

"Also trespassing," said Zack.

"It's a cemetery; the worst they do is kick you out," said Osgood.

"Osgood," said Sandy.

"Yeah?"

"The end of the Graveyard Game, if you do it right, is supposed to tell you how you'll die," said Sandy. The trio turned to her. "And as you seem to be connecting it to a bunch of murders and suicides... Could it be true?"

"Why do you think I want to find out?" asked Osgood.

"Well, sure," said Sandy. "But if it *is* true..."

"Maybe I'll find out how I'm going to die," said Osgood.

ELEVEN

"This *isn't* the Graveyard Game, yunno," said Zack. He showed her his phone, which featured a step-by-step text document detailing the various twists and turns and searches required for the TikTok game. Osgood calmly shoved the phone away and continued to walk into the dark.

Sitting on over 350 acres just west of the Andersonville neighborhood on the North side of Chicago, Rosehill Cemetery was one of Chicago's oldest and most prestigious collections of the dead. The tombs, mausoleums, and monuments spanned centuries, from the very earliest deaths in Chicago to the dawn of the new millennium. Osgood had spent many hours walking along the various paths through the graves, always finding it a peaceful place. The lawn was well manicured, the trees blossomed beautifully, and the groundskeeper never left flowers out past their prime. She'd increased her thinking walks after she'd returned from ... outside. And had COVID not interrupted, well, everything, she would likely still have been doing it regularly. But now she couldn't walk more than a few blocks without getting winded. That recent multi-mile trek had probably taken full years off her life.

With a waxing moon in the sky, the quartet didn't need flashlights, all the better because security had grown tougher since the murders began. The North Side Ripper, real or not, was having an outsized effect on policing. The wind rustled through the trees, carrying an icy chill along with it. Osgood had donned her maroon leather trench coat before they went out. *At last*, she thought, *my armor is complete again.*

"I just don't see the point of doing this unless we're going to follow—"

Osgood cut Zack off with a guttural hiss that startled him. "Shush, will ya!"

Zack stood, forlorn, as Osgood and Audrey pressed on. After a moment, Sandy put her chin on his shoulder and gave him a kiss on the cheek. He perked back up.

"*We* could do the full thing," suggested Sandy.

"No," sighed Zack.

Osgood knew when you got right down to it, the important bit was at the center. The preceding shenanigans seemed to be fail-safes. Ways to excuse why the game hadn't worked. Not ways to make sure it did. Regardless, Osgood wanted to look into the Guardian's eyes. She wasn't quite certain why. Well, no, that wasn't true, was it? She wanted to prove it was nothing. The statue had no power, just like every other "haunted" object she'd ever encountered.

"You're really going to look?" asked Audrey, scooting up next to her. Osgood watched as she checked the map on her phone, then checked it again. The hour was late, they were all tired.

"Why wouldn't I?" asked Osgood.

"I would think someone who's died might play a little less fast-and-loose with something that could be connected to other deaths."

"That's a lot of supposition."

"What do you want from me?" asked Audrey. "I got dumped tonight."

"What?" Zack asked, walking fast to catch-up.

"Yeah, Kent and—"

"He couldn't handle that Aud and I used to suck pussies."

"*Wow*, Pru," said Audrey.

This brought the quartet to a halt.

"It's true," insisted Osgood.

Audrey stared at her, mouth agape, for what seemed like a full minute before looking down at her phone and turning away. "This way."

As Zack passed Osgood, he clapped her on the shoulder. "Tactful as always, Os."

Sandy came up last, leaning into Osgood and whispering, "*I* thought it was funny," before walking on.

Osgood watched them cluster together. Zack and Audrey quietly commented to each other. Sandy moved in next to them. Here again was the thread, the one she kept picking at and cautioning herself not to pull: the expendable nature of her own contributions to the Spectral Inspectors. *But no,* thought Osgood, Audrey and Zack had worked their asses off to find her when she was

(in the territories)

gone. They'd done so without blaming her, either. And when she'd put them all in danger, because she had little doubt about her responsibility for the way it had all ended, they'd stood by her. They loved her. They supported her. Why now would things change? *Exhaustion,* she told herself. Frankly, Osgood was exhausted, 45 next year, and the myriad pains her body produced weren't getting any better, just moving their stabs around, hiding more effectively from pain meds. Combine that old chronic bullshit with being a long-haul friend of the 'rona, and Osgood wondered if her mental exhaustion finally matched her physical. If she was this tired, why wouldn't they be? Audrey had somehow managed to avoid the plague entirely, and still masked up when indoors. Zack had got it way back at the beginning, or so he thought. He'd definitely gotten sick in February of 2020, but had never lost his sense of smell.

Their exhaustion wouldn't be physical, though, she thought. It'd be the stacks upon stacks of drains on their attention, emotion, and affection for her.

Quit being a fucking baby, Spooky, said Goddard. *They haven't left you yet, and you used to be a much bigger dick.*

"Thanks, Sam," whispered Osgood as they approached the center of Rosehill Cemetery.

As though cued by some unseen global stagehand, the clouds parted and the lunar reflector seemed to point their way to a small hill. There, not twenty feet in front of them, was the Guardian. The statue was covered in similar patina as Lady Liberty, and many others, but the Guardian's green was deep and mossy, somehow wet, and overlaid a base both polished to reflection and black as pitch. The Guardian was a representation of cloth, without a visible figure beneath. A robe or cloak, from top to bottom, the hooded countenance in darkness. The arms of the cloak hung empty at the ends. It reminded Osgood of an art class her freshman year, when Mr. Pinley had tried in vain to explain to her that she wasn't to draw the model, but the space around it; to focus on that gesture and essence. Now here she stood, looking at a gesture and essence that hinted at something beneath. But that something wasn't human.

"'Sculpted between 1902 and 1903, the Guardian, was intended to watch over industrialist Ambrose Ballard's 6-month-old daughter Samantha, who died of the flu in early '02,'" Audrey read, squinting at her phone. "'By the time of its completion, the Guardian stood over both Samantha and

Ballard's second wife Cora, who, in early 1903, the Chicago Tribune claimed died of a broken heart.'"

"That's grammatically odd," said Sandy, quietly.

Both of Zack's hands held devices. An EMF detector in the right, and one she didn't recognize in his left.

"It's taller than I thought it'd be," Sandy said, breaking the quiet again.

Osgood wanted to assure her that it was okay she had joined them, and she shouldn't feel a need to comment every few minutes. *Is that bitchy?* she wondered.

"Twelve feet, including the base," said Audrey.

Osgood looked into the dark shroud at the top. She wondered if the statue even had a face deep within that shroud, or if she'd just find a blank plane. Whichever she'd find, Osgood knew she desperately wanted to climb up and look into its eyes.

"How are people ... doing the thing?" asked Zack. "The eye thing." He didn't lift his own eyes from his devices.

"There's a bench," offered Audrey.

Turning, Osgood saw it, an old elaborate cast-iron bench, small, probably made for a child. "That could work," said Osgood. "Only need a two-foot boost or so."

"You don't seem to have a good grasp of size, Os," said Audrey.

"We can..." Osgood looked for any other option, until, finding none, she blurted, "turn it on its side." She nodded to herself. Yes. That would do it. She approached the bench and was met by Sandy, who smiled at her.

"Braver than I am," said Sandy.

"I'm sure that's not true," said Osgood. But wasn't it? As the two of them hauled the bench over to the Guardian, and up onto the platform, Osgood glanced at Zack's instruments. "Anything?"

"Nothing interesting," he said with a shrug, "But also not sure what to look for."

"Fair," said Osgood. She reached up and grasped the arms of the statue, spreading her own arms wide to reach, then stepped up on the bench. Nearly there. Her eyes came right about to the base of the facial opening.

"Not quite," said Audrey. She resumed scrolling on her phone.

"How about y'all boost me?"

"Os," asked Zack.

"Yeah?"

"If our working theory is that this Graveyard Game is somehow responsible for both murders and suicides..."

"Yeah...?"

"I didn't think I'd have to continue," said Zack. "Why would you want to chance doing something that would point whatever's happening at you?"

Osgood, on her Chuck Taylor-clad tiptoes, face against the cool metal of the statue, arms spread wide, flicked her eyes to him. "'Cuz it's there?" she asked. "The same reason we played the *Ramparts Over the Hinterlands* album. Somebody has to. At least this way, we'll be going into it with eyes wide open. Now c'mon, boost me!" Out of the corner of her eye, she thought she saw him nod at her reasonable point, then felt three sets of hands boosting her.

As she rose over the neckline and saw into the dark face of the Guardian, she was impressed that her eyes wouldn't adjust to its darkness. She wondered if the true face of it was simply the backside of the hood, a concave inky blackness. With groans and strains that Osgood thought a bit much, they managed to raise her a few more inches, and there she was, eye to "eye" with the Guardian. For a moment, she even thought she could see eyes, but reasoned that was just pareidolia, a desperate attempt to see something in nothing, a face where there was none. In any case, face or not, eyes or not, Osgood saw only darkness. "No prophetic vision of how I'm going to die," she called down to them.

"Can we put you down, then?" asked Audrey.

"Wait!" exclaimed Osgood. She dug in her pocket for her phone, then remembered she'd moved it to the inner breast pocket of her leather coat. She felt the world lose stability for a moment as those below her shifted. Phone up, flashlight on, camera open, she pointed the light into the void, seeing just that. "The Guardian doesn't have eyes," she told them. "Or a face. It's blank." She stared into the hood a moment longer and then felt her stomach lurch as they brought her back down, bypassing the wrought iron bench and returning her all the way to the ground.

"Maybe it's metaphorical eyes," offered Sandy. "Like look into the statue's gaze."

Osgood shrugged and pointed at it. "My face was right in front of it. Eyes, gaze, whatever it's supposed to mean, I think the myth about seeing your own death when you look in there is just that. A myth."

Dejected, perhaps, and some grumpier than others, the quartet left Rosehill Cemetery at just after 3 a.m.

TWELVE

"You feel as though you're losing your relevance."

Osgood ponders that for a moment and agrees. Remy Yeagher gives her a solemn nod, and they descend into the subway station. As they move down the stairs, the heat below hits like a wave, breaking upon the stone steps. "Holy shit," says Osgood. This time, Remy's nod is less solemn and more playful. When their feet hit the subway platform, the temperature feels 20 to 30 degrees warmer than the surface streets above. It's night again; there's no reason these temperatures should exist at night! Osgood feels beads of sweat beginning just under her hairline, sliding down her forehead. "I don't like sweating in front of people. I..."

"What?" asks Remy. The grief counselor's hair hangs in lazy curls. Her makeup is subtle to the point it looks nearly like she has none on at all. The light dusting of freckles feels intentional, but Osgood knows it isn't. This isn't a woman who'd spray them on, or, as Osgood once did, flick henna at her face off a paintbrush.

"People I like," says Osgood, a note of finality to the statement. *Well, there it is,* comes into her brain, absurdly in the voice of Emperor Joseph II. But not the *actual* Emperor Joseph, of course, the one played by redheaded pedo creep Jeffrey Jones.

"Are you telling me that you like me, Prudence Osgood?" asks Remy. She steps closer, and Osgood can smell her, a mixture of lavender and tea tree oil. Not even a note of sweat, even though Osgood, personally, is seeping. Remy leans into Osgood's ear. "That you ... *like me,* like me?"

Osgood feels at a loss for words, so she giggles in a way most unlike herself. She looks up at the screen displaying train arrival and departure times, hoping for a distraction, any distraction. *Why is this so difficult?* she asks herself. But she knows why, doesn't she? Because Remy has already told her why. She'd gotten a real sense of "stuff going on" from Osgood. Osgood underlines the word <u>stuff</u> in her brain. She can see the stuff. Piles of it, in fact. Heaped into the trunk of a 1982 Buick Skylark she hasn't owned in decades. The 1982 Buick Skylark she totaled. The 1982 Buick Skylark she died in.

But Remy died, too, remembers Osgood. In fact, Osgood thinks she can see the faintest trace of that scar through the sheer black top Remy wears over a black bra. Surely, she must be too warm in that. It has long sleeves, after all. But Remy shows no indication that she's warmer than usual.

They stand in silence, side by side, at the blue stand-back line that rims the rail pit. Osgood wonders where they're going, why she can't remember, but the concern is only fleeting, replaced almost immediately by the calm warmth radiating from Remy Yeagher. Osgood looks at her and smiles. Remy smiles back. Osgood wants to kiss her, thinks that if she were able to, to just lean in, to go up on her tiptoes just the slightest, that so much of her stress and anxiety would go away. Somehow, she feels, Remy could replace that *stuff*.

Bing-bong!

The Red Line L train sits in front of them. How is that

possible? Did it just slide in when Osgood wasn't paying attention?

Doors opening.

Osgood steps toward the open doors of the seemingly empty train but feels Remy's hand on her arm.

"We'll get the next one," whispers the woman.

That makes sense to Osgood, who nods and steps back.

This is the Red Line train, bound for— a moist static replaces the destination, and Osgood frowns. She looks to the left, looking for the front car, but can't see it. The L seems to go on an astonishing number of cars in that direction, disappearing all the way into the darkness of the tunnel between stations. The right reveals a similar revelation: an endless train. *Doors closing.*

The hiss of hydraulic fluid always makes Osgood think the L train is being hermetically sealed, but of course, she knows that's not true. It was on this very train line that Osgood had exposed herself to the 21st century plague, after forgetting her mask and deciding to risk it after a night of very heavy drinking. She'd gone out with Nora that night. Poor Nora, sweet Nora. All the girl had ever wanted was her affection. Didn't even need it to be monogamous. But that'd been too easy, hadn't it? The promise of being able to do anything

(anyone)

she wanted and only need to come home to a gorgeous college-aged girl in a tight college-aged body with an optimistic college-aged mind and, what? Love her. Love her, just a little bit. Too easy. "Sometimes I think I self-sabotage," Osgood tells Remy.

The woman nods and takes Osgood's hand. Again, she leans in, spa scents wafting into Osgood's nose. "You most definitely do," says Remy.

Osgood starts at that. Feels harsh, doesn't it? After all, friends aren't supposed to just agree with you when you say bad things about yourself, are they? They're supposed to defend you. That's their job. But is Remy her friend? She's most definitely not her lover, much as she might want that. But *does* Remy want that? Or is she using "no" as an excuse to be friend-playful? Osgood knows friend-playful. It's the line she has to walk with Audrey. Especially since ...Kent. Friend-playful is talking about how sexy she is. Talking about wanting to eat her out is decidedly *not* friend-playful.

"I promise to never lie to you, Osgood." Remy fixes her silvery eyes on Osgood's. They shine in the strange bluish fluorescent light.

Seems an odd thing to say, thinks Osgood as she watches the Red Line train blast forward out of the station. But it doesn't leave; it just ... continues. Car after car after car. Most are empty, but then they start to fill up. She sees dark silhouettes. People reading newspapers, people with backpacks, people sporting 1940s-style fedoras. The windows flicker by her like a zoetrope until, at last, the train cars are packed to the gills, seeming to bulge outward with the excess mass of their passengers. And just as Osgood is about to gasp, to question, to say something, anything, about this strange phenomenon in front of her, it's finished. The final car moves past her and into the tunnel. She can see a reflection of herself in the back window, and then it's gone in the dark. A shower of sparks kicks up behind it, and they lazily circle before wicking out.

That reflection of herself. That bothers Osgood. There's no way she should've seen a reflection of herself in that window. The angles don't match. Besides, the image of herself in that window had been different. That one was wearing her maroon leather trench coat. Osgood, standing here on the platform, is wearing only a T-shirt and jeans. Suddenly, she feels underdressed, looking over at Remy Yeagher in a sheer top that shows her modest chest and taut belly. Remy in wet-look leggings, the kind that you might mistake for leather or vinyl. No wonder Remy doesn't want to date her. It's not the stuff, is it? It's *her*. Everything about Prudence Osgood is a mess and has always been a mess.

"I'm a messy bitch," says Osgood to herself quietly.

"You are," confirms Remy.

Again, Osgood feels a pang of pain, thinking that friends are supposed to disagree. Even if they promise never to lie, they don't have to volley the insult back. There are any number of ways to make someone who has just called themselves a messy bitch feel better about it. But looking into Remy Yeagher's face, Osgood *does* feel better. She's not sure why, but the woman's eyebrows slope gently, her eyes are wide and open, and the hint of a smile on her lips suggests no malice. Never malice. Only a refusal to coddle. And really, what has Osgood done lately to deserve being coddled?

Bing-bong! Doors opening.

"The fuck!" Osgood jumps back from the new L train. This one is only two cars long. Far more appropriate for... What time is it? Osgood cranes her neck back but can't see the clock hanging in the center of the platform. It feels early. Not the middle of the night, no. That had come and gone.

"This is our train," says Remy. She puts a hand on Osgood's shoulder, and both of them step into the empty car. They move to the front seat, the view that could be horrifying or exhilarating, depending on how one felt about motion. Osgood loves the feeling of careening out of control into the darkness. Of course, she knows the L is very much under the control of both the driver and the tracks before them, but the sensation still falls into that glorious space between driving really fast and a roller coaster. The women sit, and the L car doesn't move.

Osgood waits for the *Bing-bong! Doors closing.* But it doesn't come. Their window overlooks the dark tunnel to the next stop. Before them, they see a short zig by their track and a zag by the other, as the two directions separated by the platform come together into two twin tunnels in the dark. In the distance, she sees an amber light lazily clicking on and off. Caution, it suggests. Osgood narrows her eyes. Hasn't it always been just green and red lights?

"I wonder why we're not moving." Osgood debates pounding on the driver's chamber door next to them but thinks better of it. What's she in such a hurry for, anyway? She's here with her new friend Remy. What could she need so quickly? Why must they leave?

"The show," says Remy.

Osgood looks at her, but Remy's eyes stay fixed on the tunnel before them. Osgood looks from the woman to the dark, woman to dark. The sparks flare, briefly lighting a bit of the tunnel before fizzling back into nothingness.

"Ooh, aah," says Remy.

"Something's wrong," says Osgood as a fresh shower of sparks cascades in a parabola before them. Osgood leans over and knocks on the driver's door.

"You'll miss it," says Remy.

Osgood knocks harder. She sees, out of the corner of her eye, a shower of blue sparks joins the orange. *Nothing weird about that,* she thinks. *The electricity is often blue sparks.*

You sure about that? Zack asks her in her mind.

Osgood isn't. She bangs on the door now, standing as she does it. Finally, unable to take any more, she grabs the handle and yanks, expecting to fight with the door, but it slides open, easy as Sunday morning. And there's no one behind it. No driver. "Maybe they're driving from the back," Osgood thinks aloud. She's about to rush toward the car behind them when Remy grabs her hand.

"You're going to want to see this," Remy says firmly. Her face is still serene as Osgood cautiously returns to the seat next to her. There's no malice there. There is not even a hint of darkness behind a façade. Her serenity is genuine. She points into the tunnel. Two clusters of sparks dance and swirl around each other like fireflies putting on a show. Maybe that's what this is. Just fireflies. Osgood has heard of something called emergence that happens with large clusters of the beetles. They'll go from flickering at different speeds and tempos to all being synchronized.

That doesn't mean they dance, Audrey tells her.

No, Osgood agrees, *that is weird.* Like the murmuration of starlings, these sparks dance.

Remy excitedly taps Osgood's shoulder and points into the darkness.

Osgood needs help understanding what she's supposed to be doing differently than she is right now. She tries looking harder but sees nothing beyond the dancing sparks and the blinking amber light.

(*cha-click*)

Nothing at all in the— But wait. That's not exactly true, is it? Emerging from the inky dark, as though Osgood's vision is getting more and more used to it, is that poor goth girl who died.

"Callie York from Ravenswood," says Remy, precisely as she'd said it at Mary's a couple of days ago. Or had that been today?

Callie's pale white face looks pleading. Her eyes are open but unfocused. Her lips hang apart ever so slightly, the way they might if the mortuary assistant hadn't sewn her jaw shut tightly enough. The girl wears a Spectral Inspectors tee, their one-step-below-copyright-infringement logo. She wasn't wearing that the other night, Osgood knew. This is different. Osgood hears herself echo back. *Something's wrong.*

"See how she dances," says Remy, as the body of Callie York from Ravenswood moves as though performing that Evolution of Dance set. She's stiff.

Of course, thinks Osgood, *Rigor has more than set in.*

"But that's not why," Remy says.

Osgood knows she's dreaming, has suspected it for a while. Nowhere but in her dreams is anyone she talks to as annoyingly opaque as this, anyway. Though Remy clearly has her own secrets in real life, this is something else entirely. Suddenly, Osgood sees the answer. She feels the tiny prickles at the nape of her neck as the hairs stand up. The prickling goes all the way across her shorn scalp. All this time she's been watching Callie, but Callie was never the show. The show is behind her, and it is almost blindingly pale. Its skin, if it can be called that, is sallow and wan, a color like purple mixed with white and pale peach. The circles under its eyes are dark and deep, and its lips, drawn back to expose long teeth, are nearly black. As before, it's smiling at her. It's peeking around Callie York, and Osgood realizes that it is controlling the dance, puppeteering, its hands on Callie's arms, something on Callie's legs that Osgood can't figure out because this thing in the dark seems impossibly long, like the L train.

"What is it?" she whispers to Remy.

Remy's eyes are filled with tears. "She's in pain."

And Osgood can feel it, radiating off Callie, the pain of loss and fear and exhaustion, not as acute as her usual pain but far more all-encompassing. She begins to cry.

That's when the murmuration of the sparks swirls and becomes something new, something Osgood has seen before. Swirling faster and faster, the sparks pulse, ramping up in speed and brightness as Callie York and the Pale Long Thing dance. The sparks start to multiply and compound atop one another, forming clusters and groups, continuing to swirl, and becoming that thing that had frightened her during a trip to the Planetarium with her father. She must've been only 5 or 6. A time when she'd enjoyed the star show for its sights but couldn't really comprehend it. Until she'd seen this. The narrator had spoken of distant objects called quasars, and the entire dome ceiling had shifted to show her an artist's impression of one. The one above her had made her uncomfortable, and she didn't understand why, but she'd grabbed ahold of her father's hand tightly. The narrator told them that it was over 600 million light-years from Earth, reminding them that a light year was the distance light could travel in a single year, and that the jets emitted from the center were often over a thousand light-years long. The scope of that horrified young Osgood, seeming both impossibly long and impossibly far.

Decades later she'd seen that quasar again. First in the space between worlds, her little private kingdom at the crossroads, and then watching over the hordes of things dying to enter our reality.

She looks to Remy and knows without question that she sees the quasar as well, may even see what it's revealing itself to be, the horrifying orange eye in the sky. Whatever Remy does see, though, the tears on her cheeks speak the volumes that the three words she actually says cannot:

"It's the end."

THIRTEEN

She awoke with tears in her eyes and the quasar eye filling her mind. Osgood groped for her glasses, finding used tissues, the wrapper for a condom she couldn't recall when she'd used, and a book with a cracked spine facing down. There, atop the book, were her windows to the world. She turned her head to her bedside clock. 4:16 *a.m. or p.m.?* she asked herself. Lately, that'd been an issue. She wouldn't get enough sleep at night, then take a nap at some point during the day. This had been fine until her hour-long naps became three- to four-hour epics matching the sleep she got at night. Osgood decided to roll the dice and guess p.m., as they'd been in the cemetery until at least 3:30, and that dream she'd had, that was no fifteen-minute REM dream, that was something altogether

(the end)

different.

Osgood, perch on the edge of her bed, pressed fingers into her eyes beneath her glasses. When she didn't find the relief she craved at first, she pressed harder, watching geometric shapes and tunnels flash in her misfiring vision. There was the pain, and then it felt better. She followed this by shoving both hands into the tangled curls on her head until she found knots, then yanking quickly enough that some hair came out by the root. "Better than coffee," she grumbled. Now she just waited, listened. In the distance, she heard orchestral music, something classical, the kind Audrey listened to as she studied.

"And as she masturbates," Osgood reminded herself with a sly smile. Osgood and Audrey didn't share a wall; the bathroom sat between their rooms and included a wet wall, but it was an old building, and sound traveled. Maybe because Aud wanted it to.

She shouldn't perch here long, she knew; the bend of her knees was already starting to throw pain sparks up both of her thighs, crisscrossed with years' worth of thin white lines of

(better than coffee)

"relief."

Years, thought Osgood, *Decades, more like!* She could still remember the day she had found her father's safety razor in her parent's bathroom, and below it a box of double-sided blades with which she had absconded. She also remembered the questions she wouldn't, couldn't, answer, when the box, with many fewer blades, had been discovered in her room. Osgood knew that wasn't the worst thing her parents could have, and eventually did, find in teenage Pru's bedroom.

She knew her pain receptors, now just waking up, would start screaming the moment she put her feet on the floor and stood. From the plantar fasciitis in her left heel to the remnants of her decades-past car accident, including a bone fragment still lazily journeying through her right calf because, when given the option of a surgery that *could* lead to permanently restricted movement in her right leg, Osgood had chosen to stick with her familiar companion, endless pain. Ever the martyr, that Prudence Osgood. Didn't help that, in the years since the accident, she'd broken her right arm, pulled her left from the socket, had a concussion, and had brain surgery to remove a

(monster)

tumor from her head. *Honestly*, she thought, *the fact that I'm still moving at all is rather remarkable.* She lifted her phone from her bedside table, seeing several text messages.

ur screaming in your sleep, said Audrey. **if u do it again, imma wake you.**

Fair, thought Osgood.

Next, from her father Basil was the measured: **Os, my dear, please do consider coming home. Your mother may not have much time remaining.** She inhaled sharply through her nose, hit reply, and then stared. She knew that if Basil Osgood were watching on his end, he'd see the ellipsis. She closed the reply. Ellipsis gone. Cancer was a fucker she didn't want to deal with right now.

did you call me? was from Nora. Osgood frowned. She looked at her call log and, apparently, she had called the young woman who once could have been her girlfriend if she'd given it more than the faintest of chances. The call had lasted three whole seconds. This text *should* be answered. Osgood wondered, though, how to best approach it. *I didn't mean to*, would be quick, say lots, and would likely end the conversation. *I don't remember doing it,* would invite further questions and, Osgood suspected, discussion of her drinking. And then there was, *I miss you.* It might be true, after all. Osgood's subconscious, at least, seemed to want to reconnect with Nora, and wouldn't it be nice to have a semi-regular companion again? Osgood honestly couldn't remember the last time she'd had—

Well, that wasn't true, of course. Audrey. She and Audrey. Dating. For real. As adults. Osgood sure as fuck remembered that. And remembered the growing conflict, her roaming urges, her—

"I would never tell you that you have to be monogamous, Pru," Audrey had said through tears, "But when you fuck..." There, she'd broken down. For good reason, too. Osgood still only had the haziest recollection of it, but, apparently, she'd been picked up by a gay couple wanting to explore some outstanding questions. Even *that* hadn't been the problem, Os knew. Bareback with the both of them, though. There was the problem. Didn't matter that both had been negative for all the big scaries. It spoke to a judgment problem, didn't it? Osgood could make that decision for herself, but not for a partner. "It's disrespectful," Audrey said. "And your self-destructive behavior shouldn't take others down with you."

Self-destructive. Osgood had never particularly seen herself as that but knew why others did. She might even tell them they were right, should they come with a list of examples. Something that friends had done more than once. Something her parents had done. She sighed and thumbed the response, **I don't remember calling, but I'm happy I did. So I can say I miss you.** She wanted to throw down the phone; wondered if that would be slotted into the pro or con side. Self-destructive or not? She supposed she didn't know, but the ellipsis that appeared under her text to Nora spooked her, and she swiped to the next one.

Dear Prudence ... it's Remy. I had the strangest dream about you...

Osgood's heart thumped. Remy Yeagher had dreamt of her. Osgood hoped that Remy's dream had been less traumatic than the one at the subway with

(the end)

the thing that danced.

a good one, i hope ;) There, thought Osgood, let the winky face do the work. Typical sentences became flirty with the winky face. Flirty sentences became dirty. *And soon, we're going to town on each other's bits.* No ellipsis below this one.

Remy clearly wasn't waiting on her phone. No surprise there. Remy Yeagher was a grown-up, after all. And not a grown-up in the way Osgood claimed the title, essentially just a taller, older high schooler. Osgood had found her look in sophomore year and never seen much reason to change. Sure, she'd gone through dozens of pairs of Chuck Taylor All-Stars since then, different colors, different styles; but jeans, a tee, and the maroon leather trench coat that she'd discovered while "garage sailing" with Nicole Cruiz, whose affection was very much platonic and had confused Osgood for so very long, these were her mainstays. Remy wore expensive jackets and dressed to impress. Her hair was done in a salon, not hunched over an apartment sink. Hell, her pussy was probably lasered bare.

I miss you too.

Momentary excitement led to resignation. The message had come not from Remy but from Nora. The perfectly delightful young woman who'd probably finished college by now, who'd worn a strap-on on their first date and made Os come while beaming wide-eyed wonder from her own face. Osgood felt that a person who wasn't wired for endless self-sabotage would call the person whose affection wasn't in question, the woman whom even Osgood had to admit was likely a sure thing. After all, Remy had explicitly said that Osgood had too much "stuff" for them to be together.

Osgood's sex drive made the argument for her, though. *Doesn't need to date us to fuck us.* Very true.

wanna get coffee? drinks? soon?

She could feel something desperate about Nora's texts, especially the final question mark, and even as she had the thought, Osgood knew she wasn't being fair. No more desperate than **a good one, i hope**, and that fucking winky face. Hell, the emoji alone screamed desperation. Notice me! Think about me! Want me more than you do! Nora didn't even feel the need to use emojis, just straightforward messages.

No subtext. No games. Just genuine desire for... Osgood didn't even know. Maybe she just wanted a friend. Perhaps she wanted Osgood to finally get around to looking for her ghost. Maybe she *did* want to fuck the way they had that first night. But regardless, she didn't tip her hand with a fucking winky face. Only, **I miss you too.**

Swiping open the keyboard, Osgood sat, thumbs poised. How to respond? Moments later, though, she pressed the power button atop her phone and put her device back into black mirror mode. "I should have breakfast," said Osgood to the room. *Or dinner,* she thought. Regardless, coffee should be involved, as the minor pain from her eyes and hair follicles was nothing compared to what was about to happen. She laughed as she stood, straining when the pain raged up and down her legs, shooting through the small of her back, up her spinal cord, and waking up every single nerve ending in her body. She felt like the lead in some ponderous French new-wave cinema, smoking a thin, unfiltered cigarette and suggesting, "Life *is* pain."

That was enough for Prudence Osgood. Dwell on the pain, feed the pain, succumb to the pain. Fuck the noise.

She snatched her cane from its hanger on the back of her bedroom door and stepped into the hall, where the Chopin nocturne was loud enough that Osgood knew Audrey's bedroom door was open. She stood, torn for a moment, then turned left and went to the kitchen. Morning or night, she had to fucking wake up.

Fourteen

At Audrey's door, Osgood offered her friend, her once-lover, her roommate, a cup of coffee. Audrey declined. "I don't want to be up all night like you." This was a perfectly reasonable and reasoned response. Osgood sipped hers. Black. Bitter.

"So," Osgood said, dragging out the *o*. "Do you want to talk about …Kent?"

"Nope," said Audrey. The word was quick and clipped, leaving no ambiguity.

"You sure, because—"

"What's to talk about, Os?" Audrey set her Kindle down on the nightstand next to her but didn't turn her head toward Osgood in the doorway. Her face and her body remained pointed at the ceiling. "He left because he learned we used to suck cunts, right?"

Osgood thought she probably shouldn't have said that. "I didn't mean anything by it." After a moment, she did want to set the record straight, though. "Though I'm pretty sure I said pussies and not—"

"I'm not even really upset by it," sighed Audrey.

Osgood waited but required clarification. "Upset by my comment, or—"

"Either. Both." Now Audrey moved to sit on the edge of her bed. Her feet were clad in the no-slip socks one was given at the hospital. Especially the *very special* kind of hospital that only the luckiest of weirdos ever get to visit. Osgood knew because the socks, pink with white no-slip treads, belonged to her. Her friend put both hands on the edge of the mattress and looked down at her legs, bare, up to a thin pair of jogging shorts. Audrey's hair hung in dirty strands, and while the look might do it for Osgood, she knew it was more indicative of laziness and depression than intent to entice. "Did you need something?"

"Are you upset with—"

"Os."

Osgood frowned, staring at the top of Audrey's head. Perhaps her least favorite element of her neurodivergence was her inability to believe that anyone *wasn't* upset with her at any given time. After all, she'd had so much practice throughout her life. It was just a few years back that this woman in front of her, Audrey Frost, would've been more likely to tell her to "fuck off and die" than say even a polite hello. "Wanna help me dye my hair?"

Audrey did look up at that. Her eyes narrowed, looking for what? Nefarious plots? "Sure," said Aud.

In the bathroom, Osgood sat on the toilet as Audrey stood above her, wearing purple nitrile gloves. Audrey concentrated, her pink tongue sticking out ever so slightly between her pale lips. With the brush coated in Voodoo Blue from Manic Panic, Audrey pulled Osgood's curls and applied the dye, bit by bit.

"Nora messaged," said Osgood. "Well, I guess I messaged her, and she messaged back."

Audrey just nodded.

"I'm thinking of having another date with her."

Again, no more than a nod.

"But I really want to fuck the self-help guru."

That stopped Audrey mid-brushstroke. She lifted her arms enough to look under and meet Osgood's eyes. Audrey's own eyes spoke volumes, clear as day, but in case they weren't obvious enough, she asked the question as well: "What the fuck is wrong with you?"

"Valid question," replied Osgood.

"No response to it?" asked Audrey. She resumed the dyeing process.

"I self-sabotage."

"You *do* do that," agreed Audrey.

"I need a therapist."

"Hallelujah," said Audrey, in the least gospel choir way possible, quietly, almost under her breath.

"So I can help you promote your book."

"*Our,*" corrected Audrey, "Our book."

Osgood nodded. Try as she might, though, she couldn't reconcile that. "I didn't write it," she said finally. "My name shouldn't be on it."

Audrey seemed irritated by the suggestion. She shook her head. "It's the Spectral Inspectors book, written by the Spectral Inspectors." She paused again, pulling a bit hard on a lock of curls. But a tug from Audrey always got her cylinders firing. "Is this why you've been so erratic?"

"Long COVID," said Osgood. Though when you got right down to it, she had no idea why.

"You can't just blame long COVID whenever you—"

"Brain tumor, dead, murderer, monster host." Osgood stopped listing.

"These are all excuses, Pru."

Osgood pursed her lips.

"You know what I think you should do with Remy Yeagher?"

"Something tells me it's not what I'd like—"

"*Talk* to her," said Audrey. "I did some research. She's a well-respected psychologist. Or at least was, before her radio show. She dropped in the esteem of Chicago's psychiatric community after she took that on, but what can I say? I chase monsters for media attention."

"So *that's* why you do it…"

That got a laugh from Audrey. "Beyond that, though, Os, I don't know what I can tell you that you don't already know, or that you won't immediately dismiss."

"What have I ever—"

"You could quit drinking. You could promise to never use that knockoff Oxy again. You could, occasionally, look after your sexual health. You—"

"If this is about John and Marcus, I—"

Audrey slapped the brush down on the edge of the sink, sending a sickly splatter of teal across the white porcelain. "You've become difficult to talk to again," said Audrey after a moment, seeming to gather her thoughts. "And I don't know what to do about that."

I've become difficult to talk to again, thought Osgood, letting the words simmer. "I'm sor—"

"I don't want apologies from you, Os," said Audrey. She washed her hands in the sink beside Osgood, who remained seated on the toilet. "Because apologies don't matter if you keep doing the same things repeatedly. And when I let you, that means I'm just doing the same thing again and again."

"The definition of madness."

"Yeah," said Audrey. "Is it my madness or yours?"

Osgood tried to lighten the mood by cracking a quick laugh and looking away. "Well, I know that *I'm* crazy."

Cold fingertips on Osgood's chin turned her back. Audrey had crouched to her level, and they looked eye-to-eye. "The real problem, Pru, is that I extracted myself from our relationship—"

"Extracted?" Osgood disliked the word.

"*Due to* your insistence on being self-destructive and feeling like I didn't want to go with or watch."

"Yes," said Osgood. "I'm well aware."

"What I should've realized then was that living with you, working with you, I'll *always* have a front-row seat to the Osgood Destroys Herself show." Audrey stopped and stood, staring into the sink as the last dregs of water burbling down the drain grew louder and then faded to nothing.

Osgood thought better of her instinctual, "Well, duh."

"I love you, Os," Audrey said, before splashing her face with water and drying it quickly. "I really, really do. But you don't. I don't think you ever have."

Hard to argue with that, Osgood knew. Perhaps the closest she'd gotten was liking herself a little when they'd been minor celebrities with their TV series. But that'd been nearly a lifetime ago and one of the pinnacle moments of Osgood's self-sabotage. What could be said? What *should* be said? She sat quietly, looking at the side of Audrey's face. She feared an apology wouldn't be appreciated, judging by Audrey's response to her previous apology in this very conversation. What else was she supposed to do? Promise to change? To be better? To try? Osgood wanted to offer all those things but knew as well as Audrey that the results were contingent on every other little thing going on. Because Osgood's stability was like a row of dominos that grew larger down the line. Little issues knocked into bigger issues, bigger issues became full-fledged problems, and problems, well, they became catastrophes. Finally, Osgood just stated the conclusion she'd reached. "I don't know what you want me to say."

Audrey sat on the rim of the tub. "I don't *want* you to say anything. You improving your life isn't for me. It's for you.

You changing or *wanting* to change is all on you. And I'll fully agree that you've had an especially rough go of things. No one deserves to have gone through as much full-throttle shit as you have. No one should be expected to function at a level even approaching normal when they've been outside the known universe."

Osgood opened her mouth to stop Audrey but got a hand to talk to instead.

"Hell," said Audrey, "I'm not well adjusted either."

Because of …Kent, thought Osgood, but no, Kent was a symptom, like Osgood's haphazard libido, casual regard for drug contamination, and bottomless repository for liquor.

Audrey put her face in her hands. "I'm not asking you to change, Osgood."

"Okayyyy…"

"Just," she began, then stopped. "Maybe don't look through people when you look at them. Through them, to whatever your momentary goal is."

Osgood considered that. She was about to promise to … what? when she was interrupted by the obscenely loud *buzz!* of the front door buzzer.

"I'll get it," said Audrey, standing. "You should rinse your hair."

Standing in the shower, Osgood watched rivulets of Voodoo Blue roll down her body. Not wanting to think about anything that had just been said, Osgood focused her attention on a droplet of blue-green that lit among the dark brown thatch of her pubic hair. She recalled her terrible idea once upon a time to bleach and dye herself down there. Oh, how it'd burned.

You should not avoid what she said, suggested her mother in her head, without adding, *Just as you shouldn't avoid me.* Osgood knew the voice, as strong as it was, was merely her imagination. As were the voices of Audrey and Goddard in her head. Just her conscience, taking on various personas. But, whether Cynthia or her internal monologue, Osgood knew the voice was right. She *shouldn't* avoid this. She knew Audrey was right, as well, and no amount of mea culpas or apologies would change what had been. Only...

What are you supposed to do? Change who you are entirely? That voice... Well, that one Osgood couldn't be certain was in her imagination. It sounded a lot like her, and most of the time she could write it off as such. Still, sometimes, like in this moment standing below the showerhead, several holes blocked by enough calcification that they flickered, spitting water only at random moments, she couldn't put aside the idea that this was ... Prudence. Not herself, not Osgood. But the avatar Prudence, the imposter Prudence. The one that lived in her

(kingdom)

dreams at the crossroads where she'd died. The one that was *really* the Lord of the Hinterlands. And who knew what *he* truly was?

With a shudder, Osgood ignored that voice entirely, shut off the water, and, shivering, grabbed a towel from the hook. Before she dressed or even dried completely, she looked in the mirror. Her scalp still had some dye on the shorn-with-a-number-two-guard left side. On the right, the curls mainly looked black, plastered against her head, but in thinner spots, and at the ends of the coils, she saw the teal, the Voodoo Blue. Having applied it, like the last color, directly atop her previous one gave it a bit of iridescence in the right light.

"To go with my colorful personality," Osgood suggested to the empty room before pulling a shirt over her head. Surprise visitors didn't rise to the level of deserving bras. With that, she went to discover who'd rung.

FIFTEEN

"And this is my partner, Prudence Osgood," said Audrey, introducing her to a familiar-looking woman with dark curly hair. The woman, with watery eyes and a red-tipped nose, held a balled tissue in her left hand. She reached out her other hand toward Osgood.

"I'm more of a wave person these days," said Osgood, holding her right palm up and shrugging with a bit of a self-conscious smile. If there was one thing she'd love to get rid of in the post-COVID days, it was the handshake greeting. The Asian bow was the way to go here, she felt, but no one had any idea what to do with you if you bowed. Not to mention her back couldn't handle it anyway.

"Oh, of course," said the woman, "Hello. I'm ... Moreau." She shook her head. "Vanessa ... Moreau. Dr. Ramona Yeagher told me to come see you." She pointed to Osgood, surprising both her and Audrey.

"Moreau. Like the Doctor." Osgood laughed at her reference, which only seemed to mystify Vanessa. How could that be? Surely, she'd heard that growing up. "Well, uh..." Osgood stammered, wishing she'd put on a bra after all. What if

Vanessa reported back to Remy how utterly unprofessional Prudence Osgood was, coming to the door in sweats and a t-shirt? At least the shirt had their logo on it. "Sure. Would you like…" Osgood noticed that there was already a mug of coffee sitting on the table at the center of the couch. The guest seat. The client seat. She and Audrey could sit on opposite sides and get the complete 180-degree impression of this woman. "Why don't we sit."

Vanessa Moreau nodded quickly and for a long time. Then turned and moved back to the couch. She sipped her coffee and smoothed her slacks. She looked at Osgood, as though waiting for *her* to begin.

Begin Osgood did. "Can you tell us *why* Rem… Ramona recommended that you come to see us? To see me?"

"You were at the memorial the other night," said Vanessa. She dabbed at her nose with the balled tissue that was clearly doing nothing at this point.

Osgood and Audrey met eyes, and Audrey insisted upon the box of Kleenex at her end of the table. Osgood slid them over to Vanessa.

"Thank you. Dr. Yeagher has been so wonderful the last couple of months. Especially considering the horrible club we belong to now."

"Club?" asked Audrey.

"I'm sorry, I'm a mess," said Vanessa. "My daughter Sophie was one of the first victims of, well, *I* think, the North Side Ripper. A year ago last week."

"Oh my God," said Audrey. "I'm so sorry."

Vanessa nodded in a way that only someone who had gone through something unimaginable could. "She was only 14. They found her and her friend Anna in the industrial park on the other side of Ravenswood. Just south of the cemetery."

"The double homicide," whispered Audrey. Her voice

took on a more professional air as she added, "I read about that one. Absolutely horrible."

Sophie's mother plucked two tissues from the box and dabbed her eyes. "I don't know what it will take for them to catch him. This city has gone to shit." Vanessa looked alarmed. "Excuse my French."

Osgood and Audrey nodded.

"The police kept this for a few months," she reached into her purse and pulled out a small rectangle wrapped in a cloth napkin. Unwrapping it, Osgood saw that it was an iPhone, the model a few years old now, in a red case complete with bunny ears. "They said they couldn't find anything noteworthy. She was supposed to meet her friend Beth that day. Well, they had been less ... friendly ... since Sophie went to high school. You know the pressure children that age feel to be part of their specific group."

Boy did Osgood know.

"At the memorial, Dr. Yeagher asked if I still had this or could get it. It isn't charged, I'm afraid. I have a, whatsit, Google phone. Anyway. She told me if I could find it, I should bring it to you."

"Did she say *why* she wanted you to come to us?" asked Audrey.

Vanessa shook her head.

After a moment of silence, Audrey's tone changed to tactful concern. "Mrs. Moreau."

"It's Miss. Moreau is my maiden name. And was Sophie's name. My ex..." She scowled for a moment, then returned to polite pleasantness. "He's no longer an issue. But no 'Miss.' Please. Vanessa."

"Of course," said Audrey. "Vanessa. Did Dr. Yeagher tell you what we do?"

Vanessa looked between them. "You ... catch ghosts?"

Osgood snorted a laugh and immediately regretted it. She

covered her face, apologizing, as Audrey gaped at her tactlessness.

"Not exactly," said Audrey. "I apologize for my partner here. We explore supernatural phenomena. Ghosts can be part of that, yes, but we don't aim to catch them so much as to understand."

"She also said you lost your sister..." Vanessa pointed to Osgood.

"No," said Osgood, shaking her head. "Actually, Audrey was the one who lost a sister. To a supernatural force."

Vanessa appeared to consider that deeply, nodding down at the phone in her hands. She ran a shaky finger along the case's ears. "I don't know much about what happened to my Sophie. And since it's an active investigation, the police won't tell me anything, either. But if there's a chance that the two of you—"

"And our other partner, Zack," Osgood quickly threw out.

Vanessa seemed confused about why that mattered. "Three of you, then, could figure out what happened. Or..." At this, the tears flowed anew, and Vanessa Moreau pressed the tissues to her eyes. "Or, *why*... I need some closure. And I don't think the regular channels will give it to me."

Reaching her hand out for the phone, Osgood mustered her best professional tone. "Absolutely. We will do everything in our power."

"I," said Vanessa, again looking between them. She waited a moment and then took out a checkbook.

Ahh, yes, here's where you give us money for our services. This part always bothered Osgood, and for the longest time, she'd forced Zack to do it, even though his stammering and circular logic had occasionally gummed up the works. Since Audrey had joined the crew, though, the money thing was going more smoothly. They actually got paid on occasion.

"We can talk about that. But there's no payment tonight," said Audrey. "We need to see if we can help first."

In other meetings, "if we can" had meant "if we want to" or "if we choose to," but this time Osgood saw clearly that Audrey had meant what she said. She wanted to help. Hoped they could. Osgood did, too.

With another nod, Vanessa Moreau handed Osgood her daughter's cell phone. Osgood nodded, smiled, and thanked her. She meant to take the phone down to Zack's dungeon immediately, but before she could turn, Vanessa touched her hand. "Dr. Yeagher thinks very highly of you."

Osgood's brow furrowed. How could that be? She barely knew the woman. And it definitely took years to think highly of Prudence Osgood. Even after that length of time, one was as liable to hate her as love her. "Well," said Osgood, a bit of a stammer in her voice. "I, I think highly of her as well."

Nodding, Vanessa opened her mouth as though she would say something further, but then didn't. Osgood met Audrey's eyes and gestured with her head toward the back. Audrey nodded. She'd take it from here. Osgood could go on ahead.

As she walked through her apartment toward the back door, Osgood tried once to turn on the phone. It wasn't completely dead, she saw the "please plug me in" indicator on the screen, but it wasn't coming back to life in her hands. She stepped out the door behind her kitchen, feeling the awful balmy air hit her. She sighed. *Remember fall?* she asked herself. Chicago didn't get much of a fall season anymore. Things went from the scorching dog days of August directly into sleet and snow. Sometimes, there was a week of rain in between. And other times, like this year, summer roared back with a vengeance at random when leaves should be falling. Osgood trotted down the back steps to the ground floor and turned the knob on Zack's dungeon. Locked.

"Fucking kidding?" asked Osgood. How could she blame

Zack for locking the door? There was a killer on the loose after all. She hit the doorbell with the camera in it. After a moment, she heard some clattering, and the back door opened. Zack waved her in, squinting at the light. "Were you sleeping?" she asked him.

"Yeah. We were out late last night," he said, scratching at the patchy scruff on his chin and neck. Zack could do anything, it seemed, except grow a beard. Osgood explained the phone to him, and he took it, walking them both over to his command center, an array of six monitors stacked three over three. "Doesn't work 'cause it's not charged."

"Thanks, dingus," said Osgood. "I figured you'd be able to handle that."

"I can," said Zack. "Dick."

Osgood laughed at the sheer lack of energy in his comeback. "Touché."

"Are we looking for anything specific?" he asked her, plugging the phone into a squid of cables snaking all over his desk.

"I don't really know," said Osgood.

"The kinds of things the police don't find," offered Zack.

"The kinds of things the police don't *look for*," returned Osgood.

Zack nodded. "Aye, aye, cap'n." He saluted for good measure.

SIXTEEN

"The Graveyard Game," said Zack. He didn't elaborate as he typed at this keyboard, then that one, then clicked through some windows on a third system.

Audrey and Osgood stood behind as Zack rolled between keyboards at the bigger-than-it-needed-to-be workstation. Osgood assumed it impressed at least one specific ghosthunter.

"We played that already," said Osgood, growing impatient. Audrey shushed her.

"Ha ha," said Zack. His symphony of clicks and clacks came to a crescendo, and he pressed enter. The six monitors went dark, and a vertical video appeared, split across the center two. Poorly framed in the way only a novice streamer would do, the bottom two-thirds of a young girl's face appeared, no more than 13 or 14. Her voice still had the cadence and sound of a little girl, even if her words were that of a teen. The light but distinct red tint on her lips was meant to evoke "older," of course. Zack slapped the spacebar, freezing the image of the girl. "Based on the," Zack sighed, "literal *thousands* of selfies on here, this is Sophie Moreau."

He hit space again, and the video played.

Shaky footage, poorly lit, but moonlight creeping through the trees here and there showed monuments. "A cemetery," said Osgood.

Zack nodded. "The cemetery." He scrolled forward through footage that showed a handful of girls indistinctly stopping and pointing at different tombstones before finally, "Our cemetery." He slapped the spacebar at just the right time, showing the imposing silhouette of the Guardian as the moon peaked through the clouds behind it.

"Alright," said Audrey. "So she did it at Rosehill."

"Just like we did," said Zack, without looking over. He let the video play. The girls, bundled in puffy winter coats, the kind not meant to be stylish, the type no fashionable young woman would be seen in, helped Sophie Moreau, fine blond hair hanging around her face, up to the statue while one of her friends filmed, giggling.

Hushed questioning. "What do you see?" "How do you die, Sophie?"

"Shut up, Anna," said Sophie.

Osgood nodded, "Anna was the other one who died that day with Sophie."

They watched as the seconds passed. Longer and longer. The girls holding Sophie up began to grumble and gripe.

Audrey pointed at the other girls in the frame. "Do we know who—"

Zack shushed her and turned up the volume.

"What?"

Sophie screamed, and the sound echoed around the high ceilings of Zack's converted warehouse. The girls holding her up fell backward, and the three girls collapsed in a giggly mess. "What'd ya see?!" Dramatically, Sophie gasped out, "I saw... I saw..." But then she collapsed into laughter again.

"Sounds like she saw what I saw," said Osgood.

Zack turned to her, eyes narrowed.

"Nothing," she reminded him.

"Right."

"And this is her TikTok?" asked Osgood.

Zack nodded. "She must not have done the required deletion step. She wasn't much of a video creator, so this is one of only five or six."

"Anything good in the others?" asked Audrey.

"Depends," said Zack. "Did you think that one was good?"

Audrey pinched the bridge of her nose. "Work with me here, Zack."

"The other videos are pretty typical little girl shit. What boys they like, what makeup they're stealing from the 7-11." He shrugged. "I downloaded all of it. My guess is that the cops either didn't see these videos or didn't care."

"Because they don't show anything," said Osgood.

"The only reason we're paying attention is because of Os's friend bringing up the Graveyard Game." He flicked his thumb at Osgood.

"Do the other girls do it?" she asked, disregarding the suggestion that she somehow had led them down a path to nowhere.

"Not on this video," he said.

"Do we know who they are?" Audrey asked.

Zack typed and tapped and clicked and moved, and the six screens sprung to life. On the screens were five girls, all about the same age. The images were mostly poor, taken from the video, but some were clearer. "I ran these all through facial recognition software that I fed from her Apple Photos and Google Photos. Found likely matches for three of them."

"And Sophie," said Osgood.

"Well, yeah. I wasn't including her." He tapped, and other photos came up next to the video screenshots. "Anna

Kolciech, who is deceased. Carolyn Lee. Jackie Tomlinson, also deceased."

"Wait, what?" Osgood leaned forward, looking at the image of Jackie Tomlinson. Dark hair in braids, the metal line of a retainer over her teeth.

Zack let his research answer for him. He typed and tapped. An obituary came up. Brief.

Audrey read aloud, "'We lost our angel this morning. She's with Jesus now.'"

"It's a lot of words to tell you that Jesus wanted this little girl back, without mentioning that she drowned in the North Shore Channel of the Chicago River," Zack grumbled.

"Was she swimming?" asked Audrey.

"It was December in the middle of the night," he said. "I very much doubt it." He clicked around a bit more and came up with a police report. "'Death by misadventure.' She was up at the Devon crossing of the river. It had frozen over at that point. She jumped, crashed through the ice, and drowned."

Osgood frowned. "Disregarding the fact that that is an incredibly inefficient and difficult way to kill oneself..."

"Should we disregard that?" asked Audrey.

"Where did she live?"

Zack brought up a map that filled all six screens. On it, they saw the northern neighborhoods of Chicago. A star sat over their location, as well as three little faces in bubbles. Osgood cocked her head. "You're tracking us?"

"I asked him to," said Audrey quickly, perhaps wanting to cut off any confrontation. "As you're now prone to randomly walking home from downtown..."

Osgood opened, then closed, her mouth. As much as it felt like a breach of privacy, what did she really feel the need to keep private from Zack? She grumbled, "Fine."

Zack said, "Okay," and began to type. A pushpin appeared on the map. "This is where Sophie Moreau lived." He reached up and pointed to the map a block away from the pushpin. "This is St. Gregory High School, by the way." He typed some more, and another pushpin popped up. "This is where her body was found, along with..." Tap, tap, tap, another pushpin. "Anna Kolciech." He zoomed out the map just a touch. "Here's where Jackie Tomlinson lived. Less than a mile, but they still bussed her in for school." He zoomed out further until it showed the Devon river crossing. "Here's where her phone was found."

"Without her?" asked Audrey.

Zack shook his head and zoomed way out so quickly that the giant screen disoriented Osgood. He dropped a pin on the map near the spot where the river met Lake Michigan. "Her body got stuck on some construction debris here." A few taps and an image popped up, a zoomed shot from across the river, of the Chicago Fire Department pulling what looked like a dark blue sack from the river.

Audrey looked away. "Zack! I asked you to warn me before—"

"I thought since it didn't look like a body that—"

"In general, Zack. I *know* it's a body."

He nodded. "I won't show you the other pictures, then."

"The other...?" asked Osgood.

"I managed to get the crime scene photos. Sophie and Anna."

"I..." Audrey seemed flustered. Osgood knew why.

This is a bit close to Caroline, isn't it, Aud? Instead of saying anything, though, Osgood squeezed her shoulder, and Audrey put her hand atop hers.

"Is there anything there that needs to be seen, Zack?" asked Osgood. "Like we won't understand the case going forward if we don't see it?"

"I," started Zack. "I mean, I don't know what the case will look like going forward."

"We're not getting you to sign off on..." Osgood started, then stopped. "You've looked at them?"

Zack nodded.

Osgood took a deep breath and squeezed Audrey's shoulder harder. "Show me."

After Audrey looked away, Zack did his tapping thing and each of the six monitors got its own image. Growing up, Osgood had always had a morbid curiosity. A book she'd bought once had a gallery of famous crime scene photos. That book had taken her from the horrible image of brutalized Mary Kelly at the hands of Jack the Ripper in 1888 to the axe murders of the elder Bordens in 1892 to bisected and disemboweled Elizabeth Short, the Black Dahlia, in the '40s. One thing the book's glossy images all had in common, though, even the more modern ones showcasing the crimes of John Wayne Gacy and Jeffrey Dahmer, was they were all in black and white. This was likely due to printing costs, not a desire to protect young eyes from the horrors of full-color crime scene photography. The photos on Zack's screens appeared nearly black and white themselves. Even the red, of which there was an astonishing amount, was muted with mud. The girl's coats, once-vivid blues and purples, were dirtied with blood and dirt. They also looked washed through by... "Did it rain?" asked Osgood.

"Between when they were killed and when they were found, yeah," said Zack.

A gasp, a gulp, a sob. Osgood turned and saw Audrey covering her mouth with one hand, the other pressed against her stomach.

"Oh, Aud," said Osgood. "Why did you look?"

Zack tapped some keys, and the images disappeared from the screen.

Osgood could still see them, though. Both girls were laid out as though they were doing snow angels, the rivulets of muddy red shooting in every direction like they'd been spun on a spirograph. Both throats had been cut, giving the appearance of an enormous gaping smile beneath their chins. Osgood knew that Audrey had seen too much here. Osgood could internalize this, compress it down until it felt no more emotional than any other horrible fact she'd ever heard. Push it down deep, like when she'd seen the helicopter decapitate Vic Morrow and his small Vietnamese companion on the set of *The Twilight Zone: The Movie*. Simply a fact. Something that had happened. No more horrible than the rest of the world, right? She hugged Audrey tightly because she knew that Audrey couldn't dissociate like that. Things hit too hard, too raw.

After all, how different were the young girls here, with their throats cut open, from Audrey's own sister Caroline, who, at the behest of The Lord of the Hinterlands, had cut out her own eyes so that she might see?

SEVENTEEN

Osgood ascended her rickety back porch steps to find Audrey leaning on the porch rail, staring at the other apartment buildings without actually looking. "Are you—"

"Yeah," said Audrey, jamming the base of her palm against her eye, then wiping. "I'm fine."

Still on the final step before the porch, Osgood held her place. Her bent knee went from "fine, we'll hold this" to "dear god, woman, what're you doing" in less than a minute, but here she could observe Audrey. "We don't have to take this—"

"We're doing it."

Osgood nodded. She looked at the alley across the way, still not upgraded to the new LED streetlamps, burning the sickly orange that weirdly felt like home to Osgood. She remembered a sleepover when she'd been 7 or maybe 8, at one of the apartments above a storefront over on Devon Avenue. Those lights had been ever-present as the giggly girls avoided sleep in the living room. *Whose birthday had that been?* wondered Osgood. All she could really remember was that they watched the movie *Bloody Birthday* because whoever's parents were far less strict than hers when it came to media. Thinking about those girls, she knew Audrey was right. They had to do this. She wasn't sure what kind of predator they were dealing with, or even if their "spectral" purview would cover it. Still, more little girls should have more birthdays where they didn't have to worry about serial killers or the type of life-crushing existential dread that leads to drowning in the Chicago River.

"I was thinking I'd drive up to Devon," she said after a long silence. "Check out the river."

Audrey said nothing.

"Zack's looking at various internet scrapers, to see if anyone is collecting TikTok. He says he's sure they are, 'cuz they collect everything else." Osgood hesitated. "And said that it's more likely, because the kids are underage, that someone unseemly is…"

Still nothing.

"Did you want to stay—"

"No," said Audrey. She didn't move.

With a laugh meant to lighten things up, Osgood held up a messenger bag. "Zack gave me a kit."

Again, Audrey wiped at her face.

"We could get McFlurrys on the way back?"

Audrey put her hands on the wooden rail and looked down over it. "You're not going to make this okay."

Osgood narrowed her eyes. "I'm not trying—"

"I know," said Audrey. She turned to look at Osgood. The light from the orange lamps reflected in her watery eyes. "I'm just telling you that this feels like Caroline. And that fucking sucks. And it fucking hurts."

Osgood nodded.

"But that's why we have to do something." Audrey's voice dropped to a whisper. "Whatever that is."

"C'mon," said Osgood, reaching out to her friend. "Let's go look at a river." Audrey took her hand, and they went.

The ride wasn't long, but it was silent. Audrey drove, after a squabble that involved Osgood saying "I'm fine" five or six times, then Audrey tapping Osgood's right knee with her index finger. The shock of the pain, while a cheap shot, made Audrey's point. Osgood was a better passenger, anyway.

Climbing out just before the river overpass, Osgood was grateful for her backup cane in the cargo area of Audrey's Honda. Devon, the road over this portion of the river, was a four-laner and busy, even at this late hour. They went up the walkway on the south side of the bridge. Here, the river was just under thirty feet wide and moved relatively slowly, when there hadn't been a recent downpour. Knowing their investigative methods differed, Osgood watched Audrey, waiting to see how she would begin. Instead of leading, Audrey stood, her pose at the side of the bridge almost identical to the one on the back porch. Looking into the middle distance.

Not wanting to be insensitive, Osgood stood next to her and looked south down the river. Large trees lined each side, their leaves—typical of a Chicago autumn—unsure whether to stay green and cling or descend into yellows and reds. On either side were steel panels, defining the shores and allowing for depth fluctuation. While some enjoyed the river for fishing or boating, this far north it became mostly utilitarian. Drainage for the north side and beyond.

Osgood looked down at her phone and opened a map screenshot Zack had texted to both of them; on it was a small phone icon. She stepped to the edge of the bridge and leaned over the rail, checking her phone once more before pointing at a small patch of dirt and weeds. "That's where they found her phone."

"So it stands to reason she jumped in from that side."

"Yep," said Osgood.

"Why that side?" asked Audrey. "Why cross the river and then jump?"

"How do you know she crossed the river first?"

"Because *we* did. And she lived on the same side as us." Audrey pointed across the four lanes as some cars went by. "Could've jumped in on the north side of the bridge. Could've gone under. Could've."

"You talking about that kid?"

Both Osgood and Audrey turned, startled. A woman pushing a shopping cart limped up to them. Her gray hair was long and dirty, and so was her jacket. In the cart, in addition to what looked like a bedroll and various other clothing, was a cardboard sign. Osgood could only read the first sentence, but it began with, **need help. mom of three kids. please**— She patted her pockets and found nothing. *Shit.* Audrey came to the rescue, a $10 bill in her hand. She handed it over to the figure Osgood would've called an "old woman" if asked, but really, who knew how old she actually was. Could be 40.

"Thank you," said the woman, tucking the money into her coat.

Osgood watched Audrey switch from melancholy into professional mode. It was a sight to behold every time she did it. Audrey was definitely not one to wallow on the clock.

"That kid," repeated Audrey.

The old woman who was probably just a "woman," nodded. "He jumped two weeks ago," she said. "I heard his neck broke."

"He?" asked Osgood.

"Yeah. Young kid. Maybe twenty?" The woman pointed to a spot in the center of the bridge. "Stood there a minute and then just..." She waved her hand over her head and exhaled sharply. "Gone."

Osgood opened her mouth to ask a follow-up but glanced at Audrey first. The perplexity on her face was intense.

"You said two weeks ago?"

"Might've been three. I dunno."

Audrey did some tapping on her phone and then showed Osgood the screen. The mobile edition of the Sun-Times described "'Another apparent suicide in the North Shore Channel.'" She turned back to the woman. "My name is Audrey. This is Osgood."

At the formality of it, the woman seemed to shrink back. She cast her eyes askance. "I don't know anything."

"I'm sure that's not true," said Audrey. She put her hand on the woman's wrist, causing her to flinch. "I'm sorry! I'm sorry." Both hands shot into the air.

Osgood looked between the woman and Audrey. "We're not cops," she said.

"Didn't think you were," said the woman.

Audrey cocked her head. "You got all—"

"You think I got a city of people offering me their names?" asked the woman. She gave them a morose chuckle and started to walk away.

It was time for Audrey to pull out the big guns—a $50 appeared in her hand.

The woman looked between them. "I'm Betty," she said, then snatched the $50 from Audrey's hand. "What do you wanna know?"

"Were you here when this young man jumped?" Audrey showed her the phone to be absolutely specific.

Betty shook her head. "I heard about it after."

Osgood watched Audrey deflate.

"I was here for the other one."

They both looked at her. "A young girl?" asked Osgood.

Betty nodded. "Such an awful thing. I have kids too, yunno."

"Do you remember when this was?" asked Audrey. She

knew it had happened the previous December, but it was always good to gently test a potential witness.

"Christmastime," said Betty. "People are more generous at Christmas, so I'm out here more."

"How many years have you been…" Osgood couldn't find a word that didn't sound offensive, so she just left it.

"Beggin'?" asked Betty. She laughed, and Osgood got the distinct impression it was at her discomfort. "Three years. Lost my job 'cuz of the China virus."

Osgood opened her mouth to ask why she hadn't gone on unemployment, but she saw Audrey's eyes on hers. She knew what that look meant. This was not about the fascinating life story of Betty the Unhoused. Each moment they kept her away from the median on the westbound side of Devon, they were keeping her from money. Audrey's $50 only went so far. *Focus, Pru.* "Did you see her jump?"

Betty shook her head. "She didn't go off the top, though." She pointed at the peak of the bridge arc, where a box containing a weather-worn orange life ring hung. "She went down below." This time, her finger indicated around the side of the bridge, where Jackie's phone had been discovered. "I saw her go down there. Told her it was dangerous. Not just 'cuz she could slip. Sometimes there's a man under there."

"A man?" asked Osgood. She could feel the little prickles on the nape of her neck, on her forearms. The *something strange in the neighborhood* prickles.

Betty nodded but didn't seem to want to elaborate. "By the time I got to the side to look, she was out on the ice. Then…" She fluttered her fingers up, perhaps suggesting the splash that occurred.

"You didn't see her once she went under the ice?"

Betty shook her head.

"And besides her and the man you mentioned, has anyone else—"

"Gone down there?" asked Betty.

They nodded.

"Sometimes I think I want to. Because I can hear the whispers."

Audrey's eyes flicked to Osgood and back. They both took a moment, trying to hear "the whispers."

"Can't hear them now," said Betty. "Too loud. It's gotta be *quiet*."

"What do the whispers say?"

Betty shrugged. "Never talk long enough for me to find out. By the time I get down there, they've stopped."

"And ... the man?" asked Osgood.

The woman stared at them blankly.

"The one you said is sometimes under—"

"Oh!" said Betty. "I haven't seen him in a while."

"When you did," began Audrey, slowly. "What did he look like?"

"What the fuck you think he looked like?" asked Betty, a note of humor in her voice. "Like a bum! He's a bum."

Osgood laughed, too, feeling the sense of encroaching concern fade again.

"I gotta get back out there," said Betty, flicking her thumb toward the road.

"Thank you, Betty," said Audrey, handing her a business card. "Please call if you think of anything else."

"Or hear the whispers," added Osgood.

Betty took the card as though she thought it absolutely preposterous, and Osgood knew they wouldn't be hearing from this woman in the future.

It took some care and cautious foot placement for Osgood to get down the embankment behind Audrey, but the two of them made it to a small walkway beneath the bridge that ran along the west bank of the river. There were, as could be expected, various pieces of garbage. Soda cans, a forty, a bottle in a paper bag, but not much else. Osgood looked up at the steel structure of the bridge's underside, hearing the vehicles moving above them, the sounds growing and fading, the faint, unsettling growl of metal moving against metal. Beneath it all, though, the whooshing of the wind; it wouldn't be impossible to believe it whispered.

"This is a stupid way to kill yourself," said Audrey, breaking Osgood's hypnosis.

Osgood looked at the water, then back to Audrey.

"The river's not deep here, not terribly wide, doesn't move very fast. If you want to kill yourself, you want to kill yourself... You go somewhere you can't change your mind at the last second."

Osgood thought of the Ts on her wrists but said nothing.

"But two people managed to do it. From the same bridge. In less than a year. Two *young* people."

"We need to see if that boy..."

"Kyle Mattoon," said Audrey, still staring at the water.

"...See if he also did the Graveyard Game."

Distracted, Audrey waved it away. "Already sent the info to Zack. Jackie Tomlinson makes some sense. Poor girl's best friends died horribly around Christmastime. Yeah, I get it. Life becomes too much, and she—" Audrey cut herself off and crouched at the water's edge. "And she jumps into a shallow river and hopes she'll drown?"

Osgood nodded. "Doesn't seem to align."

"Nope."

"Especially not with an additional suicide."

"Nope." Audrey took one last look at the river, then climbed back up the embankment.

Osgood's last look took longer.

EIGHTEEN

When Osgood looked into the river, she felt a pull, one she'd felt before in her life. Many times, in fact. Describing it to a counselor whom she'd been reluctantly dragged to see, it'd been given a name: the call of the void.

"It's not just suicidal people who feel this way," Dr. Barbara had said. "We all feel the call of the void. At night, when driving, there's that momentary questioning that asks, 'What would happen if we swerved into traffic?' or when we're at the top of a precipice and wonder about leaping off. Our brains ask these questions, not because we necessarily want to do it, but because that idea is something that we cannot completely comprehend."

Osgood had answered the call of the void. First, a T along her right wrist and forearm, and then, thankfully (or not, depending on her mood), a much shallower T on her left. The shallower T had saved her life. There were times after that the void had called, and she'd answered again. She'd wondered occasionally if her accident at the crossroads had been another answer. She should've seen the semi-truck coming, right?

There'd been nothing but prairie and darkness, after all. The semi couldn't have hidden behind anything. There weren't any problems with its lights. How could Osgood have driven into the intersection and only *then* noticed the truck about to T-bone her Buick Skylark? It made no sense. Osgood knew there'd never really been a point in her life, not since her adolescence had begun in earnest, when she could consider herself emotionally stable. Most of her adult life had been about plugging holes in the dike, desperately trying to keep the onslaught at bay. Some plugs had been more successful than others. There had even been periods here and there when she would've been described as "doing markedly better" by any of her therapists. *Three out of four doctors give Prudence Osgood a clean bill of health,* she thought, staring into the murky brown of the North Branch. But always that last doctor ... well, they were the ones who were being pragmatic, sensible. They were the ones who'd seen the oncoming storms.

"Maybe I *should* get back into therapy," she muttered. Even at this low volume, she heard her words reverberate against the overpass.

So what was this here? This void pull?

Osgood had managed to avoid a therapist's office for seven or so years, getting by instead on a steady diet of denial, sex, whiskey, and self-loathing, bolstered with a bootleg OxyContin tincture for when her pain was too much. Osgood didn't much care if that pain was physical or emotional; the tincture tended to work either way. However, once Chicago had legalized marijuana, even her oxy dealer had suggested she explore the relief of cannabis. She couldn't understand why every dealer had turned into an evangelist. Maybe because they could grow their own without as much fear, and oxy still had a stigma (and laws) attached. Her emotional turmoil would ebb and flow against her physical, sometimes in tandem and other times at odds. She never quite knew when either would flare up but understood enough about how to treat both that she could exist in a haze of pain, and the masking thereof. Unhealthy, she knew. But she'd never been a healthy specimen.

Given all that, the call of the void here interested her. Standing above the river, she thought about drowning in it. She considered how it'd feel when she couldn't hold her breath any longer and gasped in the putrid water of the Chicago River. How it'd fill her lungs, and she'd panic, scrambling, desperate to find the surface and oxygen, but even then, it'd be too much, wouldn't it? Because surfacing with lungs full of water would continue to drown her. This would not be a pretty way to go.

Or easy, Osgood thought again and wondered if it'd only been the ice cover that had made this work for young Jackie Tomlinson. *But what about the other one?* She supposed someone with no swimming ability whatsoever could drown in this river, but even then, most people have an instinctual doggy paddle that'd likely get them over to the side. She thought Jackie would've had to actively work against her survival instincts to permanently end herself here. The white rubber toes of Osgood's beat-up yellow Chucks poked over the edge of the concrete platform. Maybe if she just slipped off close to the platform, her head might whack against it as she submerged, the impact could knock her out. Unconscious, she could drown here. If she hit her head hard enough, she might even get some internal bleeding.

She could die here.

"What the fuck?" she asked of the thought, shaking her head. "Aud!" she called.

Audrey leaned over the rail above her and looked down. "What?"

"Did you..." What should she ask? What did any of this mean? "...Feel anything weird here?"

"Weird, how?" asked Audrey.

"Like." *Just ask. No need to sugarcoat it. Just ask her what you want to ask her.* "Did you want to kill yourself?

"Ummmm." Audrey's word was drawn out, concern wafting off it. "No."

"Okay," said Osgood. "I'm coming up."

Audrey met her around the side of the embankment, leaning down with an outstretched hand. Looking up, Osgood saw that concern in Audrey's eyes. *Well, great,* she thought. *Now it's gonna be a whole big thing.*

Back in the car, there was silence for a while. Osgood watched the streetlamps go by. Out of the corner of her eye, she could see Audrey's quick glances in her direction. Occasionally, her friend's mouth pursed to speak, but nothing came. Halfway home, Osgood could stand it no longer. The silence was worse than conversation. "I don't want to kill myself."

Osgood could almost hear the ellipsis in Audrey's "...Good."

"Your 'good' sounds like a 'but,'" Osgood grumbled.

"It wasn't," said Audrey. Now that the talking had begun, she kept her eyes firmly focused on the road ahead. "You understand how concerning it might be for someone to ask, 'Did you want to kill yourself?' at a spot where at least two people have killed themselves, right?"

"I thought it might be relevant," said Osgood, a tinge of defensiveness in her voice.

"It would absolutely be relevant if I'd felt that urge," said Audrey. "Did you?"

"Did I what?"

"Feel the urge to kill yourself?"

"That's different," said Osgood, though she couldn't figure out why.

"Different how?" asked Audrey.

"Because you're... Not..."

"What, Os?" Audrey turned to her. "Is this the part where you tell me you're crazy, to get me to say, 'No,' and reassure you that you're not?"

Do I do that? Osgood asked herself. But she only said, "Now *that's* crazy!"

"You're not crazy, Os," said Audrey. "You're right, self-destructiveness is one of your cornerstone traits, so I'd imagine the thought of suicide presents itself a bit more frequently to you than others." She fixed her eyes on Osgood for a moment. "But you don't have a monopoly on suicidal tendencies."

"Oh, I didn't..." *Wait,* thought Osgood, *are we about to fight over who's more suicidal?* "I didn't mean for you to take the question personally, Aud."

"I'm not taking anything personally," said Audrey.

"Apparently denial is as strong as suicidal tendencies..."

Audrey shook her head. "You realize there's a reason I might be concerned about any suicidal thoughts you're having."

"Yes, I know. Because I have people who love me," said Osgood, realizing she'd made it sound like a burden.

"I mean, yes, you do," said Audrey, shaking her head. "But more pressing to our current investigation..."

Osgood waited.

"You don't see it?"

Osgood shook her head.

"Jesus, Osgood," laughed Audrey. "What the hell are we investigating?"

"A girl who was murdered."

"Because?"

"Because she and her friends—" There it was. "Because she and her friends played the Graveyard Game and saw how they would die."

"And some of them were murdered, and others killed themselves."

Osgood frowned. "I'd just assumed they killed themselves to avoid dying the way they'd seen, not that they killed themselves *because* that's what they saw."

"You're still sure you didn't see anything when you looked into the eyes of the Guardian."

"Still sure it didn't have eyes."

"Less glib, please."

Osgood took a moment and a breath. She pictured the statue in her mind. Rising up to meet it, courtesy her friends' hands. Seeing the ridge of the hood, then looking into its darkness. There'd been nothing inside. She'd seen nothing. Right? She tried to scan deeper, to do the TV "enhance" thing and see what, if anything, she might be missing. Then it came to her, obvious in its suggestion, but something she hadn't considered. "They didn't see anything either."

"They didn't?" asked Audrey.

"I don't think so."

"Then, why?"

"We thought a vision would happen when you looked into the statue's eyes," said Osgood, shuffling to get more comfortable in her seat, though of course the comfort wouldn't come. "That in looking you'd see, or feel, or understand, or whatever, in the moment, how you would die. Then, cursed with that knowledge, you'd decide to stick around or do something about it."

"Right."

"But when I looked, I saw nothing."

"Because you did the game wrong."

Osgood made a *pssht* sound and shook her head. "You think the game actually matters? It's a meme, for fuck's sake. The bit that matters is the statue. And it doesn't show you how you'll die, but it gives you the knowledge. How your brain shares that with you is up to it."

Audrey sat with that for a moment. "So you think that, tonight, when you felt—"

"The call of the void."

"Sure."

"Yeah," said Osgood, more and more confident. "I think my subconscious was telling me to jump because that's what the Guardian showed it."

"Now what happens, since you didn't die when the statue wanted you to?" Audrey asked, her tone still skeptical.

"Maybe that's why some of them are murdered," said Osgood, speaking the thought aloud as it occurred.

They both sat in silence at the implications about what life in the short term might hold for Prudence Osgood.

Nineteen

"Os! What? What're you doing here?" The surprise in Nora's voice belied annoyance, as though the woman was trying to mask one with the other.

Truthfully, Osgood didn't remember how she'd gotten to Nora's apartment in Wicker Park. A quick pat of her leather trench coat didn't reveal car keys to her, though thankfully, a phone was there. But despite having a phone, she didn't appear to have called ahead. So, Osgood improvised. "Text never really gets across what you want to say."

Nora leaned against the hastily stained and re-stained door jam. "I agree." Her candy apple red hair hung to her cheekbones, wavy and unkempt. This had been an unexpected drop-in. That would also account for the smudgy black mascara beneath Nora's chocolate-colored eyes. Osgood couldn't deny that this messy look was doing it for her.

"So, I thought I'd come and say it in person."

Nora nodded.

Osgood couldn't really blame her for her standoffishness. After their first one-night stand, Osgood had all but ghosted her until their second date. Just after they'd fucked that time,

Osgood—well, there was really no better way to put it—had vanished into the margins of the spirit world for just over a year. When she'd returned, Nora had been away at school. Then, a handful of dates that were glorified booty calls, and Osgood was back to ghosting. It was her thing, after all. Not just because she was a ghost hunter, of course, though Osgood did enjoy the wordplay, but because it was often just easier to say nothing than to say anything hard, or real.

"At 12:40 in the morning?" Nora folded her arms.

Looking around, Osgood sought confirmation. "Is it?"

"It *is,*" said Nora, a frown on her face. But Osgood could see, somewhere deep beneath the scowl and folded arms, the little bit of Nora that found messy bitch Osgood irresistible. If only that bit could be coaxed out. After a silent moment, Nora asked, "And what might be important enough to say at 12:40?"

Osgood was still uncertain why she'd gone there in the first place (desire for the distraction of a sexual escapade?), and she didn't truly know what she wanted to say to this woman, whom she'd met as a college freshman, when Osgood's college days had been long since passed. "I *did* miss you," she said finally, hoping she'd be invited in so that, even if they didn't get naked right away, she at least wouldn't be afraid of the door behind her opening and whomever lived in 3B poking their head out to find out what all this chit-chat at almost 1:00 in the morning was about.

Nora waited for more, but when it didn't come, she wiped her hands down her face, drawing streaks of the smudged mascara down her cheeks. "I shouldn't have to be the mature one in this relationship, Os. You're *two decades* older than me."

Osgood nodded, reluctantly acknowledging that truth.

"As a 24-year-old woman, even *I'm* too old to be showing up unannounced looking for pussy."

"You're never too old for that," said Osgood with a laugh.

"Yes," said Nora, and the seriousness and maturity in her voice overwhelmed Osgood. "You are."

A warm and unsettled feeling of embarrassment began to crawl up in Osgood's chest. She scowled and began to turn away.

Nora caught her. "I'm sorry." The woman sighed and refolded her arms. "Look, if I didn't have to be up for work at 6, I'd be thrilled to see you."

"But," said Osgood.

"But," agreed Nora. "Text next time?"

Osgood agreed that she would. Nora dropped a quick kiss on her cheek and stepped back inside her apartment, closing the door.

Stepping back outside of the three-flat, Osgood found her battered old Mustang parked in front. Again she patted her pockets, and this time found the keys that had somehow fallen down into the liner of the coat. The engine roared, and she gunned it down the backstreets of Wicker Park.

She threw the radio on seek, hearing snippets here and there of songs and talk radio. Briefly, she thought she heard *The End of What's Real* by Rhapsody in the Shallows. A few seconds later, it was lost in static, thankfully. Then a voice caught her attention. She stopped the radio from seeking onward.

"—Dr. Ramona Yeagher taking your calls for another ten minutes before we call it a night for **Feel's Good** *on WGN Chicago."*

"Remy," said Osgood. She felt her mood instantly lighten.

TWENTY

"I shouldn't have come," said Osgood, her hands stuffed deep into the pockets of her coat. "Should've at least called first."

Remy Yeagher smirked and shook her head, her curls bouncing in the loose ponytail she wore. "I have exited the studio to far worse people waiting for me, Osgood."

"Yeah?"

"You'd be surprised how many people want to shoot you for the crime of suggesting that people ought to feel good."

Osgood was, admittedly, surprised by the suggestion that *anybody* would want to shoot this woman. Looking at her NYU sweatshirt and quilted leggings, Osgood felt a swell of, well, lust, yes, but also... Not even just affection. She wanted Remy Yeagher. In every way that one could.

"You broken?" asked Remy with a laugh.

Broken. Osgood thought the word apt, and she nodded solemnly.

"Oh, Os," said Remy, putting her long, manicured fingers on Osgood's arm, "I meant because you just stopped and stared. Not— I don't believe you are broken."

The assurance relieved Osgood, but her internal voices disagreed. Especially the one she called Mother.

"C'mon," Remy told her. "Let me buy you pie. But you have to drive. I took an Uber today."

As she always seemed to be doing, Osgood apologized for the state of the passenger seat before moving her junk to the back seat, then apologized again for that. Remy watched with a bemused expression on her face. The last thing Osgood transferred to the back was her cane. She held it a moment. Had she not used it to climb the stairs at Nora's apartment? To make the walk down the street to the Hancock Building? "Huh," she said, dropping it in the back.

"You appear to be juggling a myriad of thoughts tonight," said Remy as they headed north.

All at once, Osgood spilled. "I wanted to get fucked. Because I thought I might kill myself this afternoon. Not because anything happened or was wrong, I just got that call of the void feeling, you know?"

With the stoic lack of surprise that all therapists seem able to muster, Remy nodded to indicate that she did know.

"So, I went to a girl ... woman's house. We're ... I dunno. Kinda off-and-on dating. But I was unannounced, and it was after midnight, and she has work in the morning, so..."

"Rejection," said Remy.

"Yeah!" agreed Osgood. "And I don't really think my partners need me anymore, they're just keeping me around because, well, I guess I technically started the company because I was a podcast host."

"*The* Spectral Inspector," said Remy.

"But they're both so much better at investigation than I am. I mean, I don't quit, so that's a positive thing, but I don't have discipline or even decent planning skills, which leads to dead ends and meandering investigations." Osgood took a deep breath, and the achiness of her lungs when she did indicated she ought to take more. "And then you sent us a client. Thank you, by the way. She really wants our help, and we really want to help her. But when I looked into the eyes of the statue, I didn't see anything."

That stoicism vanished, replaced with concern. "You looked—"

"But then today, when I was feeling that urge to kill myself, I wondered if it was connected."

"That's a lot of stuff, Osgood," said Remy.

"It *is*," agreed Osgood. She turned and watched as Remy leaned her back against the passenger door. Osgood realized she wasn't wearing her seatbelt and was about to mention it when Remy's calm voice took over the space.

"You say you wanted to get fucked," said Remy.

"Yeah," said Osgood with a quiet laugh. She felt redness on her cheeks.

"Is it the connection with other people or the—"

"When I'm fucking..." Osgood took a moment to clarify her own thoughts. "It's the only time I can forget about..." She waved her hand around in a circle. "The noise."

Remy waited.

"Everything, you know? The pain I have in my legs and back. The migraines I get. Chest pain. It's all noise. Add to it the desires, and the regrets, and the yearnings. Hatreds and loves."

"The stuff of life," said Remy.

Osgood nodded.

"It's not about reassuring yourself of your place in the hierarchy of their lives, then?"

That took Osgood a moment to parse. Did she do that? "No," she said, then agreed with herself. "No, I don't think of sex as being that high a priority for people."

"You don't? It's a priority for most."

"But it's disposable, isn't it?"

"Tell me more about that," said Remy Yeagher, leaning forward in the seat.

"Like, if I have a one-night stand, I have it, and then it's done."

"Interesting," said Remy. "You don't linger on it? Reflect on it later? Masturbate over it?"

Osgood shrugged. "If it's excellent, I might."

"How often is it excellent?"

"I..." Osgood wasn't sure. She wanted to continue that sentence. Wanted to say usually. Wanted to explain. "The sex... I don't know that it's been excellent. Some *people*, though."

"Turn here," said Remy, pointing down a side street. Osgood didn't ask why; she just did it. "Now park." Again, without question, Osgood parked on a side street off Lincoln Avenue. Quiet, multi-flat houses and apartments lined the street. Parking was surprisingly available for the time of night.

"What're we doing," asked Osgood. Then the hope hit. "Are we going to mess around?"

"You are," said Remy. She leaned forward further, bringing her legs up under her butt on the seat. Her head touched the black fabric ceiling of the Mustang.

All at once, the mild flush Osgood had felt, the wave of embarrassment, grew to an astonishing level. She felt the shame in her stomach. Here she was, spilling her heart to this woman she didn't really know, and—

Remy's fingers were cold as she slid them onto Osgood's forehead. They felt like an ice pack, in fact, to tend her fever. How very strange. But with Remy's hand there, Osgood took two slow breaths and controlled the growing embarrassment.

"That's better," said Remy.

"What do you want from me?" asked Osgood.

Remy cocked her head, bouncing her curls again. "Not a thing," she said. "Believe it or not, and I sense you're more 'not,' I'd just love to help you feel better."

"But you're not going to mess around with me?"

"I'm not."

"And, just for my, uh, edification: why not?"

"Because you have 'stuff.' As I told you. And as you reminded me." Remy smiled, though, and the smile was gentle and unthreatening. "But I want you to masturbate."

Osgood snorted. "Fuck you." She laughed.

"I'm very serious."

Narrowing her eyes, Osgood studied Remy's face. Her silvery eyes sparkled. There wasn't even a hint of the thing Osgood had seen before, that mean girl bullshit look. The "what can I get you to do?" expression. "Well, Dr. Remy, I assure you that I masturbate plenty."

"I've no doubt," said Remy.

What the fuck is with this woman? asked Cynthia in her mind, using a word her mother never would.

"Do you trust me?" Remy asked.

"No!" said Osgood.

Remy laughed. "Fair. But do you think you might, someday, trust me?"

"I..." Osgood had to be honest with herself. She couldn't put her finger on why and was self-conscious about the foolishness of trusting someone so quickly, but she did, in fact, trust Dr. Ramona Yeagher. Add to that the fact that Osgood was dying to figure out where this was going, what was going to happen. She'd only had one *actual* mutual masturbation session in her life, and that'd been in the early exploratory days with Audrey. Every time since had been just a prelude to the "real thing." Osgood opened her mouth to ask more questions, protest more, suggest this was some kind of prank, but nothing came out. So, with a shrug, she slid her hand into her jeans, down the course curls of her bush, immediately feeling enough wetness that she thought she'd probably leave a stain on the car seat. She spread her lips, found her clit, and went to town.

"Close your eyes."

She didn't have to be asked twice, clamping them shut. No neighborhood out the windshield. No woman strangely perched on the seat next to her. Just Osgood. Just clothed-for-some-reason Osgood diddling herself. Just doing it in the car. Just—

"Stop overthinking it." This time Remy's voice came closer, and Osgood felt warmth from her breath.

That was enough to shuffle the deck, and Osgood could feel the pleasure begin to rise from the wet warmth between her legs.

"There you go," said Remy. "Take yourself back. Find those people, those pleasures, those moments you don't think you deserve."

Osgood opened her mouth to tell the woman to stop bringing her own elements to this, as Osgood knew what she was doing, but she felt an overwhelming urge to go with it. She found the moments very quickly. That one when both she and Audrey, both 16, had realized that the other wasn't, in fact, asleep, and their masturbatory privacy had been an illusion. Audrey had been the one person whose pleasure Osgood had given herself to. Their sexual relationship hadn't been long the first time, or the second, or the recent third, but it had always felt different than the others. So many of them were just genitals, practically a sex toy Osgood could use to get off that night. So many of them had so little value at—

"Don't judge yourself, or your choices."

How did she know? wondered Osgood, but she shook it off and tried to acquiesce. The one-nighters, the pickups, they were all hazy, most often accompanied by some sort of reality modifier, be it drink, drugs, exhaustion, or just steadfast refusal to allow reality to be reality. Genitals, yes, of many shapes and sizes. A glorious plethora of vulvae, individual orchids all. And despite Osgood's amusement overall at the design and appearance of penises, she did enjoy when they hit in just the right place.

A wave of pleasure hit. *Woah!*

"There it is, let it come."

Again, a question appeared in Osgood's mind, but she refused to engage. She pictured those she'd come upon in her time on this earth, as well as all of those who'd come upon her. She was amused by the bon mot and knew that she hadn't created it, only plucked it from something delightful she'd seen, something that—

Holy—

That—

Osgood immediately regretted the volume of her orgasmic ululation but couldn't sit with the feeling long enough to engage in shame. Instead, she felt reality flowing back to her. Her back against the leather seat of her Mustang. A place where she'd fucked, but never fucked herself. She slid her hand from her jeans, marveling at the wetness and wishing she'd worn underwear. With every sigh of breath, she felt herself sink lower and deeper into her seat in comfort.

"A cathartic expulsion," said Remy Yeagher, whom Osgood had, somehow, forgotten was there. She looked over at the woman next to her, the self-help guru, the strange therapist who'd just told her to masturbate in her car. Remy leaned against the side door again, palms flat on her thighs. Her face had reddened, a flush ran from her forehead down the left side of her neck, where it grew splotchy and less pronounced. There was a sheen of sweat on her brow.

"You're a strange therapist," said Osgood.

Remy flicked her eyebrows up slyly. "I'm not *your* therapist."

At the doorstep of Remy's house in Evanston, the suburb just north of Chicago, Osgood asked if she should come in.

"You shouldn't," said Remy, and Osgood had the barest inkling that the reason for "shouldn't" was that Remy herself wanted to fuck Osgood in this moment but was staying true to her word. "Os, if you go home now and go to bed, I can honestly say you will have the best sleep of your life."

"'Cuz of your magic masturbation."

"The only thing magic about masturbation, Osgood, is that the human body is capable of it." With that, Dr. Ramona Yeagher blew Osgood a kiss and walked up the steps to her front door. She stopped and turned back to the car, pointing past it to the lake, where the first faint blues had begun to pierce the veil of night. "A new day, Prudence Osgood. Make it a great one."

Then the door closed, and Remy was gone.

Osgood looked out at the waters of Lake Michigan. She still felt the contentment and pleasure in her stomach and below. Nothing felt wrong. Weird, perhaps, but not wrong. No pain either. Which really emphasized the "weird." Osgood supposed that her sexual openness made things like this... "What, normal?" she asked as she began to head south toward home. "There was nothing fucking normal about that." It was true. Sexually open or not, what had just happened, happening without further explanation, was really fucking weird.

That said, Remy was right; Osgood's sleep into the early afternoon was both dreamless and some of the best rest she'd ever experienced.

TWENTY-ONE

Only thirty seconds or so passed between the knock that wrenched her from sleep and the opening of her bedroom door. Going from the blackout-curtained bedroom fully draped in darkness to a room with this cutting shaft of hallway light sent a stabbing pain into Osgood's head. Almost immediately, all her pain receptors came online, not wanting to give the migraine a head start. First her head, then the arm she'd broken diving out of Sampson Goddard's vehicle into a snowbank, then the spot in the center of her chest that appeared to have nothing physically wrong with it—but Osgood knew better than the doctors, as this was where several creatures had clawed their way into this world, and where Prudence Osgood had turned herself inside out. Next came her oldest pain: lower back, upper legs, and knees; the pain of having been crushed two decades and change ago.

"I made coffee," said Zack, almost as an apology.

"For someone so horrified by my naked body," she said, "you're sure playing a dangerous game, opening the door without being asked in, friendo."

"Noted," said Zack. He held out his hand, showing an oversized mug bearing the *Ghostbusters* logo. "I even added a little Irish."

"Cream or whiskey."

She heard Zack sigh. "Cream."

"It's a start," said Osgood, swinging her bare legs around to the side of the bed. The pain was excruciating, yes, but it tended not to get more so if she did things quickly. "It's definitely a cane day," she told him, sitting with her head down, doing deep, full-body breathing. The cane days had been more frequent of late, hadn't they? But so had her random walks.

"Where is it?" asked Zack. He looked at the empty broom holder mounted on the back of the door.

"It's..." Osgood wasn't sure. She must've had it when she came to bed early this morning, right? There was no way she could've been out so late without excessive pain. A suggestion popped into her head, one she quickly denied. In the years since she'd discovered how good it felt to rub herself on things, Prudence Osgood had managed nearly every type of orgasm possible; there was no way she'd discovered a new one that wiped away the pain. No way at all. Discarding the idea, though, definitely left questions about where she'd left her cane. "Maybe you can grab one from the hall."

Zack nodded, walking away. "Crow's head?" he called back.

"Whatever!"

When he reappeared, he had the mug in his left hand and Osgood's antique cane with a carved onyx crow's head on top in his right. She didn't use this one often, keeping it mainly as a conversation piece, but always thought, should she need to defend the apartment, that beak on the crow's head could do some damage.

Hobbling out to the living room with Zack just steps behind her, Osgood felt the throb of her headache and yearned for the oxy tincture, sitting empty in her medicine cabinet. She paused for a moment and stiffly looked over her shoulder at Zack. "Gummies?"

"Hmm?"

"Would you find the pain gummies? The CBD ones?"

"Uh, sure," said Zack, disappearing again.

(Essential.)

She stumbled a bit from a sharp stab through her calf as she entered the living room, but Audrey was there to guide her to her chair and then sit across from her. When Zack returned, he'd brought a single gummy, not the tin. Osgood thanked him, keeping the "don't you trust me?" question to herself, and chewed on the vaguely dirty-melon-tasting hunk of sugar and cannabis. They both looked at her, waiting. She cocked her head at them. "Why does this feel like an intervention?"

"Oh, uh," said Zack, going and sitting on the couch. Audrey's side of the room. "No. We're just concerned."

"Hence an intervention."

"Audrey said that you—"

"Oh, is this about the suicide feels?"

"Yes, Osgood," said Audrey firmly. "This *is* about the suicide feels."

Osgood shook her head and waved dismissively. "It's nothing. I'm no more suicidal than usual." They stared, not blankly now, worried. "So... Not very," she added.

"Being glib about suicide is concerning," said Zack.

"Is it?" asked Osgood. "I'm sorry you feel that way."

Audrey put her hands up. "Alright, we've expressed our concerns."

"Your concerns have been noted."

"And with this case involving suicide, you will tell us if..."

Osgood chortled. "Yes, I'll tell you if I'm ever seriously considering offing myself."

"Maybe even casually considering it?" asked Zack, his voice high and quiet.

"Sure." Osgood looked between them. "Speaking of our case?"

Zack nodded and picked up his tablet. "Deeper investigation of the EMF spikes in the subway did show some unusual properties. If we didn't have another investigation, I'd say we devote some resources there, but as we do—"

"I want to know what I saw," said Osgood.

"We don't have the time or the..."

"Can't you send your girlfriend?" Osgood suggested to Zack, then immediately regretted putting it like that.

Zack scowled. "Sandy would be happy to help because she is a dedicated paranormal investigator, *not* because she's my girlfriend."

"Right," said Osgood. "You're right. I'm..."

"Sorry?"

"Yes, if you'd allow me to say it."

"Just seems like you trailed off there, notably *not* saying it."

Osgood and Zack stared at each other.

"For now," said Audrey, breaking the silence. "Our primary concern is a mother hoping we can learn what happened to her child."

"Agreed," said Zack.

"So we're ignoring the phantom I saw in the subway, then?"

"When you were drunk and tired," said Zack.

"I see how it is." Osgood fixed a tight grin on them. "If our primary concern is Sophie Moreau, let's discuss her. Zack, have you found any other interesting videos from her TikTok account? From any of her social media, in fact?"

"I was..."

"And Audrey, you were interested in identifying that other

girl in the video. Perhaps she could be found in one of those other videos."

"Well, I'd—"

"You both forget, before there were Spectral Inspector*s*," she made sure to give the pluralization a bit of extra English, "There was *a* Spectral Inspector. And I was a lot drunker and higher back then."

"No," said Audrey. "I remember."

"I'm really fine." Both of them just continued to look at her. Osgood shook her head. "As it appears I need to prove myself to y'all now, here's what we're doing: Zack, please continue to go through her phone. Take a look at location data on the day of her murder."

He nodded sheepishly.

"And Audrey mentioned you might be able to find some scraper friend who saves TikTok videos before they're deleted."

"Creepy people gonna creep," said Zack. "They're *not* my friends."

"Audrey, I think you and I should visit Jackie Tomlinson's parents."

"Oh God," said Audrey.

"I can go myself if you—"

"No," she said with a shake of her head. "It's just... It's just going to be a lot."

Osgood flicked a finger in Zack's direction. "Zack brought out the edibles."

"No, Os," said Audrey, firm. "I'd prefer to have my wits fully about me for this conversation."

Osgood, who rarely had her wits about her, agreed.

"You know we're just concerned about you." said Audrey later, as she drove them toward the neighborhood of Edgewater, just north of Andersonville on the Chicago grid.

"I know that," said Osgood. "You've said."

"And yet you continue to act in a concerning manner," said Audrey with an exhausted laugh. "Walking home from the Loop in the middle of the night, falling asleep in the shower, completely decimating your sleep schedule, talking about killing yourself at the location where other suicides took place."

"These *are* all concerning things," agreed Osgood.

"Well, I'm glad we agree," said Audrey. This time, her laugh held real humor.

"Believe it or not, Audrey," said Osgood, leaning over a bit. "I feel better than I have in years."

"The pain is—"

"Excruciating," said Osgood. "But my mind is clear."

Audrey nodded and looked back to the road. It was evident she didn't exactly believe Osgood.

Ed and Marissa Tomlinson lived in a rare single-family home on a street off Peterson Avenue in Edgewater. Their unlisted house phone had been disconnected earlier in the year, and the investigators had only found Ed Tomlinson's cell phone number after tracking down an old car repair business of his. Going by their current presence, the Tomlinson didn't want to publicly exist. Osgood knew that even if she and Audrey got through the front door, the conversation would be difficult. *Don't you want to talk about your 15-year-old daughter's suicide?*

"No," was the answer from a woman inside when they rang the bell. The single word came from right behind the door, and a moment later, a hint of light in the peephole said they were no longer being observed. Osgood looked at Audrey and then down at her own outfit. Sure, the maroon coat was a bit garish, but she certainly didn't look like she was selling anything. Hell, look at her hair. Sales folk didn't dress this way. Reporters might.

Audrey sighed and knocked a commanding knock. Not an

"open up or else" knock, but a "this is quite important" knock.

Now came a man's voice. "Go away."

"Mr. and Mrs. Tomlinson?"

"We don't do interviews," said the woman inside, surely Marissa.

"We *do* call the police," said Ed.

Osgood leaned into Audrey and whispered. "Maybe we should let them; I've got some questions for them as well."

"I'm not going to let you suicide by cop, Osgood."

Shocked to laughter, Osgood did her best to stifle it in front of the peephole. "Dark AF, Aud." She put on a smile and polite tone. "We've been hired by Vanessa Moreau." With no response from beyond the door, Osgood knew she at least had their curiosity. "We know there's more to your daughter's death than—"

"The North Side Ripper," said the woman in a harsh, clipped manner. "Nothing to do with us."

Osgood turned to Audrey and shrugged. Audrey pursed her lips and leaned forward. "Mr. and Mrs. Tomlinson. My sister Caroline disappeared when I was younger. I know how it feels to lose someone so young and full of potential. Part of my mission is never letting that happen to someone else."

"Not much you can do about Jackie," said the man.

"Maybe not," said Osgood. "But if we find the right connection, maybe we can stop this from happening to other families."

The door opened a crack, and two sets of eyes peeked out, one above the other. Osgood was struck by the absurdity; it could've been a moment in a cartoon. She marveled at how strange real life so often was, though she knew, especially after the last five years, she shouldn't be surprised anymore.

"You're agents, then?" the man asked.

"No," said Audrey, then lied with astonishing comfort.

"Private investigators." She pulled a small leather flip folio out. "My license. Feel free to check it—"

Both pairs of eyes seemed to sag in resignation, and the door slowly opened, revealing a couple in their late 30s who looked exhausted. Ed's beard was patchy and too long, and it grew untrimmed around his neck and cheeks. The woman had a distinct line of gray at the root; a good deal of time had passed since she'd gone to the stylist or touched up at home. *No wonder they're so apprehensive*, thought Osgood. The Tomlinsons clearly spoke to people infrequently.

"Can I get you anything?" asked Marissa, her hands clasped tightly. "We don't have ... coffee or—"

"Water would be fine," said Audrey.

After staring at them for a moment without blinking, Ed said, "Nah, I can make coffee," and then shuffled off toward the back of the house.

"Really," called Audrey, "It's—"

"I'll get your water," said Marissa, and she followed Ed.

"Wow," said Osgood quietly.

"They're broken," said Audrey, and Osgood could hear the pain in her voice.

Osgood nodded and looked at the wall immediately to the side of the door, covered with framed photos in different sizes. 4x6, 5x7, 8x10. All showed Jackie Tomlinson, a little dark-haired girl with a wide grin, some with friends, some with her parents, but she was the clear focus in every photo.

"She looked happy," said Audrey.

"So did I," said Osgood.

They waited, patient and nervous, for the parents to return.

Twenty-Two

The lamp on the table beside Osgood, an ornate piece made of clay or some china simulacrum, buzzed and flickered nearly imperceptibly. But Osgood could percept like a son of a bitch. As their conversation with the Tomlinsons went on, not for long, only a handful of minutes, the sound of the electric insect began to burrow into her brain. In front of her, on the coffee table, sat a tall transparent glass of water and a short mug filled halfway with dark coffee. The mug had Woodstock on it. Snoopy's little friend had a heart bubble above his head that made Osgood wonder who he loved. Snoopy? Her?

What the hell are you even thinking about here? That voice in her head belonged to Audrey, but Osgood heard it so vividly that it may as well have been said by the actual Audrey Frost seated beside her on the sofa. What the hell *was* she even thinking about here? It was an excellent question. They were here to discuss a teen suicide, and here she sat, trying to distract herself from the buzz of an incandescent lightbulb by considering the love life of a small, yellow, cartoon bird.

She cleared her throat, hoping to clear her mind, and for a moment, the buzz subsided.

"—had so many friends suddenly, Ed and I were over the moon," said the woman.

"She wasn't the most popular kid in junior high," said the man.

Audrey nodded in that way that encouraged stories to continue. Osgood had always been impressed by that. Her own conversation style often bordered on interrogation, a brute-force method of gathering information. No wonder she rubbed people the wrong way. People loved Audrey.

"Did you know her friends well?" asked Audrey.

"Well, we..." began Marissa Tomlinson, suddenly very focused on the tissue in her hand. She didn't continue. But Osgood saw fresh tears forming in the corners of her eyes.

Ed took over. "Jackie had them over for a sleepover here one night. Late September, I think. We..." Now, he also trailed off.

Osgood suspected and saw her suspicion reflected in Audrey's eyes that something was being left unsaid. Audrey looked down, pursing her lips. *Here come the probing questions,* thought Osgood, just before a *tink tink tink* flicker of the bulb and the electric buzz returned, somehow louder and angrier this time, roiling, snarling at her, burrowing through her gray matter into the deepest recesses of her brain. She wondered if the Tomlinsons had any Excedrin. She stood, suddenly enough that it surprised her. "If you'll excuse me a moment, I need to use the restroom."

The Tomlinsons looked startled and began to point and describe the location downstairs. Osgood had no intention of going to that one, so she immediately started up the wooden steps covered in a thin carpet runner.

"You don't have to use the one—"

Osgood cut Ed Tomlinson off, saying, "I've got this, thank

you." Then she pointedly turned to at Audrey. "I'm sure you have more questions for them."

Audrey nodded. The gambit. In their early days of ghost hunting, this was how they would find the con. The secret behind Discovery Channel's ghost shows was that most hauntings are phony. Frankly, Osgood thought that faulty wiring could explain 75-80% of them. Higher-than-typical electromagnetic fields (EMF, the holy grail for dubious ghost hunters) can cause feelings of nausea, disorientation, and, at certain levels, even hallucinations. Couple bad wiring with an old, noisy house that creaks when the wind blows, and you've got a recipe for one exciting, but very false, haunting. Their gambit usually involved separating the homeowners from the haunt and, in most cases, was accomplished just like this. (These days it was easier, as her cane made her far less potentially threatening. A thief with a cane would be easy to catch.) Audrey would move into information-gathering mode, and Osgood would go hunting, not for ghosts, but for proof of *no* ghosts.

Today, however, Osgood had her sights focused on something else. She moved down a skinny hallway, common in turn-of-the-20th-century houses like this. Bedroom, bedroom, bathroom... She was gambling on a master bath, an iffy proposition. The oldest houses in Chicago often had only a single bathroom. This house, though, felt somewhat modernized. Probably not by the Tomlinsons—the upgrades felt turn-of-the-21st-century modern, all calming colors. Osgood opened a door at the front of the house and found a room with a queen bed and two nightstands. Definitely an adult bedroom. She saw a red Target prescription bottle on the left side table. Daridorexant. Osgood knew that one. Sleep aid. Unsurprising. Opposite the bed was a wall where an effort had been made to replicate the ornate Victorian crown molding, but they hadn't quite matched the vintage handy work. In that wall, a door, and behind that door, a master bath.

She caught a glimpse of herself in the mirror—something she tried not to do at all, if possible. The circles beneath her eyes were profound. Osgood felt she might be transitioning into a heroine in a Tim Burton film, as her skin grew paler and her eyes more sunken. She must remember to eat more. Or at all. She couldn't recall the last meal she'd had, actually. That was concerning. She banished the ghoul in the mirror by opening the cabinet. Glory of glories, rows upon rows of prescription bottles. Some were in the red of Target pharmacy, but most were in the older translucent orange bottles. She peered down the row, noting names, both generic and not. Escitalopram, buproprion... Generics for Lexapro and Wellbutrin. Osgood wondered if Marissa downstairs would appreciate that they seemed to be medicine twinsies. Though, Osgood noted, her personal dosages were much higher than the grieving mother's.

More important, though, was the bottle she found in the back on the lower shelf. It wasn't oxy, no, as pharmacists had made it incredibly difficult to acquire that, but codeine in 30 mg doses wasn't bad. Osgood popped the top off and saw only four pills at the bottom. Momentarily, she wondered if she should take them all. She looked at the label; the script had been written by a DDS and filled over a year ago. Someone had some dental work done. They wouldn't miss it. She dumped all four pills straight into her mouth, filled a hand with water, and did her best to swallow them down before replacing the cap and the pill bottle in the medicine cabinet. Before closing it, though, another name caught her eye, another generic: quetiapine. It'd been a long time since she'd seen that old friend, first prescribed to her in high school, when, at her parent's insistence, she'd gone to an incredibly homophobic psychiatrist who'd suggested it to treat, among other things, bipolar disorder and possible schizophrenia. This bottle had Jackie's name on it.

Osgood considered this. Indeed, the fact that Jackie had been on antipsychotics was relevant to the discussion being had downstairs. Still, "What exactly were you doing in our medicine cabinet?" Osgood snapped a photo of the label and closed the mirror. It showed her turquoise curls floofed out like a fright wig, her buzzed side badly in need of trimming, and her lips beginning to crack from a combination of dryness and a refusal to stop nibbling on them. *Portrait of the artist as a bitch,* thought Osgood.

She flicked the light off and went to the stairs, stopping for a moment and listening to the discussion below.

"—trying to be supportive. We're modern, of course," said the man.

"The school wasn't as accepting," said the woman.

"Did you consider other potential schools?" asked Audrey.

"We've. Well, I—"

"We've been a part of St. Gregory's parish since we both were young. Grew up nearby on Catalpa Avenue. It..."

As the man trailed off, Osgood moved away from the stairs. She kept her cane up and tried her best to lighten her footfalls. The pain seared but had begun to mute. As well it should; she'd taken double the maximum dose of codeine for a healthy adult, and she was anything but.

The bedroom called to her, the one in the middle of the hall, across from what was likely the original bathroom. Osgood flipped the switch and stepped inside.

A preponderance of cute boy posters on the wall made Osgood snicker. Several of them were Asian. Jackie had been a K-pop fan. The bands in other posters may as well have been in another language for all Osgood knew of them. They appeared to be cute, manufactured pop groups, like the Back-street Boys and *NSYNC in her era. All the girls had loved them, and they'd seemed so non-threatening because they were never "spotted going into a club with…" How girls she'd known had been crushed to learn so many of them were gay. Osgood remembered the looks she'd get when she'd say sure, "Sure, *that's* why you're never going to date Lance Bass."

The books on the shelves made Osgood like the kid more. She had several Stephen King paperbacks to go along with her Judy Blumes, including the seminal *Are You There God? It's Me, Margaret.* The battered paperback copies of *The Exorcist* and *Jaws* were even more amusing. Osgood lifted *Jaws* and looked at its cover. Had she read the book or only seen the movie? She couldn't remember. She opened it, finding the spine broken at a specific point, and skimmed the page. Matt Hooper and Ellen Brody were having lunch and talking about an affair. Osgood laughed, surprised, especially when she read Ellen's concern that, if they fooled around while driving, they might get in an accident, and she'd be found without her underwear, legs spread, and, Osgood couldn't help but read the next bit aloud, "'vagina yawning open for the world to see.'" She laughed, then flicked her eyes toward the door to the bedroom. The hall beyond it was still silent.

She could imagine Jackie in here, snuggled on her bed, paperback in hand, reading this. Her young 12- or 13-year-old libido just coming online, enough to make the confusing feelings palpable. Osgood had a similar moment when she'd discovered *Wifey* at the library after completing Judy Blume's early and middle school works. Thinking the only difference would be that it was longer, young Prudence had settled in to read, discovering the story of a sexually frustrated wife told with the same kind of graphic detail that Judy had used to explain periods in *Are You There God* or the frank descriptions of boners and masturbation in *Then Again, Maybe I Won't.*

She'd felt the tingles in her private parts. And from then on, those bits in books, and eventually movies, helped her recognize that her interest in girls wasn't an interest only in Audrey, but was broader.

Osgood pulled *The Exorcist* down from the shelf, finding its spine also cracked in a specific spot, one she suspected before she even opened it. The horrifying sexy and religiously confusing moment where little Regan, possessed by the demon Pazuzu, masturbates with a crucifix.

"Os?" called Audrey from downstairs.

She slapped the book closed and fumbled it back onto the shelf, feeling her face flush and her heart race. *Ahh, sexual embarrassment; I haven't been acquainted with you in quite a while,* she thought. "Be right down," she called back. Looking at the other books, she suspected she'd find much the same. Subtle indications that certain pages and passages had been read more than others. Noting *IT* down at the end, she suspected there'd been all sorts of puberty confusion reading that one.

Hobbling back down the stairs, Osgood found the three of them waiting on the landing for her. Both mom and dad looked mildly concerned, while Audrey's eyes held judgment, seeming to ask, "What the fuck took you so long?" As she descended, though, she thought of the question she'd wanted confirmation on. "Mr. and Mrs. Tomlinson," she began. She reached the moment the stairs made a final turn toward the landing and stood, resting her hand on the newel post. "Was Jackie gay?"

The parents' eyes widened, and they looked toward each other, then at Audrey, then back at Osgood.

"She..." began Ed, but he didn't continue.

"She was too young to know *what* she wanted," said Marissa.

There it was. Osgood had heard that from her mother as

well. As her father had disappeared into other rooms, discussions with Cynthia involved *trying* boys, like it was something she'd just have to get used to. Of course, she would later discover she enjoyed dick as well, but *bisexual* just wasn't really an oft-discussed concept in the mid-'90s.

"Why?" asked Ed. At that moment, while Marissa reminded her of her mother, Ed reminded her of her father. Judging inwardly but trying to be supportive. It wasn't fair, though, assigning that to either of them.

"I was looking in her room, and—"

"You went into her room?" shrieked Marissa.

"Well, yes, I—"

"Get out!" The shriek turned into a wail as Marissa pressed her hand to her face. Ed put his hands on her shoulders, clearly trying to help reign her in, but to no avail. The wailing grew and grew. She began to shuffle them toward the entryway.

Osgood leaned into Audrey. "Did you get anything?"

"Before you fucked this up?"

"Seriously."

"Not much," whispered Audrey. "I think we—"

"I'm sorry for what I'm about to do," whispered Osgood. She took a breath and whirled on the Tomlinsons. Marissa's eyes were wide and wild, and she was startled by Osgood's turn. "Did your daughter kill herself because you didn't accept her for being gay?"

As though Osgood had slapped her, Marissa actually reeled backward. Thankfully, Ed was behind her to stop her from sprawling on the foyer floor.

"How dare you!" said the woman. "We may be Catholic, but we're progressive Catholics."

"I didn't say—" began Osgood. She noticed Audrey's eyes very wide, gaping at her. "While Catholics and Christians often have a problem with gay people—"

"Not *all* Catholics," said Ed angrily.

Good, thought Osgood. *Nice to see him show some emotion here.* Another voice prodded her, a voice from deep within. Her conscience, maybe? *Why are you pushing so hard with people who just went through a traumatic—* But Osgood ignored it and pressed on, moving toward the Tomlinsons, away from the door. "My parents resented me for being queer. They thought it was psychological. They put me on antipsychotics."

"Wait," said Ed. "Did you look in—"

"And I want to know what you might have done that had something to do with her death?"

"Os," said Audrey, putting her hand atop Osgood's on the cane. It wasn't a gentle *let's stop this,* but a death grip *you're out of your mind.*

The thing was, Osgood felt it, too. She'd lost a bit of that tether that she always relied on, the centering bit of herself. She was floating in a weird netherworld where she identified far too much with a 14-year-old girl who'd killed herself, enough to attack her grieving parents as proxies for her own.

"No!" screamed Marissa through sobs. "We loved her so much. Every bit of her. Gay or straight didn't matter to us." Osgood resisted the urge to suggest that maybe their psychiatrist didn't agree with them on the pro-gay stance. "She was on medication for other reasons. She'd had difficulties in junior high. With the kids there. Not us."

"Kids in junior high can be brutal," said Osgood. "Especially if you're different."

Marissa's sobbing ebbed a bit as she nodded.

"High school is better, but weird is still weird. Was she weird?"

"You need to—" began Ed, but he stopped when Marissa put her hand on his arm.

"Yes," she said. "Very."

"Gothy weird? Band weird?"

"Horror. Books mostly."

Osgood nodded. She moved toward the now-sniffling mother. Her voice was low and calm. "Not just school, but the world is unkind to kids who are different. Like Jackie. Like me."

Still looking at Osgood with questioning eyes, Audrey quietly added, "Like me."

"Me too," said Marissa. Ed was quiet.

"And in a world where people can be cruel, especially young teenagers, as their puberty-addled brains are still in soft sociopath mode, it is especially tragic when young people are desperate for companionship. Desperate to find a place to fit in." Osgood reached out a hand to the woman, who yanked her own back on reflex. Osgood continued to move hers forward until she touched the wrist hem of Marissa Tomlinson's sweater. "Because when we try so hard, especially if we think we're broken, if we think we're unworthy of love because either a psychiatrist or priest told us so, we tend to make mistakes."

"I didn't like her friends," said Ed quietly.

"Why not?" asked Audrey, matching his energy.

"There was, uh, a mean girl—"

"Little bitch," said Marissa under her breath.

Ed nodded and remained silent.

"That little bitch Anna," said Marissa. "I'm tired of pretending she wasn't awful just because she died. 'Cuz they're all little angels now, right?" The woman expelled a laugh-sob that came out like a guffaw. The shoulders of all four in the foyer released a bit of tension.

"What made Anna a bitch?"

Ed just shook his head.

"You know the type, always wanting to stay out later than

curfew, asking if we have any beer." Marissa's face scrunched with distaste. "She stole my makeup, too."

Looking at Marissa now, a harried grieving woman, face as clean as the morning, it was hard to believe that a high school freshman would have wanted anything she had.

"Can we sit back down?" asked Osgood. "Just for a few more minutes. As you may have guessed from my hobble, I have leg problems. And back problems. And head problems. You name it, I've probably broken it."

Ed looked at his wife. A moment passed between them, and Osgood saw them for what they were. Young parents who'd gone through a tragedy. Young adults, no longer allowed to be young because of that tragedy. "Yeah. Okay," he said. The reluctance made Osgood feel good. It showed concern for his wife, who had just been confronted by a yelling lunatic who now wanted to stay longer.

"Do you need something for pain?" asked Marissa as they sat. "We might have some heavy-duty stuff upstairs."

Osgood tensed and thanked them, but no. She found herself seated again next to that table lamp with the buzzing bulb. She eyed it, irritated, wondering what they'd say if she just snapped the fucking lamp off.

TWENTY-THREE

"As we told Miss Fro... Audrey," said Marissa. "She had her ups and downs but didn't seem different."

"Did Audrey ask you about the Graveyard Game?" asked Osgood. She tilted her head at them, hoping that a change of angle would reduce the horrid crawling buzz beside her.

"No," said Audrey, calm but firm. "*Audrey* thought that might be a question for—"

"What is the Graveyard Game?" asked Marissa, concern on her face.

Audrey sighed, throwing another tension-filled glance at Osgood, who wondered why she wouldn't have asked about it in the first place. Maybe she was worried about giving up their private investigator cred by throwing in some supernatural mumbo jumbo? Well, the cat was out of the bag now. Osgood opened her mouth to explain, but Audrey gave them the CliffsNotes. "It's a social media thing. Kids are going into Rosehill Cemetery to look at a statue."

"And that's ... fun for them?" asked Ed.

"You remember Bloody Mary?" Before they could ask if

she meant the drink, Osgood added, "Or Candyman." *That* they got. "The Graveyard Game is a scare challenge. Something people, especially teenagers, try to convince each other to do."

"Why are you asking about this?" asked Marissa.

Osgood saw Audrey open the video on her phone but then hold the phone face down.

"We have video of your daughter participating in this game with some other girls her age, including the two who were murdered,"

The buzzing grew louder. Osgood couldn't understand why the others in the room weren't bothered by it, why the Tomlinsons didn't change the bulb. Time to go green, get some LEDs in there. If she came back, she'd bring them one. Zack had scads in his warehouse, and Osgood suspected they'd fallen off a truck at some point. Audrey showed the concerned and bewildered parents the video. If the buzzing hadn't been so loud, Osgood could have heard the video, too. But she knew what it showed, she could imagine the girls, see the Guardian statue in Rosehill. See them climb on up to look in its—

(it showed me)

What? It had shown her nothing. It didn't have eyes to look into, only a blank surface not meant to be seen. The sculptor had clearly intended light to never penetrate the hood's depths, so the shrouded figure might never be known.

(now i can see)

Osgood shuddered at that memory of what the Lord of the Hinterlands had done, had convinced his followers to do. "We've cut out our eyes, now we can see." They'd discovered the message hidden in pages and pages of text. *This isn't the same,* Osgood assured herself. *But it might have implications.* That second voice in her head, the one Osgood didn't know. Her brain had always been wired to create personas for her own thoughts, and very occasionally it gave her someone new, someone worth listening to. She wondered what kind of implications and, as though she'd asked it the question, the darker voice answered. *You don't know what you saw.*

But she did know, didn't she? She'd seen nothing. Just a sculpture, a monument atop a tomb. Surely she hadn't seen her death or anyone else's. Surely she—

The whiteish T on her left wrist split, first up her forearm and then, as though crossed with a sword, across her wrist. The ripping sound was loud enough that everybody in the room should've looked at her, but they hadn't. For a moment there was nothing, only a slight split like an elongated papercut, then the blood began to flow. Still, no one else looked. Osgood clamped her hand down on that wrist, trying to hold together the edges of the old wound. Even this, this panicked grab, called no attention to her. And still the buzz from the light droned louder. *It's not real,* she told herself, adding it again under her breath for good measure. That got a bit of attention from Audrey, a side-eye as she held the phone in front of the Tomlinsons. A second rip and now Osgood's right forearm and wrist gushed blood as well. Real or not, Osgood began to feel lightheaded from the blood loss, but she couldn't very well ask for first aid for something that no one else could see.

Purple splotches began to float in her vision. She wondered if she was about to pass out. The signs were there. Light-headedness. Nausea coming on. She wondered if the codeine had gone bad. No, drugs just got less powerful. They didn't suddenly become hallucinogens. Though she couldn't remember the last time she'd used codeine. After the doctors had stopped prescribing her the good stuff, she'd learned to stop asking them. The light-headedness grew. Her eyes began to swim. She looked at her hands, so pale, especially compared to the bright red blood covering her lap and the floor in front of her. She watched Audrey sip from her water glass, not noticing the red tinge and the fresh droplet of blood slowly trickling down the side. That was enough. Her swimmy vision began to narrow to a tunnel, then a point, then black.

But she hadn't passed out, had she? Osgood felt fully awake and aware, here in the dark behind her eyes. That said, it wasn't at all unusual for her to drift away, so she didn't feel much concern. That is, until the pressure in her chest. Overwhelming pressure, not just down from above, but from all around her, as though she were wearing a blood pressure cuff around her entire torso and it'd steadily begun to tighten. First it was only the pressure, but soon enough she felt as though she couldn't breathe deeply or long enough to get the oxygen she needed, and with each expulsion of breath the internal volume of her lungs grew smaller. Her heart pounded hard enough she imagined she could feel it against the inside of her chest. It reminded her of the strange sensation she'd experienced in the moments just before an orchid-like creature had crawled out of her body. Somehow that had been less concerning. This felt like every panic attack she'd ever had rolled into one, and boy howdy, did she feel like she was dying when those happened.

Maybe I did look into its eyes, came the fleeting thought in the darkness, a momentary suggestion that she was still functioning normally. And again, the feeling that

(it showed me)

there was something beyond her reach. Something behind the veil of the world that she couldn't lift. Something dark and hidden. Of course, that made it incredibly enticing; even as she felt this endless constriction, could barely take in a breath, she wondered about the forbidden knowledge. Wondered if she could get to it, capture it somehow. Just see a little further, a little deeper into the dark. Because there lay understanding. There were the answers to all of her questions. Who wanted the mortal realm anyway? It was in her own darkness in the margins she'd built her kingdom; why return to a world of agony and evil?

Wait. What? That voice was Cynthia, in that level of polite fury her mother had perfected through decades of board meetings and fundraisers. *You will* not *resign yourself to* not *living!*

Osgood wanted to point out the weird double "nots" in the sentence she knew her mother would never say, but her brain felt scrambled, and the pressure on her chest, which surely should've crushed or killed her by now, continued to grow.

Snap out of this nonsense! Now, Prudence!

And at once it was gone. All of it. In its place, the simple living room of Ed and Marissa Tomlinson, and she was sitting next to Audrey, who was leaning across the coffee table to show the Tomlinsons her phone. Osgood looked down at her wrists and saw nothing out of the ordinary, just her mismatched T scars and her semicolon tattoo. The Tomlinsons sat back after the video ended, and Audrey closed out of her phone and put it in her pocket. The three of them continued to talk, and slowly the buzzing of the light next to Osgood began to ebb, restoring the sounds of the conversation before her and the streets of Chicago outside. After another moment, all was as it had been before.

Wide-eyed, Osgood asked herself, and her version of her mother in her head, *What the fuck was that?* Of course, neither of them knew the answer.

TWENTY-FOUR

They regrouped as night fell on Clark Street, October finally bringing in a chill. By the time the sun had entirely disappeared behind the buildings to the west, the blue evening had dropped into the 40s, enough for the radiators in Osgood's apartment to wake up. The *tick tick tick* of freshly risen steam flowed through it, as did the smell of reheated old building. There was a musty warmth to it, a comfort Osgood found, just as the harsh orange streetlamps offered reassurance. *What we grow up with can become what we love, no matter how awful,* thought Osgood. It wasn't a stretch to assume that her love of Scotch, whiskey, and bourbon, all facets of the same elixir, had come from watching her father drink it as she grew up. She'd come a long way from when it had tasted like fire and dirt, and the surface spirals and machinations in a glass with no ice, just a droplet of water, were beautiful to behold.

Osgood sipped and looked over the glass as Audrey brought Zack up to speed. She pushed aside her foolish annoyance that they'd moved on without her. She'd been gone for over a year, left no trace; of course they'd moved on. No matter what Osgood's ego might want to believe, if she were to well and truly go, there'd be some consternation, some tears, some mourning, and then the world would bounce back. Life is flexible like that. One can only create so big a divot in the world, and even then, the moment one is removed, the divot begins to shrink. The more horrifying, the longer the shrinking takes, as had happened with the Tomlinsons. Who knew if they'd survive, continuing to scratch at it. Some divots become scars. Caroline Frost's disappearance had made a scar that Audrey had torn open over and over, enough for it to become gangrenous. But they'd cut out the poison—a creature, an entity, a thing called the Lord of the Hinterlands. And once it'd been excised, the scar had finally begun to heal, so that now it was nothing more than those scars on the insides of her thighs.

"—should we be?"

After a moment, Audrey asked, "Osgood?"

She focused again, outside her head this time, and found that Zack and Audrey were looking her way. Both faces were full of concern. Osgood hadn't heard the conversation, but she knew the question. She'd been to enough actual interventions, even been the guest of honor at a few, to know that this was an assessment of risk. Could this party be trusted on their own? She thought she could, but the interventionee always thinks that. "I will..." began Osgood, but then she thought a bit more. What was this? What was it really? "Acknowledge." There, diplomatic. "That I haven't been myself..." A deep breath. "Since we were at Rosehill."

"We're not ganging up on you, Os," assured Audrey. She put her hand on Osgood's knee.

Shit, this is serious.

"Look," said Zack. "I will never restrict your autonomy."

"Okay," said Osgood, concerned about what might follow that ominous phrase.

"But let's look at the facts as we know them." He took a deep breath and leaned back in his chair before counting off said facts on his fingers. "First, several young people are dead, both from suicide and from murder."

Osgood nodded.

"Second, at least some of them played the Graveyard Game, which purports to show you how you'll die or your future, depending on who tells it. Third, you looked into the statue's face. Playing not the game, but the end."

"And it was blank," insisted Osgood.

"I'm not sure that's what matters," said Audrey.

"And fourth, now you're having suicidal ideations and fantasies about your old suicide attempt."

"I wouldn't say fantasies," said Osgood. She knew she was deflecting. Of course, all those things were true. Of course, they should be concerned. She was worried herself, wasn't she?

Zack looked to Audrey, who nodded, then back to Osgood. "We want you to tell us how to proceed."

"With the investigation?" asked Osgood.

"With you," said Audrey.

They stared at her, and she stared back. After a moment, she laughed, unable to think of what else to do. "Like, should I be on suicide watch?"

"We have no idea how this works, Os," said Audrey.

"All I know," said Zack, "is at least half of the people who've died did the Graveyard Game. We don't know about the rest, and we don't know if they did it online. Something is happening here; even marking these up as coincidences doesn't make much sense. Statistically, we could suppose the North Shore Ripper is real, and that's *why* the murder rate of young adults is high in this area. But there's nothing that could explain these unrelated suicides."

"The world is pretty shitty right now," said Osgood.

"Well, agreed," said Zack, "But you see what I'm saying, right?"

She did, and it frightened her. Looking down at her hands, she couldn't help but see the gushing blood coming from her wrists, still as vivid as it had been when she was at the Tomlinsons' place. "So..." She laughed again. "What do we do?"

"Well, I mean. We keep researching. Keep investigating," said Audrey. "I'd like to see if the schools have an on-staff psychologist who may have some insight."

"It probably *wants* me to kill myself," said Osgood with a mirthless laugh.

Again, they looked at each other. This time, they appeared to be attempting subtlety, but Osgood saw it, could've seen it without her glasses. She knew the look, too, so how could she blame them? Unearned false confidence in the face of unknowable danger? That was the Spectral Inspector way. Osgood's laugh came out as little more than a puff of air. "What's the difference between those who kill themselves and those who are murdered? Like, killing themselves only requires the statue to influence one person, but the others..."

No one had an answer for that.

Zack changed the subject. "While you were out, I did some digging about the statue." He lifted the remote for the TV above their decommissioned fireplace and turned it on. After it came to life, he pressed the small remote in his hand, and a black-and-white portrait appeared on the screen. The portrait showed a man with an elaborate mustache and long, well-groomed mutton chops. "Ambrose Ballard, born 1857, death unknown."

"Oh! School!" said Osgood.

"Hush," said Zack.

Osgood waved her hand at him to get on with it, but she also just wanted the picture to go away. The man's eyes seemed too pale for his face. Objectively, Osgood knew that portraits taken during that time needed more light, which often resulted in tightly constricted pupils; the colors of a subject's iris didn't always photograph well, either. Despite this knowledge, Ballard's picture unsettled her.

Zack nodded and popped forward to another slide, this one an old photograph of the Guardian and the flat stones at its feet. He drew digital pink lines on the screen using his remote, outlining the area directly below the statue. "This is the grave of Samantha Ballard. Her stone doesn't have dates on it, but she's thought to have been six months old when she died. Next to her," he said, drawing another outline, "is Cora Ballard, the man's second wife, who died in February of 1903 at the age of 19."

"46 and 19, eh?" said Osgood. "Big daddy."

"We got all this when I looked it up, Zack," said Audrey. "Did you find anything new?"

"I thought you enjoyed my color."

"I do, just—" She repeated Osgood's hand wave, which made Osgood snicker.

"Alright then, unique things about Ambrose Ballard. He was a very wealthy industrialist, though the exact origins of his fortune are unknown. Interestingly, he created Ballard Drug and Ballard Department Store, both usurped by others in Chicago, namely Walgreens and Marshall Field's. He also dabbled in candy, outdone by Brach's and Wrigley. And he opened a hotel along Grant Park, quickly overtaken by the nearby Congress." Zack flipped through slides, some featuring photos of these locations, others of brand names and sketches. "No matter what Ballard did, it seemed someone else did it better and more effectively."

"Sounds like the kind of thing that makes someone go broke," said Osgood.

"That's what's curious," said Zack. "As I mentioned, there's no known sources of income, though it's long been thought his main sources of money were from playing the stock market exceptionally well."

"Maybe he bet against himself," said Audrey.

"This guy was in Chicago during the Chicago fire; he contributed to the 1893 Columbian Exposition. Who knows, he may have crossed paths with H.H. Holmes." Zack's enthusiasm for lore was boundless, especially regarding Chicago's storied history. While New York and Los Angeles may have eclipsed it in other ways, neither of them had a psycho who'd built a murder hotel to off guests of a World's Fair. H.H. Holmes, the titular Devil in the White City, was a Chicago exclusive.

"I appreciate your color, Zack," said Osgood. Audrey threw her a look.

"But," said Zack, anticipating what was to come.

"But as interesting as Ambrose Ballard may be, the statue is really—"

"Right!" Zack exclaimed. He popped an image of the Guardian back up on the screen. "So, I found that the Guardian was sculpted and cast with the intent of being put in a fountain on the Ballard property at..." He elongated the word "at" to find his information. "Well, I can't find the address. But it's inner Lake Shore Drive, now in Lincoln Park."

"He wanted this in his yard?" asked Audrey, staring at the screen.

"Front yard, actually," said Zack. "He had a koi pond in the walkway leading up to his house, and the Guardian was intended to watch over the pond and the house, presumably."

"But the sculptor didn't complete it in time?" asked Osgood.

"No," said Zack. "The original sculptor ... Giovanni Rossi, died six months into the creation process. As did his apprentice Salvador..." Zack looked over his notes. "...Something. I can't find his last name, but he followed his master into the grave two weeks later. It's not known who finished the statue, but the popular belief is that the hooded face—"

"There's no face; it's blank," said Osgood quickly. She wondered why she was so insistent on that point.

Zack looked at her, uncertain what to say. "They call it the face. I don't know."

"It's blank," repeated Osgood under her breath.

He took a minute to find his place. "...the 'face' was completed by an artist who drew a salary from one of Ballard's wealthy cohorts. In any case, the statue was about to make its debut at the Ballard house but was redirected to Rosehill Cemetery when the news came that Ballard's wife and daughter had died."

"Wait...," said Audrey.

"Yeah," agreed Zack. "So, I'm finding conflicting reports here. While most reputable sources, including the Chicago Tribune, separate the deaths of Cora and Samantha, listing causes of death as flu for the daughter and broken heart for the mother, other sources suggest that Cora died in childbirth." He put down his tablet but left the image of the Guardian on the screen. "Those other sources also go back and forth on whether she was legally Ballard's wife. I found one essay that suggested the first Mrs. Ballard, Lavinia, had employed Cora Coleridge as a maid." He gave them both a nod and a smile. "And that's all I've got." He sat for a moment, then leaped to his feet. "Wait! No! I just found..." He rushed over to the side table that the three of them had designated for ongoing investigations but, over time, had become overwhelmed with closed inquiries and, eventually, catalogs and junk mail. But it only took Zack a moment to find a torn piece of paper with a note in his scribbled handwriting. "'The Luminous Brotherhood of the Eternal Flame.'"

Osgood snorted a laugh and then thanked the gods she'd

swallowed down her Lagavulin before he'd mentioned it. "Wait," she said, pressing the back of her hand to her mouth to suppress a hacking cough. "The Luminous..."

"Luminous Brotherhood," said Zack.

"Luminous Brothers of the Eternal Flame."

"Brother*hood*," corrected Zack.

Osgood looked to Audrey, who pondered, "I wonder what made them luminous."

"Do you two want the information, or will you just make fun?"

"We're not making fun of *you*, Zack," assured Audrey.

Osgood nodded, then shook her head, then nodded again, uncertain which response would be assuring. "It's just such an..." She wasn't sure what it was.

Audrey picked it up. "Grandiloquent title."

"I was going to say ornate, but grand... That's better." Osgood looked back at Zack. "It sounds like the kind of club that would have a weird, overtly sexual initiation, but they wouldn't let any women in, so over time, it devolves into circle jerks around some arcane altar."

"Wow," said Zack. He looked back at the piece of paper in his hand. "The Luminous Brotherhood counted among its members Daniel Burnham, the guy that basically designed Chicago, and Richard Warren Sears, who, well ... Sears, so..."

"Okay," nodded Osgood. "Decent pedigree. What else do we know about them?"

"The last lodge, number nine, is in Willowbrook and is still open."

"Holy shit!" Osgood exclaimed. "Can women join?" She cackled, momentarily forgetting why they were here, what they were even doing.

Zack just shook his head at her, and at Audrey as well, who'd joined in the laughter. "Well, I'm gonna go downstairs," said Zack, standing again.

"No," said Audrey.

Osgood put her best reassuring face on. "This is good information, Zack. Really."

"I prefer it when I'm tech."

"But you find information better than anyone," said Osgood. She reached out toward him but felt her body sway. How many Lagavulins had she had? One when they got back, and another while Zack set up. Three? Four? Couldn't be more than four. Looking at the one in front of her, she didn't know when she'd poured it, but her pours looked heavy tonight. "And we love you."

"Okay, drunkie," said Zack. "But really. It's late, and I need some sleep." He flung a finger pointedly at Osgood. "And so do you."

"Oh, boo," said Osgood.

TWENTY-FIVE

When Audrey returned from what she'd claimed was a trip to the bathroom, she brought with her a rocks glass, which she set on the coffee table next to Osgood's three remaining fingers of Scotch.

"You're drinking with me?" asked Osgood.

"Seems as good a time as any. Kent dumped me. You're suicidal. We're investigating the Ancient Secret Lodge of the Flaming Brothers..."

Osgood laughed. She didn't need any further explanation. She splashed an oversized draft into Audrey's glass, noting the ice cube Aud had nabbed from the kitchen.

"Sorry if I'm ruining it," said Audrey.

Osgood shrugged. "It's alcohol. If you like it, there's no wrong way to drink it." She watched as her friend lifted her glass and tipped it toward her. Osgood brought up her own to clink. As they sipped, Osgood watched Audrey through narrowed eyes. The apartment's lighting was low, and the lights on the wall behind the couch lit the edge of Audrey's hair. Her icy blue eyes met Osgood's.

"What?"

"Nothing," said Osgood with a smile.

Audrey's sip grew long enough to consume the entire glass. She set it back down with a louder-than-usual but not concerning *thunk*. Her eyes, though, confused Osgood.

"Are you trying to get me drunk?" asked Osgood.

"How? You're like four drinks ahead of me," said Audrey.

"Fair point." Osgood cocked her head. "Just ... you're looser than usual."

"I thought you liked that," said Audrey.

"I do. I just—"

"Os," said Audrey firmly.

Osgood stopped and waited.

"Shut the fuck up and pour me another drink."

Osgood obliged. "How are you doing?"

"I'm fine. Stop," said Audrey. "Are you going to pour or what?"

"Yes, fine," said Osgood, and she obliged. "I meant, how are you doing about ... stuff."

"By stuff, you mean Kent."

"Yes, Aud, by stuff, I mean Kent."

"Fuck it," said Audrey. "Maybe I'm just not a relationship person. I thought about that for a while, after my divorce."

"The divorce was because of your focus on Caroline, though," said Osgood. "Wasn't it?"

"I mean, divorces can never be boiled down to a single why. 'Irreconcilable differences' covers so much." Audrey threw up her hands and flopped them back down. The stretched-out collar of her tee fell off her shoulder.

Osgood felt her gaze drawn like a magnet to Audrey's newly exposed clavicle. Sudden focus, sudden attention. Her friend's skin had the same pallor as hers, of someone who didn't spend much time outside, but Audrey's was dusted with the lightest freckles Osgood had ever seen. So pale they could vanish, and they never stood out or called for attention, only ... were. The fact that Audrey had gone sans bra after returning from their interview didn't surprise Osgood. Almost inevitable, their post-investigation wardrobe of sweats or shorts and t-shirts. Osgood, too, was braless, but her obnoxious tits didn't poke out the way Aud's did. At 44, her nipples had begun to point to her feet. Audrey's little titties, though... Osgood sighed and Audrey glanced at her sideways.

"I've never *not* had something else going on, something else pulling me away, something else on my mind." Audrey sipped this glass. "What I have had is a string of people who won't allow for that. Like the book."

"Kent didn't like that you wrote a book?"

Audrey's sigh was deep. "He wasn't crazy about any of this." She waved her hand floppily around her. "The ghosthunting. You."

"So, it's not my fault?" asked Osgood with a sly smile.

"I never wanted you to think it was your fault," said Audrey. She considered a moment. "Maybe a little."

"Cunt," said Osgood.

Audrey laughed so hard she snorted, which made her laugh harder and harder, which made her snort more. She tried desperately to stem the flow of snorts, but her hand wasn't mighty enough. She rolled onto her side on the couch, bringing her face so much closer to Osgood's, though, miraculously, she managed to keep the final finger of her drink upright. "Well done," she said to herself, when she regained a semblance of composure. From here, with her right ear pressed against the faded fabric of their couch, she turned her face up to Osgood's.

Knowing she'd regret it physically—if not shortly, then definitely in the morning—Osgood slid out of her Barca-Lounger to her knees. The radiating pain shot both upward and downward, screaming about what the ever-loving fuck she was thinking. But Osgood's mind was lucid despite all the

Scotch, and she wanted one thing: to kiss Audrey Frost. The first kiss was gentle and quiet, bringing their lips together at nearly the same angle, but they didn't part. The dryness of autumn gave the kiss a sound like the rasp of papers sliding together. Far from an uncomfortable or discordant sound, it made Osgood happy enough that she held to Aud's lips as long as she could, before sliding away with a barely audible *aah*.

They said nothing for a while. Long enough that Osgood's ears adjusted, desperately searching for sound. Sound on such a busy street in Chicago wasn't challenging to come by. Still, she'd lived here long enough that the random sirens and car alarms, the shushing back and forth of commuters, and the rattling thuds of fools who thought their cars needed to get low had woven themselves together into a tapestry of sound that was her baseline. This sound was background, omnipresent. Had been, was, would be. But in the silence after that kiss, the other sounds of the apartment came to life. She'd absconded with the pendulum clock in the hall from her parents' basement, the first time they kicked her out. Its regular chimes were a part of her youth in this city, and they sounded so much better here than in the dreaded suburbs. Beyond the couch, through the cracked door to the office, she heard the whir of Zack's powerful upstairs workstation in harmony with the higher pitch of her desktop fan and the intermittent fan on Audrey's laptop. Deep inside the cushion of sound, the fridge droned down the hall. Far from irritating, these were the sounds of her life, far better than when it had only been a single computer. If she concentrated and sank deep enough into silence, she could usually hear the disco/pop of Mary's below her. But even they'd toned it down post-COVID. Another sad change—

Audrey's kiss interrupted this train of thought that was rolling without destination down the tracks. Her friend, her once-lover, her Audrey, had also moved to the floor on her knees before Osgood. This kiss began with lips parted. The small transfer of breath between them pulled Osgood's mind entirely away from the noise in the world and the noise of the pain in her body. It brought her to the present with alacrity, where her tongue found Audrey's and rolled for a moment, circles on circles, before the proper dance began, waltzing between each other's mouths. Audrey's hand found the short-shorn side of Osgood's head, and she slid her nails lightly across. Audrey didn't have much to speak of when it came to fingernails, as a lifetime of chewing had made them weak beyond her fingertips, but they were long enough for this job, and they sent shivers through Osgood's body.

What're we doing? asked Osgood's version of Audrey in her head. She was hoping that voice would tell her. Would explain it. But as much as Osgood craved an explanation for what was happening here, making out with Audrey for the first time in years, since before COVID had crashed the party, she didn't want to risk bringing it to a premature halt by saying something. These flashes of sexual attention from Audrey could feel like a quantum state, and observation only hurt it. But one should have observation and thought for this type of thing, shouldn't one? The kissing continued, growing both more passionate and delightfully wetter, but the niggling issue ricocheted around Osgood's brain. For every wall it hit, it asked questions like, *Is she trying to keep me from killing myself by fucking me?* and *Does she just miss Kent?* or *Does she just miss cock?* But the one that concerned Osgood most, and the one she felt most angry at her inner voices for, was, *Is she just drunk?*

Osgood sat back with a sigh, and as she did so, Audrey's face momentarily trailed hers, like magnets being pulled apart. Osgood looked at her friend closely; the redness in her eyes suggested exhaustion; the flush on her cheeks could be arousal, sure, but it could just as well be the drunken flush that Osgood had long since stopped getting. After all, Os was a professional drinker, not a lightweight. Once she'd thought the solution to hangovers was the obvious but mind-numbingly stupid answer: just keep drinking. Someone who was never sober would never face consequences for their actions. *Of course,* thought Osgood, *we know how utterly asinine an idea that is.*

"Aud," said Osgood.

"Oh, Os," said Audrey, sliding her hand up under Osgood's shirt, along her belly, until Aud found a handful of tit. Audrey's thumb crossed her nipple and back, and the wetness between Osgood's legs was immediate.

Whenever the frustration grew too great, the multi-faceted voices of her inner conscience collapsed downward into just one. Just her. And this voice screamed *Fuck!*

"Aud," repeated Osgood. She pressed her hand atop Audrey's from over her shirt and smiled at this woman who, at many times in her life, had been the Platonic ideal of perfect. Osgood's true love. Her person. Who she loved and liked. And she could kick herself for having let it end. This last time, over such petty shit. One drunken fuck when you said you'd be home, and non-monogamy wasn't fun anymore. Osgood could understand it, probably more than Audrey thought she could, but at the same time, she'd never "get" it.

What she did get, though, was that whatever Audrey was feeling now, it wasn't the same thing she was feeling. No. Osgood would be using Audrey for the pleasure of love and Audrey using Osgood for the joy of sex. And while mutual usage might seem commensurate, it most certainly wasn't. Osgood wasn't about to allow herself to take advantage. "Another time." Perhaps the most challenging words she'd ever said.

Audrey stopped and looked down at Osgood's hand over

hers. She momentarily took stock of the situation and then began to nod. Her head bobbed as she pushed herself back on her butt, then returned to the couch to sit, not making eye contact. "I'm sorry," she whispered.

"No, no, no, no, no," said Osgood. She leaned forward and put her hand on Audrey's knee. "Nothing to be sorry about, I promise."

"I just thought you'd—" But she didn't continue.

"I know," said Osgood. She wasn't sure, of course, what the next word would've been, but she thought Audrey was likely about to say something like, "...you'd fuck me, because you're a slut." It didn't bother her to be called one, Osgood never hid her sluttiness, but she knew that if Audrey said it aloud, it'd be the one thing she remembered most about this otherwise lovely moment. "I forgot what a great kisser you are," Osgood lied.

Audrey expelled air from her nose in a tiny laugh that didn't match the rest of her face at all. "I should go to bed."

Osgood nodded and agreed.

Then Audrey was on her feet, heading for the hallway, leaving behind the last finger of Scotch. She hesitated in the entryway and Osgood could only see her in profile. Audrey didn't look over her shoulder or make eye contact. "I love you, Prudence."

"I love you too, Audrey," said Osgood. She waited a while longer, until she heard the light switch flip off in Audrey's room. Then Osgood, feeling the pain now charging interest, finished both glasses of Scotch, went to her room and fucked herself to sleep.

TWENTY-SIX

Osgood awakens to the scents of lilac and sex. Both come from Audrey who has joined her in the darkness, which Osgood knows from the scents. The lilac aroma from Audrey's nighttime face cream and the warm and inviting smell emanating from between her legs. In the dark and silence, they're just bodies. Audrey slides into bed, her toes brushing against Osgood's legs. Osgood feels the tickle of hair against her fingers and realizes that Audrey has slid herself up against her and is asking for those fingers. Osgood feels sober. Sober*er*, anyway. Maybe Audrey is, too. Perhaps it's okay now. Their tongues find each other in a kiss, one that moves past any pretext and false suggestions of modesty or chastity. The kiss is deep, and the kiss *is* lust. They probe each other's mouths with the tips of their tongues as hands begin to wander and grope in the dark. While Osgood often wishes her fuck-buddies would touch her less—sometimes going so far as pointing out that the one part of her body that *doesn't* hurt is her pussy—she wants Audrey's fingers and hands everywhere. And everywhere they go. As Os's fingers move through the small wisp of Audrey's bush, enthusiastic but hesitant, excited to reacquaint herself with the treasures within, Audrey wastes no time, no hesitation, and her fingers slide deep inside Osgood, causing her to moan louder than she has in ages.

For Osgood, sex is typically a quiet affair, a practice ingrained in her from the beginning, when she'd tried to hide her newfound interest in her developing body. Masturbatory exploration required silence, as the old house's walls were thin, and her parents' bedroom had bordered hers. As she'd moved forward into maturity, her quiet enthusiasm had continued. She would only ever be loud when she was choosing to put on a show, which was usually reserved for folks who didn't deserve it. The louder and more obvious an orgasm was, the less chance she'd be asked if she'd had a good time, the sexual guest star would leave, and she could move on. For Osgood, an especially loud exhalation of breath was a more honest show of pleasure than the most vociferous of verbalized orgasms.

The covers fling off, and Osgood lies on her back, exposed, though still cloaked in the complete darkness of her bedroom. She feels Audrey's movements on the bed, knees lifting and dropping next to her, up and up, until the glorious fragrance of Audrey's body alights directly above Osgood's face. She opens her mouth, slides out her tongue, and waits. Audrey lowers herself onto Osgood, sliding both of her arms under Os's butt and thighs to draw her pubis upward into Audrey's face. Osgood feels the soft tongue slide from her mons down to her clit, parting her lips, penetrating, going deep, and then she feels the full-court erotic smother of her partner's pussy.

They devour each other.

Audrey isn't silent but is reserved. Osgood can feel her gasps can whispering through her bush, inviting a chill occasionally onto her wet body. Little *oh*s of joy; little *oh*s of pleasure. Osgood thinks this moment, while incredibly erotic in its spontaneity and silent synchronicity, is so comforting. Such a wonderful affirmation of their connection, even if not as actual girlfriends, as true romantic partners. Because here they are, both feeling adrift due to circumstance, coming and cumming together in the best of—

Thighs clench around Osgood's face. The Audrey in her head asks what the one outside isn't verbalizing: *Do you think you could focus up and eat my pussy like you mean it, Os?* She can and does. Osgood reaches around Audrey's small ass cheeks and grabs at her lower back, pulling her pussy closer and thrusting her tongue deeper. For an absurd moment, all Osgood can think is, *I'll give you an orgasm you can't refuse,* and she forces herself to stifle the laughter, as she's afraid the rapid expulsion would wind up creating an embarrassing raspberry sound. Maybe Audrey knows because, again, her thighs demand attention. Osgood feels the whisps of the incredibly fine blond hair of Audrey's upper legs. They tickle ever so slightly. *But we can't focus on that now, can we? We've got a pussy to eat!*

This time, the thighs distract when they contract. Osgood feels the pressure on her skull. As much as she enjoys the sense deprivation—Audrey's thighs press hard enough that all sound is blocked—as well as the dominating aspect (surprising as it was, since Audrey has never been one to dominate) Osgood knows her body well enough to know that a few more minutes of this and the migraine will start. And once that begins, the fun will be over. All Osgood wants in the world is to prolong this moment. Because in the morning, the real morning with the sun up and everything, there'll be the discussion around the table, beginning with "Soooo..." and ending with "Probably shouldn't." And they'll both agree that, while last night was a lot of fun and was perhaps what they both needed then and there in that moment, going forward, they probably—

Osgood taps Audrey's butt as she squeezes again and the

headache begins. Sure, it's still low and slow, but it'll grow and grow. *Fuck.* Audrey doesn't loosen her legs; in fact, she doubles down on the squeeze and begins to rub herself against Osgood's face. She's discontinued her own licking and begins to sit up, giving her a better position to ride Osgood's face. Os's joy turns to surprise and discomfort as the woman atop her bears down, rubbing her greedy vulva up and down Osgood's nose and chin. Her first attempt at saying her friend's name is too muffled to hear, but the second time, she gets out, "Audrey, stop." The grinding continues, and more and more weight seems to be applied, much more than could be on Audrey's frame. Far from stopping, Audrey speeds up, and her small *oh*s have become bellowing moans, rising and rising in tone to near screams. Osgood feels a hand grasp her pubic hair and take it in a fist, and she's suddenly sure Audrey is using it as a bridle as she rides. Again, Osgood tries to get her to stop with taps and talk, but when that doesn't work, she grabs Audrey's waist to yank her off. Audrey comes at the same time as this attempt at interruption does, yelling an extended "Fuuuuuuuuuuck" into the darkness and expelling a virtual tidal wave of ejaculate into Osgood's nose and mouth.

As Osgood coughs and chokes on this near-waterboarding experience, she marvels at how much she wants it, no matter how unpleasant may be. She drinks deeply from the font of her friend, mostly because she has to, but partially because there'll always be that wretched self inside, desperate to be confronted for her whorishness. But no, this feels wrong. She shouldn't do this. She shouldn't let Audrey... Osgood squeezes Audrey's waist and shoves. She feels the woman tumble off her in the black, hit the bed next to her, and then suddenly the bed is empty. The silence of the room feels loud. As Osgood coughs fluids out of her sinuses, she turns on her bedroom light and finds herself...

Alone.

"Don't worry," says Sam Goddard. He emerges from the shadows at the other end of the room. He's naked, and his penis juts out, down, and to the left. He walks to the end of the bed, and Osgood pulls back her toes from this phantom. "We can all fuck. I'm not jealous."

"This is a dream," says Osgood.

"Sensible thought," says Goddard, as he snatches her right ankle, pulling it back toward him. She shrieks. As he comes closer, his pallor grows more ashen. His eyes grow milky. A bead of fetid black dribbles from the end of his cock. "Unfortunately..." He grabs at her left, and Osgood feels him spreading her legs. "That doesn't really matter, does it?"

Osgood tries to use the power, the ability that she supposedly has, to create her space, to adjust it. Even the dream world should bend to her control.

"This isn't your kingdom," he tells her. Now he's on top of her, and his entire body feels waxen. She can't move her arms to shove him off, but she turns her head to avoid his putrid breath. She feels the head of his rotting dick push through the patch of her pubic hair. "This is mine," he says and bites down on the side of her neck. It's not a love bite. Goddard's teeth, jagged and rough, go so deep she can feel them snap together. She screams.

A spasm shoots through her, and she turns her head away, feeling the wetness from her new bite wound begin to spread onto her pillow and bedspread. She sees, by the lamp, a straight razor lying open. How inviting is its glisten. She scrambles and twists below this creature that is somehow still Goddard, not the monster he became, but the man she once tried to live a happy, straight, suburban life with. The one she eventually got killed.

Her fingers curl around the razor's handle.

Goddard pushes himself up, both hands on the bed on either side of her. His teeth and lips are stained with her blood.

"Go ahead," he tells her. "You remember how easy it was. It's nice and sharp, too, so you're only a couple Ts away from quiet."

Osgood sees the scars on her arm puckering as though wanting to be rent back apart. So easy, to open her radial arteries and loose the rubies within.

"You can be a part of things again. Essential. And you won't ever be alone; HE will be there."

At the word HE, the name HE, the ceiling above her becomes transparent, revealing a sky full of cold and distant stars. But those stars aren't her own. They're the stars of the crossroads. *My kingdom.* HIS *kingdom.* She tries to look away, to close her eyes, but she can still see as the aperture in the sky opens: the blazing orange iris, the jagged, inky pupil. The thing in the sky sees her, oh yes. HE sees her. And HE will be there.

Osgood screams now, though the void above her swallows most of her sound in its vacuum. She draws the straight razor quickly across, not her own wrists, but Goddard's throat. The arterial spray drenches her, covering her naked body in his blood, orange-red like melted Crayolas, thick and cold all at once. His hands go to the slit, his mouth falling open as though nothing is keeping his jaw shut any longer. He leans, then falls from the bed.

When Osgood looks back up, HE is gone from the sky, and the roof of her apartment and the ceiling of her bedroom have returned. She takes gasping breaths, realizes that she's sobbing. She turns and looks over the edge of the mattress, steeling herself for the vision of whatever Goddard's body has become. But she's in no way prepared. Goddard has vanished, and in his place is Audrey, a second, yawning mouth below her chin, a bib of red down her

(little titties)

chest, her eyes staring blankly at the impartial ceiling.

Osgood's sobs turn to screams. She refuses to live in a world without Audrey. She can't! She won't!

Not again.

She begins to hack away at her wrists, starting atop the semicolon tattoo.

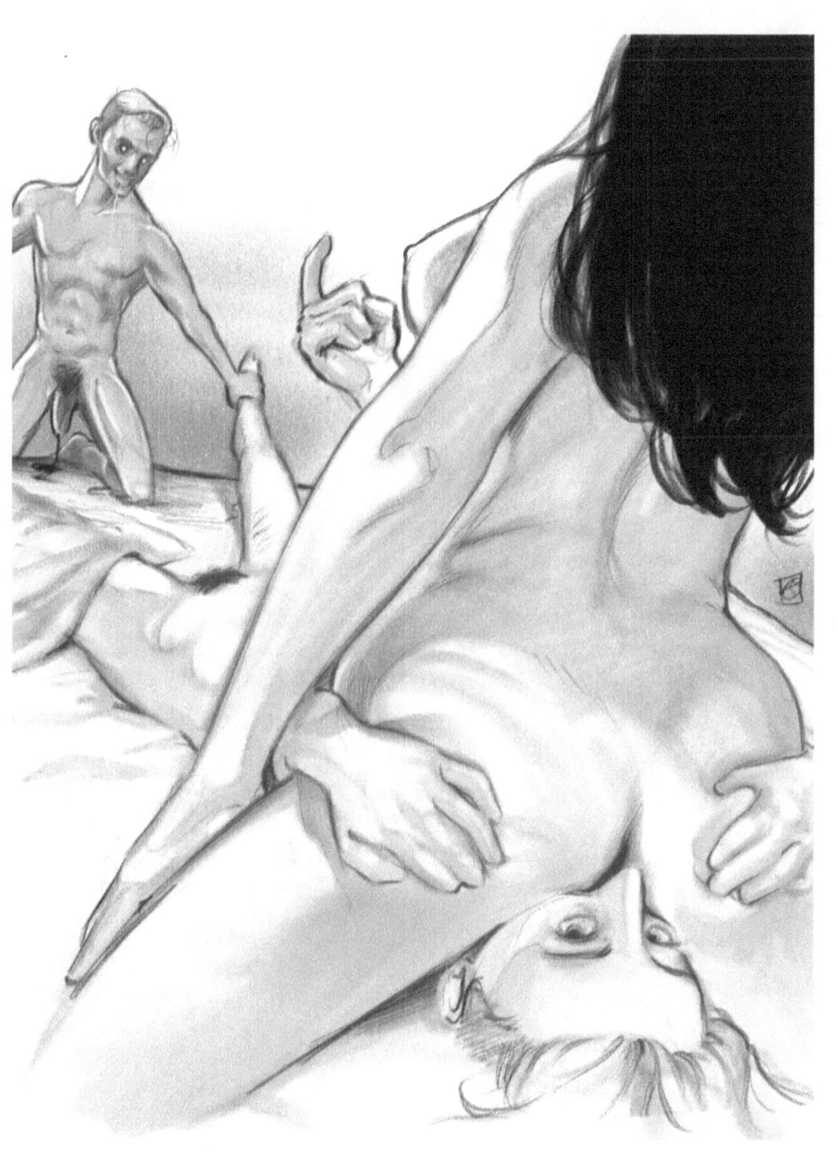

TWENTY-SEVEN

The screaming woke Osgood. A few moments passed before she realized that the scream belonged to herself. She jumped to a stand on shaky legs, wrestling with the sheet, soaked with sweat, that clung to her naked body. Osgood let out a choked sob—the blood, the blood. She grabbed again at the sheet but couldn't pull it away, couldn't get away from what she'd done. She screamed again, a guttural wail that began so deep within her it may as well have been from below her, from hell itself. She fell to her knees, resigning herself to being smothered for her crime. But then the door opened. And the light switched on. And there stood Audrey, in her t-shirt and pajama pants. Her hair a mess, her eyes wild with concern.

Osgood heaved her way through breathy sobs, staring at Audrey, who ran to her, kneeling next to her. Her very-much-alive friend pulled the tangled sheet from her body. Now fully nude, Osgood shivered and pulled herself closer to Audrey, grabbing at her t-shirt, pulling the woman toward her, feeling her heat, her breath, her heart still beating. Now Osgood truly sobbed, letting the tears flow so hard that the moans caused her to gasp over and over. She went down to all fours, heaving her way through the agony of the loss of this woman next to her and the paradoxical joy of having her still alive. "Aud... Audrey..."

"What happened?" Audrey's voice shook. Tears were in her eyes as well. Osgood didn't want that.

"Just," she said, trying to catch her breath. The heaving had become an involuntary spasm, each one throwing her whole body forward. "Just a dream," she finally got out.

"Oh, Os."

"I dreamed I killed you."

Audrey processed that, then nodded. "Well," she said with a small laugh. "Happy to see you're broken up about it, anyway."

Osgood turned back to her, hands shaking. She put her hands on Audrey's face, holding it. Their eyes met. Osgood thought hers must be blazing, wild. *Crazy eyes.* "I love you so much," she said.

Again, that small laugh, Audrey reacting to the intensity of a moment she'd not been a part of. "I love you too, Os. Focus on breathing." She began to demonstrate in deep, slow breaths. *In. Out. In... Out...*

It took Osgood a few minutes, but she managed to match that speed. She felt the terror and regret slowly ebbing as the dream began to fade. Audrey held her gaze the entire time. *In... Out...*

"Why don't you put some clothes on," said Audrey. "Your bush is unruly."

Osgood looked down and laughed. Naked and covered in goosebumps with her billowy brown bush. "Cunt."

Audrey laughed for a moment, true and genuine, but then her tone turned graver. "There are updates." She stood slowly, holding onto Osgood's hands as she did.

When Audrey helped her up, Osgood felt every bit of it.

Her knees screamed, and the scream shot through her thighs, through her pelvis, to her spine. She felt every bone as though they were rubbing together with no buffer. A grinding feel, like brakes on their last legs. She supposed she was on her last legs, too, but she didn't tell Audrey that. The last thing she needed right now was more indications of suicidal ideation. There'd be another intervention, and Osgood'd had quite enough of those, thank you very much.

Emerging from the bedroom took far more time than expected. The agony of pulling on sweatpants and a shirt over her head tempted her to just go out there naked. Or in a robe, maybe, just a robe. Her nerves, all wide awake, fired sensations at every movement, and even the fabric from the shirt and sweats became somehow painful. She couldn't remember the last time she'd felt this bad. Even tumbling down a thirty-foot rock-covered extradimensional hill in the Hinterlands hadn't knocked her down like this.

Down, thought Osgood. *Down but not out.*

Because that was her thing, right? Prudence Osgood, the universe's punching bag. Dead for over eight minutes but got back up. Cut her wrists in the bathtub in a dramatic gesture of teenage woe but got back up. Got so horribly damaged by a demigod that she'd vanished from reality for a while but fell down and out of that otherspace into the foyer of her once-mentor Donald Albrecht's house, and then she got back up. Her chest split as creatures literally tore her open, but she got back up. Had a brain tumor the size of a baseball, covered in teeth and hair and a single sightless eye, but she got back up. Six days at Swedish Covenant Hospital on a respirator because she caught COVID before anyone knew what to do with it, but, even after all of that, Prudence Osgood got the fuck back up.

She lumbered down the hall, thankful for Chicago apartments' turn of the 20th-century design that provided such skinny hallways as she could hold her palms on both walls simultaneously. It took an unfathomable amount of time. But Osgood thanked the absent gods for helping her choose the right direction, the kitchen, not the living room. She found Audrey and Zack in there. Audrey stood at the corner of the kitchen cabinets, Zack at the table with a newspaper. Audrey had seen her moments ago and knew where she was emotionally, but Zack's face shone with horror at the sight of her.

"Not dead yet," she told him.

"You know I don't find that funny," he told her.

"But I do." She kicked a chair away from the table and flopped into it, and again, her body screamed. At its worst, the only thing that could even come close to quelling this pain was her OxyContin tincture, but her source had dried up. Or gone to jail. Or maybe died of COVID, for all she knew. Regardless, that number didn't answer anymore, and the brown bottle with the O on it in silver Sharpie was long since empty. "Zack."

"Yes."

"I don't need a lecture," she told him.

He looked confused, his boyish face more youthful than ever despite the patchy growth of stubble. "I wasn't planning to—"

"For what I'm going to ask."

"Ah." He held out a hand that Osgood was fairly certain was an indication to proceed.

"I need oxycodone."

"Yeah, I thought—"

"Zack," said Osgood firmly. "I'm not addicted to it. I'm actually in pain. I cannot even begin to explain to you the amount of excruciating pain I'm in. You know that addicts have made it utterly impossible for people like me to—"

"I know, Os, but—"

"Please," she begged him. "Just this once. Because you love

me. Talk to that network of reprobates you run with on the dark web and find me *anything.*"

In the years since Osgood had met Zack in the parking lot of a ghosthunting convention, being roughed up by fellow hunters he'd scammed on EMF detectors, they'd had an unspoken rule: Zack didn't judge her for how she dealt with her pain—though his silent judgment on her drinking and fucking and oxy had come through anyway—and she didn't ask him to participate in it. But this was too much. Surely he could see that. Surely he didn't think she was just trying to use him for another—

"Okay," he said. He gave her a long look, sadness in his eyes. Osgood wondered if it was disappointment that she'd finally asked or concern for her that ran so deep he'd go down that path, but he picked up his phone, scrolled through a few things, typed some words with his thumb and then set it back down. Within seconds, there was a *ping*, then another, then another. He looked again, then up at her. "You'll have it in an hour."

"I'm sorry, Zack," she said.

"You have nothing to be sorry for." His smile was weak but there. Almost the same one he'd given her after she'd bashed her old cane into the skulls of the ghosthunters hurting him. Sure, she'd come down on the side of the scammer, but she'd come to love that little scammer. Zack was, after all, essential.

Osgood sighed, then looked down at the paper. Today's Chicago Tribune. The headline was a screamer of the type that the Tribune didn't usually do. **FIVE STUDENTS DEAD IN APPARENT SUICIDE CRASH.** "What the fuck?" she asked, then looked at the two of them.

"That's one of the updates," said Audrey.

"The newspaper doesn't name them," said Zack. "But bizarrely didn't have any qualms about saying the driver appeared to do it on purpose. I... Asked the right people. They're all students at Marchand Prep, on the other side of Clark. The oldest was 17, and the youngest was 12. The little sister of the driver. I have names here, but what's important, Os, what's essential, is that before their accounts got scrubbed by parents or whatever, three of them, including the driver, had played—"

"The Graveyard Game."

Zack nodded. "And not just any. The Rosehill Graveyard Game."

"Face to face with the Guardian," said Audrey.

"This isn't coincidence. Like, it can't be, right?" Osgood looked at the photo beneath the banner headline. An upside-down SUV, on fire. Firefighters on the scene. Gruesome.

"It could be," said Zack. "But I'd be rather astonished."

"Tell her," said Audrey.

Zack's face seemed to fall inward, and, for a moment, Osgood thought she was looking at his skull. "I got the rolls for St. Gregory's, junior high and high school. Marchand Prep's are coming. In fact, they might be in now, downstairs. But the real headline here is that since the Graveyard Game first appeared on these students' radar just over thirteen months ago, it has steadily increased in popularity. Seventy percent have done it."

Osgood laughed. "Seventy percent of what?"

"Of the student body."

"Wait—"

"My friend," said Zack, but then he seemed to reconsider the term. "Well, my—"

"We know how your sources work, Zack."

"He's been scraping TikTok since he first heard the US wanted to ban it and has been compiling hashtags and themes. He believes the social network might be some sort of emerging intelligence." Zack shook his head to dismiss it. "Doesn't matter. What matters is the Graveyard Game is a nationwide phenomenon, but everywhere else hasn't had this crazy uptick in death."

"Only *our* Graveyard Game," said Osgood.

"Only our *graveyard*!" said Audrey. "The kids further south are going to Graceland, further north to Calvary. But this one swatch of kids is going to Rosehill to see the Guardian."

"And it gets worse," said Zack. "The meme is growing and evolving."

"It's *what?*"

"When people say things 'go viral,' it's because internet trends behave like a virus in many ways." Zack stood to refill his coffee but didn't make it to the machine, instead giving himself over to the speed and movement of his words. "The more people feed it, the more power it has. But the longer it lasts, the weaker it gets, so it must evolve into new strains to capture the same number of people. But the best viral content does that *while* it's going viral in the first place, so by the time one bit of it doesn't work, that's okay because a dozen are there to take its place. The first versions of the Graveyard Game were ridiculous; they involved complex steps, doubling back, and fun math problems, and only then did you get somewhere. Rosehill's version had already been simplified to ten or fifteen steps. But in the year since then, it dropped to a six-step variation, to a four-step variation, to, now, one."

"One step," repeated Audrey.

"Look into the face of the Guardian," said Osgood.

"That's the one," said Zack. "The other issue is that *our* version of this viral phenomenon is far more dangerous than others. Just think if you'd heard someone you knew distantly had *actually* been murdered by Bloody Mary."

"I'd still try it," said Osgood to herself. She knew, though, what Zack was getting at. The truth was that she'd be *more likely* to try it.

"These kids know there's a chance they might die, which has been exacerbated by the presence of the North Side Ripper, so their willingness to, I dunno, *defy death*? Is huge." Zack shrugged. "And I don't know how to stop it. I asked some friends how difficult it'd be to crash TikTok, and ... let's just say we're not crashing TikTok without accidentally starting a war with China. But even if we did, they don't have to film it to do it. I..." he trailed off, seeming incredibly disappointed with himself. "I don't know what to do."

Reaching across the table was excruciating, but Osgood did it anyway, putting her hand on his. He looked down at it, then up at her. "It's not your responsibility to fix this," she told him.

"Someone has to."

"We're... We're going to do everything we can," said Audrey.

Zack nodded. Osgood thought she saw tears in his eyes. "Oh," he said after a moment. "Sandy drove by the Luminous Brotherhood of the Eternal Flame, Lodge 9." He pulled up an image on his tablet and pushed it across the table to her. The squat building looked like a strip mall more than a temple or lodge, but the front was all brick except for the door. Only the number 9 appeared on the building, elaborate and ornate, on the front door window below a much smaller address number. "Said a couple people were coming and going. The Lodge doesn't have an online presence and is just called Lodge 9, from what I see in the registration details."

"Actual Brotherhood members?" asked Osgood, surprised.

"Don't know. It may just be a social club at this point, but, notably, it's active."

Osgood nodded. "Who wants to go for a drive?"

Twenty-Eight

Too much OxyContin was an abstract concept. Osgood knew her body, and she knew exactly how many milligrams it'd take to make it stop screaming without overdosing. Unfortunately, that amount was nearly half of what had been delivered in a nondescript paper bag inside a Pizza Blast Pringles container. The delivery had been made without fanfare, only a *bloop* from Zack's phone. Osgood shared the remaining Pringles with Zack. It was only fair. He expressed his concern only once, noting that this had cost him $2K in bitcoin. Half was the rarity, half was the speed, plus some markup for a "new customer" or some such bullshit. Regardless, for the first time in a long time, Osgood was sailing along on a buoyant sea of fuzziness, feeling just enough pain to know she was still alive but not enough to make her want the opposite. She'd need to get more, sooner than later, but that was a problem for Tomorrow Osgood or Next Day Osgood. How Today Osgood loathed her.

With Zack behind the wheel and Audrey riding shotgun, Osgood could lounge across the Jeep Cherokee's back seat. Just in case, she buckled herself into the center and right seats.

She drifted in and out on the drive that took just over an hour into Chicago's south suburb Willowbrook. Amid her drifting, she heard a voice, a dark one. The one who once upon a time had pretended to be her younger self. *Wouldn't it be nice to be rid of all this? You're gonna need more pain meds in three days, at most. You can't afford that. Easier to just lean forward. Lean forward and grab the wheel.*

Osgood looked at her hand, outstretched, just to the edge of the console between the front seats. She stared at it, hovering there, perhaps preparing to do what the version of her who had unzipped her face wanted. With a yelp, she pulled it back. This drew attention from both Zack's via the rear-view mirror, and Audrey.

"Hey," said Audrey.

Osgood volleyed the "Hey" back.

"Any better?" asked Audrey.

"Notably," said Osgood. She unbuckled the side seatbelt and sat up, still buckled in the center. "Should we visit Resurrection Mary while we're down here?"

"I think I'm done casually visiting cemeteries for a bit," said Zack. Audrey nodded emphatically.

"Fair enough," said Osgood. Willowbrook had been one of the first areas she'd gone to when she got that '82 Skylark. Within a small radius were two notable cemeteries, Resurrection, which was the supposed home of Resurrection Mary, Chicago's variation on the hitchhiking ghost, and Bachelor's Grove, once thought to be the most haunted cemetery in the United States, where around two decades later a beacon would be lit by something pretending to be Sam Goddard. Neither of these cemeteries had what Rosehill did, though—a game that caused rampant destruction in a community of young people. Osgood wondered what playing the Graveyard Game would result in at Resurrection or Bachelor's Grove. *Maybe your place is as special as your pain.* Osgood ignored the voice, hoping that if she did, it'd go away. But like most problems, it probably wouldn't.

In person, Lodge 9 looked a bit nicer than it had in Sandy's photo, but it still felt rather rinky-dink for a brotherhood that stretched back to the 1800s. The building had two stories and took up so little space that Osgood was shocked upon seeing that the side wasn't much longer than the front. At midday, they only found three cars in the lot next door.

"Members only," said the man who held the door shut when they tried to pull it open. His white scruff glistened in the fall sunlight, shining through the door into the cavernous space beyond. His blue chambray shirt clashed with his almost identically-toned blue jeans.

Audrey flashed her wallet, quicker than Osgood see what she was flashing. "We're private investigators."

The man looked from her, to Osgood, to Zack. He took just as much time to scowl at each. "No women."

"Very progressive club you got here!" said Osgood. She banged on the window for good measure, causing the man to flinch back.

"Os," said Audrey calmly. Without looking away from the man inside, she put her hand on Osgood's, pulling it back down. Then, she reached into her own pocket and pulled out a hundred. She pressed it, Franklin-forward, against the window and said nothing.

The man's eyes betrayed his desire for it, but the rest of his face remained stoic. After a moment, he unlocked the door, opened it a crack, and grabbed the bill from Audrey. She let it go and waited. He examined it—looking for forgery, Osgood presumed—then opened the door to them. "Bought yourself ten minutes."

Osgood opened her mouth to tell him they'd bought themselves all the time they wanted, but Audrey squeezed her hand. Instead, she nodded as her friend and Zack thanked the man. They went inside.

The Luminous Brotherhood of the Eternal Flame, Lodge 9, looked like a rec center trapped in 1987. The floor was tiled in dingy red and brown checks, and the walls were tiled a yellow that Osgood thought may have once been white. The man threw his hand to the left of the front door, at a set of double doors festooned with regal purple drapery. "That's for ceremony," he said. "And you ain't fucking going in there."

"Okay," said Audrey.

He pointed to a couple of doorways ahead. "Offices. Men's room." He turned to Osgood. "We don't have a lady's room."

Osgood widened her eyes toward Zack, who nodded back.

"Can I get your name."

"Leland. You don't need my last name."

"I might," said Audrey.

"Well, that's tough shit."

"Alright, Leland," said Audrey.

"Y'all can come in here," said Leland, pushing another set of double doors open. "Fellowship," he added, almost as an afterthought.

The room was indeed a fellowship room, but more accurately, a dive bar. The floor had crumbles of peanut shells atop even dingier red and brown. A smattering of Formica-topped tables bordered a line of booths along the back wall. Along the wall with the doors, though, was an elaborate bar in a large semi-circle with stools abutting it. The bar shone, a lacquered cherrywood, replete with brass foot rest poles and corners. Only two stools were occupied: a woman with a coiffed do in a blouse and slacks and an angry red-bearded gentleman who got up from the bar and walked to the booth in the far corner.

"Reggie doesn't like visitors," said Leland. "Bev..."

"I thought you said no women," said Osgood under her breath as the woman, presumably Bev, turned to them and raised her beer. Her face was creased with years, and Osgood thought she likely shared a similar number with Leland.

"I also said no guests, Miss."

"Please don't call me Miss," said Osgood. "You can call me Osgood, or Os."

"Funny name," said Leland. He opened his mouth to add something that the growing smirk on his face indicated he might think was funny, but Audrey cut him off.

"I'm Audrey Frost; this is Zack Nguyen."

"Win?" asked Leland.

"Close enough," said Zack.

"Private investigators," said Leland, pointing to the three of them. "Sit down."

They did, taking the spaces next to Bev while leaving a polite single stool gap. He went behind the bar and filled three beers, setting one before each of them. "You get one on the house," he said.

"What're you investigating?" asked Bev.

Osgood turned to Audrey. Zack opened his mouth, then closed it again. Even Audrey seemed unsure how to begin this. Osgood stabbed in the dark. "You have kids?"

"We do," said Leland. "But they're hardly kids anymore. Youngest is 44."

"Hey," said Osgood, "I'm 44."

"And you still dress like that?" asked Leland, giving her a disdainful look.

Osgood gaped. Sure, her tee and sweats weren't "private investigator" proper, but her coat was très chic.

Again, Audrey saved her from tanking the whole thing. "We're looking into a rise in murders and suicides of kids between 12 and 18 up on the north side of Chicago."

"Oh, yeah," said Bev. "I heard about that." She shook her head. "Shame."

Leland nodded and then added his own, "Shame." Then he looked back at them. "What led you all the way down here? We're a long way from the 'north side.'" Somehow, his emphasis on the location felt disdainful in and of itself.

"You're going to think it's silly," said Audrey.

"I already think y'all are silly," said Leland with a grin, this time without overt hostility.

"Fair," said Zack.

Audrey smiled back. "Well, this lodge of yours is a part of a Brotherhood that—"

"You don't need to tell me our history. All brothers know it." He sipped his own beer.

"Sisters, too," added Bev.

Leland nodded.

"You had a lot of notable members in the late 1800s," said Audrey.

"Some of their portraits are around." Leland made a pointing gesture that seemed to point through walls because they saw no portraits in the fellowship room.

"Can I use your restroom?" asked Zack. It was a long drive.

"I suppose you're a man," said Leland.

"Thank you?" He hopped off his stool and headed toward the door.

"Don't bother trying to get in anywhere else," said Leland. "Everything's locked tight. Part of my job is to keep it that way."

"I really just need to use—"

"Well, go!" said Bev. "Don't piddle yourself talking to us!"

Zack disappeared from the room.

"Does the name Ambrose Ballard mean anything to you?" asked Audrey. She played it lightly.

"Young lady, you must not have done your research."

The smallest scrunch on the bridge of her nose indicated to Osgood that this man had finally gotten Audrey's goat. She wasn't sure if the "young lady" comment had done it, or the suggestion that her research had been poor.

Leland didn't wait for a response, though. "He founded this Lodge." He gestured with his beer toward the far wall, where a portrait they hadn't noticed before hung. The Ballard in that picture looked younger, healthier, than in the one Zack had found. Osgood also didn't get the crawly feeling from his eyes.

"But what does Ambrose have to do with missing kids?" asked Bev, fixing Audrey with a hard stare.

Audrey turned and looked at Bev for a while. "When you're dealing with such an expansive case, with such precious little ones at the center, you run down every crazy lead you hear, right?"

Bev nodded solemnly.

Well played, Aud, thought Osgood.

"Look, ladies," said Leland, leaning on the bar. "You gave me a hundred, so that ought to be worth some honesty, right?"

"Please," said Audrey.

Leland leaned forward on the edge of the bar. "Lodge 9 is the last lodge of the Brotherhood. And besides Reggie, Bev, and I, we only see a handful of regulars in any given year. It's here because the influential people who built it shaped laws that keep it here and free. We couldn't maintain with membership dues."

"Then why so secretive?" asked Zack from the doorway.

Sighing, Leland scratched at his beard. "What's the point of a secret society without secrets?" He laughed, and Bev joined in. "I don't know what you could want from us about those murders, but I can tell you it ain't no one from here."

He knocked on wood on the bar top. "I know everybody who sets foot in this bar, and they're all as old as God, like me. All they wanna do is drink in peace and think about the times they were relevant."

Audrey took that in and stood. "Thank you, Leland. Bev."

"Don't wanna finish your beers?"

Osgood shrugged and knocked hers back, then looked at Zack and Audrey, who stared at her.

Leland guffawed. "Well, hell, maybe I judged you too soon, sugar."

"Maybe you did," said Osgood with a smile. She was sure to make it the most minuscule bit genuine.

Climbing back into the Jeep, Osgood buckled herself into the seat behind Zack. He was, after all, the shortest of them, and Osgood needed to unbend her legs before they began to get stiff. "I think I want to...," said Osgood. "Rush? How do you join a secret society."

"Blood oaths, probably," said Audrey. "But I don't think Leland was lying to us."

"Maybe not," said Zack. He pointed at the building. "But that's a second floor. And there are no stairs."

"Maybe they're in the ceremony room," suggested Osgood.

"Please," said Zack. "I peeked into all of them." He held up a gadget that looked like a miniature screwdriver. Zack's lock pick, the electric key.

"Nothing?" asked Audrey.

"They have two tiny offices; one has a layer of cigarette tar so thick it felt sticky," said Zack. "The ceremony room is basically storage. Some flags, a stage of sorts. Ornate chairs. But also rolled carpets and stacked tables. Rec center shit."

"But no stairs?" asked Osgood.

"But no stairs," said Zack. He grinned. "But I'm pretty sure I know where they are." He turned his phone toward them and unfolded it, extending the screen to a 6″x6″ square. A small image resized and rotated itself to fill the screen. Between two office doors was a case. Inside were plaques and portraits. Groups of men.

"Okay," said Audrey.

Zack shook his head, his grin widening. "You don't see it?"

They didn't.

He fiddled with brightness and contrast settings on his futuristic screen, but they still didn't. With a sigh, Zack said, "Bottom left."

Osgood narrowed her eyes and leaned forward. The bottom left of the photo was the checkerboard floor. She still didn't see what he was— Wait. "No fucking way!"

"Yep!" exclaimed Zack.

"I still don't get it!" Audrey shook her head.

Zack traced with his finger, starting with the bottom left corner of the trophy case, an almost imperceptible line in an arc. A scuff line on the floor. Audrey's eyes widened in under-standing, but Zack told her anyway.

"It's a hidden passage!"

TWENTY-NINE

The urge Osgood felt to explore this secret—she was more confident than she'd ever been in an investigation that whatever was behind that wall was critical to this whole thing—only grew in desperation on their drive back north. Zack and Audrey insisted that they rethink and regroup.

"Actually *plan* an attack, Os," Zack had said with an almost audible eye roll.

From the back seat, Osgood had swatted at his head, missing it entirely and only blowing a tuft of his black hair up. She'd felt the sway of her oxy haze and had realized that they were likely right. She was certainly not fully lucid at this point. A phantom irritant had begun in the pocket of her jeans. She knew nothing was there, she hadn't even bothered to bring her wallet, but it still insisted upon itself. Ignoring that, her concern, though, began as an itch. First physical, then mental. The physical aspect reached out to some old familiar places. The mismatched Ts on her wrists, the raised white slits on her inner thighs and shoulders. At first, it was no more than a tickle, but that began to grow and change until Osgood grasped her knees, panicked that, if given the chance, she'd tear her wrists open to make it stop. She took long, slow breaths, focusing only on the filling and emptying of her lungs and her chest's rising and falling. In through the nose, out through the

(rip 'em)

mouth. In through the nose, out

(tear 'em open)

through the mouth. She looked between Zack and Audrey, who seemed much further away than just the front seat. She felt as though the Cherokee had elongated, row upon row between her and her friends, like those transport vans she'd ridden at summer camp when she was young. Here, in the way way back, she wouldn't be bothered, could only be seen the tiniest bit in the rearview, and anyway Zack seemed wholly distracted by Audrey, by planning, by things *other* than Prudence Osgood. Was she upset about that? That her friends didn't seem to notice or see

(or care)

what was going on with her? That they couldn't be bothered to ask, "Os, are you okay?"

She knew why, though, didn't she? Osgood had spent her adult life learning to hide her tells. The only way for someone with chronic pain to live free, to not be inundated with impotent offers of aid, is to do one's best to fully mask the symptoms. After all, what does back pain look like? Is it a walk, a waddle, an expression? Sometimes she couldn't help the visible signs, but the cane was a mask. When someone comes upon another with a cane, a strange walk, a limp, the first thing they do, out of ostensible politeness, is attempt to ignore it. The longer they ignore, the closer they come to simply not seeing it. Then, only the face is a giveaway. Osgood knew she couldn't hide the sharpest of pains, like when she stepped down on her heel and her plantar fasciitis drove a railroad spike upward. But she could limit the duration. It's a flinch, not a gasp; it's a moment, not a drawn-out sigh. Everything else, though, was more manageable. After all, if one's baseline is pain, it doesn't take a lot to mask the minor fluctuations.

So it wasn't that they couldn't be bothered, she reminded herself; it was that this was how she'd taught them to respond to her pain. To wait for her to mention it. To not stare. To not ask. Because what's the point of asking if there's anything you can do when you know damned well there isn't? Osgood also recognized that, though this itch was growing, it still was nowhere near topping out her pain levels and her tolerance.

"So, bring it on," she mumbled to herself.

The Jeep collapsed back down to two rows, and Zack's eyes met hers in the rearview mirror. Audrey turned to look at her. "What'd you say?" she asked.

Osgood shook her head and squeezed out a smile. We're all normal here. Fine and dandy. Right as rain. Nothing worth being concerned about, certainly. Not like I want to

(tear my wrists open)

do anything. She slumped a bit. That errant thought. Intrusive as ever. No no no. The call of the void. That's not what this was. The call of the void was abstract, not concrete. It certainly wasn't posing: "I wonder what'd happen if I ripped open my wrists and loosed the blood."

She knew what would happen, after all. Right here, tearing at those scars with her fingers: nothing. She couldn't get in, couldn't separate the skin. When a wound heals and scars, it becomes stronger. There'd be no getting into her wrists with nails as short as hers. And she had to keep them short, both for finger-fucking new friends and so she couldn't commit suicide.

"What the fuck?" she asked herself, again low enough to be a mumble.

"Should we be concerned?" asked Zack.

"Aren't you always?" returned Osgood.

"Fair," said Zack. "What do you think of our plan?"

Osgood had no idea. She hadn't caught more than a snippet here or there. She knew that, overall, it had something to do with breaking into Lodge 9 and that actually sounded like fun, but logistically, she knew nothing. Nothing, that is, except that Zack's logistical planning abilities far outweighed her "what happens if I do this?" approach, so she felt pretty comfortable just nodding and giving a thumbs up. He smiled and nodded back. Audrey watched her for a moment, then resumed her conversation with Zack.

I have no reason to kill myself, said Osgood to herself.

(the endless pain)

None at all.

Sure, if you wanted to go for low-hanging fruit, her chronic pain was a reason. After all, people killed themselves all the time over pain that never abated. Why shouldn't she be one of them? A statistic. *Prudence Osgood died today, unable to keep the pain at bay.* Osgood snickered morosely at her inner poet. Mostly, though, she felt thankful that this moment hadn't happened at home, alone. She thought she could keep the urges down, especially when she didn't have the means to do anything about it. She shuffled uncomfortably at the thing in her pocket. It poked a dull end into her thigh, and then, with a quick seating adjustment, it poked into her belly.

Fine, she thought, giving in to the phantom sensation. She reached in and pulled out ... the straight razor.

Not just any straight razor, either. The one she'd used in her dream to cut Goddard's

(Audrey's)

throat. And here, in the light of day, she recognized it from another place and another time. The origin of her wrist scars. Because this razor, with its pearl inlay and its silver edging, had belonged to her father. She ran her thumb over the etched monogram BAO, Basil Allen Osgood. During the good times, she'd called him Daddy Dumpling. Only because it irritated him. Feeling the relief of the monogram sent a shudder through her. This shouldn't be here. She hadn't seen this razor in person in decades. Not since she'd used it for purposes beyond its charge. She was reasonably sure her father had thrown it out or put it away in some deep and secret spot. She knew he no longer used it for shaving.

The itch in her wrists grew to maddening levels, as though all sensation in her body had refocused itself there.

All you have to do is let it out. Just a few swipes and you'll let out the itch. Let out the pain. All will be soft and quiet. Finally, we can sleep.

That voice again, the one Osgood didn't know. Pitched high, layered atop an undernote, a lower, darker tone.

Or, it offered.

Osgood didn't move, just waited. Or? Or what? Was this voice about to make an offer? The voice was surely only in her head, a product of her ongoing psychosis. Maybe it was an effect of the oxy mixing with her elaborate cocktail of mind meds. *Or maybe,* thought Osgood, *I've actually gone full-on toys in the attic crazy.*

She thought about Audrey's suggestion that she see a therapist. Probably right, after all. Her phone appointments with her psychiatrist four times a year, the ones where he'd ask, "Anything new? Any symptoms?" and she'd say no and get her prescriptions sent through, they certainly didn't have a talk aspect to it. She thought about Remy, who'd told her, "I'm not *your* therapist," just after coaxing her to masturbate in front of her. Remy, despite being a mélange of mysteries, was the only person Osgood knew in the mental health field who didn't immediately make her wonder what they *really* were after.

Her right hand seemed unwilling or unable to drop the razor, so she fumbled with her phone in her left, managing to wake it, unlock it, and bring up Remy's number. She texted, simply **SOS**.

Within seconds, it seemed, a return: **Here. What can I do?**

Meet? Hour? asked Osgood.

Mary's?

yes.

See you then.

Osgood dropped the phone onto the seat next to her. Alright, that was proactive. She'd taken a real step there. Sure, the idea of telling Remy about her suicidal desires, or about that dream she'd had, filled her with warm discomfort and embarrassment. Still, it was better than the alternative, supposed Osgood.

The alternative, just now, had stopped trying to pull the razor to her wrists and had begun to lead her, without saying a thing, to the idea that all might be better if she slit Audrey's throat.

THIRTY

Upon arriving at their apartment, Osgood realized she was no longer holding the straight razor. Before climbing from the rear seat of the Jeep Cherokee, she felt between the cushions and around the floor, but her father's razor was nowhere to be found. Osgood wondered if it had ever actually been there. And if not, what would have happened if she'd tried to cut her wrists or, dear god, Audrey's throat. At the doorway between Mary's and the building next door, she told them she was meeting someone.

Zack narrowed his eyes with surprise. "You don't want to plan our—"

"A therapist," she said.

She saw Audrey stop Zack from asking more, a hand on his arm. Audrey smiled at her. "That sounds like a good idea."

Of course, it does, thought Osgood. *A therapist might be able to tell me I'm going crazy. And you already know that, don't you, Odd?* Osgood herself couldn't explain the anger of that thought, so she decided to say nothing, only nod.

"Well, you'll come back after?" asked Zack.

Of course, she would. It was her apartment. If she didn't, that would indicate a far bigger problem.

"Yes," she said. "Back and ready to break into Lodge 9."

Zack loudly shushed them, looking around like some random bystander on Clark Street, over thirty miles from the decrepit Lodge, might overhear and want to do something about it.

Osgood shooed them upstairs and then walked to the corner, the door to Mary's Diner and Bar. She reached out to open it when she saw Remy's Trans Am on the side street. The beautiful woman sat behind the wheel, looking at Osgood. Remy threw her a mild smile, which Osgood returned. Then she beckoned Os over with a head tilt that made her curls flutter. Osgood climbed in.

"We going to your office?" Osgood asked.

"That depends on what you want from me," said Remy.

That question had myriad answers, but Osgood knew one was more important than the others just now. "I need to know if I'm crazy," she told Remy.

Remy snorted a laugh, then covered her mouth. "Sorry."

"No," Osgood said, "It's a wild way to start a conversation, I know."

"Well, that and any good psychologist has long-since retired the word 'crazy' from their diagnosis vocabulary."

Osgood fixed her eyes on Remy's. The therapist's silver eyes looked back, inviting, welcoming, paradoxically warm.

"I've wanted to kill myself," said Osgood.

Remy nodded.

"But not really? Like, I absolutely don't want to kill myself. I just feel urges." Osgood leaned her head back against the headrest. She felt tears beginning and wiped them with the back of her hand. "Could we drive or something?"

Remy said nothing, but her Trans Am roared to life and took off north on Clark Street.

"Osgood," said Remy as they drove.

"Yes," said Osgood.

"We both know I can't be a regular therapist for you."

"Why not?" pled Osgood.

"First," said Remy. "Because I don't think you need a regular therapist just now."

"What does that—"

"And second, because I know too much about the situation to be objective." Remy hit her turn signal and spun them up Sheridan Road, the street that wound its way into the northern suburbs right along the lake's edge.

Osgood waited for Remy to continue, but she didn't. "I'm going to need you to explain that further."

Remy sighed. "To do that, I'm going to tell you that I knew of you long before you knew of me."

Osgood narrowed her eyes.

"Nothing sinister, I assure you."

"I'll be the judge of that," said Osgood.

Remy nodded and laughed, the horses under her hood propelling them north faster. "I first discovered you on *Chicago Haunts.*"

Now Osgood laughed, though she felt discomfort creeping.

"I was watching that live show," said Remy, then broke. "*The* show."

Osgood knew *the* show well, of course, would've known it without the emphasis. The show broadcast live on Halloween night from the haunted Waverly Hotel. The show on which she'd betrayed Audrey's trust, faking a ghost with her producers. The show that had destroyed their relationship for over a decade. The show that had changed everything. It was also the thing Osgood held deepest, closest, as the single most significant example of what an awful human she was.

A hand on her upper arm. Cool, soft. Remy squeezed and

drew Osgood out of the self-flagellation. "I bring it up," said Remy, "Because I'd like you to focus on it." The doctor drove faster north, and Osgood wondered how they were managing to avoid all lights and stop signs.

"Well, babe," said Osgood. "I've never *not* focused on it, so—"

A sharp squeeze now, enough to distract Osgood from completing her sentence, then Remy returned to her soft grip on Osgood's upper arm. "I want you to think of every horrible thing you've ever said about yourself. Every bit of self-doubt and torture that you've inflicted on yourself. Every time you thought yourself unworthy of trust, of love, of affection."

Osgood opened her mouth to ask why but couldn't. Her mind was abuzz with the answers to Remy's prompt. The profound hatred of herself that Osgood kept just barely covered, hatred of this body, of this mind, of everything she'd ever—

Floating. She blinked. She was floating. Above herself. She saw, below her, the exquisite corpse of Prudence Osgood. But, no, that wasn't right. She wasn't dead. And this wasn't an out-of-body experience; this was just a—

The Trans Am screeched to a stop before Dr. Yeagher's Evanston house, and Osgood looked at her in a daze.

"How do you feel," Remy asked.

"What did you do to me?" asked Osgood.

"How do you feel," she asked again, ignoring Osgood's question.

Osgood thought about it. There was ... a lack of something. An emptiness of ... what?

"It can be disorienting when it's that direct," said Remy. "You'll feel like you lost something critical."

"Did you drug me?" slurred Osgood.

"No," said Remy.

"Then what did—"

"I took it," said Remy. "I took it and kept it. Not the memories, not the context or content, that's all there. It feels empty because I took the pain of it. The regret. The horror. The guilt. You offered it up, and I took it."

Osgood looked at her for a moment, her head swimming. Maybe it was the oxy, still, perhaps it— "What the *fuck* does that mean?"

"I'm going to ground you," said Remy.

"Have I been bad?" asked Osgood, feeling like she was drunk.

The woman pulled Osgood to her and kissed her, holding herself against Osgood's lips. Again, Osgood asked herself what the fuck this was, but she didn't much care about the answer. Remy's lips were warm and soft. Osgood wondered how her tongue would taste, tried parting her lips, but it was too late. Remy sat back and stared at Osgood.

Sure enough, though, Osgood did feel more grounded. She was here, in her body, more emotionally sound. Not upset, betrayed, or the victim of her own hatred. She was just ... being. And that was something that hadn't happened in a very long time. "So... You're like a witch, then?" asked Osgood.

"No," said Remy. "There's not really a name for what I am."

"Well, you're really working the mysterious woman angle," said Osgood. "If I didn't want to fuck you before, I—"

"Os," said Remy, putting her hand on Osgood's.

"What?"

"We have a problem."

Osgood sighed and waited.

When Remy talked, she talked fast. "Theo Brautigan, the alderman of the 48th ward, called an emergency meeting today."

"That's our ward."

"It is. The meeting was for parents, to address the growing epidemic of suicides, as well as the looming specter of the North Side Ripper."

"Finally going to try to do something about—"

"Osgood."

"Sorry."

"I went, as always, to help," she told Osgood. "In a crowd, I can siphon off the pain. I don't take it fully from anyone, but I can make them feel ever so slightly better. I needed to show you, so you'd understand."

"You give me a lot of credit, thinking I understand any of what's happening right now."

"You understand," said Remy. "You're just rejecting it."

Osgood frowned.

"The parents begged for resources that the area doesn't have, beyond therapy in schools."

"And you?" asked Osgood.

"I can only rarely do what I just did," Remy said, indicating Osgood's arm. "I'm ... not strong enough."

At that, Osgood noticed Remy's silver eyes were ringed in pink. Strained. Stressed. Perhaps near tears herself.

"I asked for the floor and asked how many of them had heard their kids or their kids' friends mention the Graveyard Game?" Remy shook her head, her hackles definitely up. "Brautigan told me not to waste everyone's time, but enough of their hands went up that I knew we'd crossed a tipping point."

"What kind of tipping point?" asked Osgood.

"The kind that will make every last one of them kill themselves or each other."

THIRTY-ONE

It wasn't late, just an hour after dusk, but late enough for Rosehill Cemetery to be closed, and the caretaker had gone home. One would think with the sheer number of kids breaking in to do their little Graveyard Game, Chicago would've afforded themselves a bit more security. Osgood knew, though, how easy it was to dismiss things that ultimately were supernatural. One could see the effect, understand it, and even link it with actions, but when they wanted to step back and see the big picture, it grew fuzzier the further back they went. On their walk to the Guardian, Osgood and Remy saw a young girl.

"Hey!" Osgood called out to her. The girl, with frizzy brown hair wearing a yellow parka, ducked behind a tombstone. "You're not in trouble," Osgood added.

The girl took a moment to rise and, even then, only lifted herself enough so her eyes could be seen. "Dr. Remy?" asked the girl.

Remy sighed, nodded, and moved toward her. "I told you not to come out here, Dawn."

"I know, but—"

"No buts!" said Remy. "You're not in trouble now, but you will be if you don't go home immediately!"

"I'm sorry, Dr. Remy!"

"Go, Dawn," Remy said, making a shooing gesture. The girl got up and ran headlong back down the path. "Tell your parents that you're safe!"

"What's your plan, Dr. Remy?" asked Osgood.

"My plan?" asked Remy. "My plan is you, Osgood."

Osgood frowned. What did that mean?

"Os!" came a harsh whisper to the right. Osgood and Remy braced, then relaxed as Zack and Audrey emerged from the darkness.

"This is Dr. Ramona Yeagher; she's *not* my therapist."

"Okay," said Audrey. She shook Remy's hand. "I know your show. It's pretty good."

"I know yours, too," said Remy, "similarly good. But your book is a masterpiece."

Audrey stammered.

"A friend of mine at the Chicago Reader passed it along."

"It's good? Really?" asked Audrey.

Osgood cocked her head. She'd never seen Audrey so in need or want of praise.

"You know it is," said Remy.

Zack seemed to be the only one in their cluster concerned about being caught, as his eyes darted around furtively. "Can we, uh, move it along?"

"Right," said Osgood. "So apparently, I'm Dr. Remy's plan."

"Please don't call me Dr. Remy," said Dr. Remy.

Osgood began a defiant reply, but then remembered asking everyone to call her 'Osgood' and redirected. "She's also magic."

Zack and Audrey looked to Remy, who shrugged and nodded. "That's as good a way to put it as any. But the reason

Osgood is my plan is twofold. First, she's already, *foolishly*, looked into the eyes of the Guardian."

Osgood balked. "I told you, it doesn't have eyes."

"I don't think that matters," said Zack.

"And the two of you have not?" confirmed Remy.

Audrey and Zack shook their heads just as the foursome crested a small hill and saw, standing before them, all twelve feet of the Guardian.

"As Osgood said, I have a sort of magic, and that sort will not allow me to get closer than ... fifteen feet or so to that thing," Remy pointed at the statue, "without a level of pain I cannot properly describe." Remy turned to Osgood with a cocked head. "Though I imagine your friend Os here can understand it perfectly."

Osgood looked at her and saw a sort of wild desperation on her face, an erratic and messy expression she hadn't seen on this woman before. But she did understand pain and would never suggest someone endure it if they didn't have to. "You still haven't told me what we're doing..."

Remy looked at her for a long while, then lifted up the package she'd retrieved from her trunk, showing it to Osgood. It was nothing more than a pillowcase, but something was inside. Osgood reached in, felt a cold handle, and slid it out. She held a hacksaw.

Zack scoffed. "If you'd told me what we were doing, I could've—"

"Zack," said Remy, stopping him in his tracks, "you know as well as anybody, I'm sure, that often low-tech solutions are best when confronting magic."

"Are you saying that—"

"That I think power tools would drain before you could use them to stop this thing?" asked Remy. "Yes, Zack, I am."

"So, Osgood has to..." began Audrey. "What?"

"Kill it," said Osgood. She'd known, from the moment she

pulled the saw from the sack, that soon she'd be scaling the Guardian to take its head. Something felt right about it, as though she'd always been meant to do this.

"Okay," said Audrey. "Let's all calm down for a second. Dr. Remy—"

"Please, just Remy."

"Fine," said Audrey, calling her neither. "I need you to step back and give us a moment."

Remy looked at them, the mania on her face growing as her eyes darted from Zack's face to Audrey's and finally to Osgood's. Their eyes held. Within Remy's eyes, Osgood could see the rightness. She saw steadfast confidence amid the manic energy, unearned maybe, but strong!

"What the fuck, Os?" asked Audrey, yanking her away from Remy so hard she nearly dropped the hacksaw.

"What?" asked Osgood.

"You tell us you're going for therapy and then call us out to help your crazy—"

"We don't like to use that word," said Osgood.

"—friend do what? Decapitate a statue?"

"If it doesn't have a face, people can't look into it," offered Zack with a shrug.

"It never had a face!" exclaimed Osgood. "You don't look into it. You look into yourself."

"Os," said Audrey, affecting a placating tone Osgood knew only too well. "We're still investigating this, we're still—"

"Five kids died this morning," said Osgood. "That crash."

"Yes, but..."

"If me taking the head off this thing can stop another one—"

"But what if it can't?" asked Audrey. "What if you do this and it does nothing? What if they just find another statue? The Guardian isn't the only hooded monument in this cemetery."

"I need to do this!" exclaimed Osgood, her panic and terror rising, her eyes filling with tears. The certainty that this was the move grew and grew within her.

"Why?" demanded Audrey.

"So I don't fucking kill you!" exclaimed Osgood.

The silence was deafening.

"What?" asked Zack, after what felt like an eternity.

"That thing," said Osgood, pointing at the statue. "It doesn't show you how you're going to die. It doesn't show you anything. You show it to yourself." She poked at her head. "Since I looked at the empty space under its hood, I've had endless urges to kill myself. But worse, I've had the urge to kill you."

Audrey stammered.

"What the fuck, Os?" asked Zack.

"Not because I want to, in any way, but because I feel like I need to." Osgood stepped away from the two of them, raising the hacksaw to point. "And if there's one chance in a thousand that killing that thing will make the urge stop, I'll kill it without hesitation."

"Okay," said Audrey, trying to bring down the heat of the conversation. "We need to just—"

"No!" said Osgood. "I'm doing this. Now you can help, or you can watch me desperately try to scramble up it."

They looked at her, and she gave them a defiant look in return. Zack sighed first and pointed. "Behind it, you can use the crypt to get pretty far up."

Osgood walked to the statue. She looked up at it, feeling like it was looking back down at her. She looked over her shoulder and saw Remy standing away from the others, giving her a small nervous wave. Osgood threw a half smile back at her. Sure enough, behind the Guardian was a long concrete crypt, not as well maintained as Ballard's plot. The crypt's stone cross had fallen and half-buried itself in the dirt. Osgood thought these two plots had once been further apart, but a steady downward movement along the slope had begun to bring them together. She wondered whose grave it was, as she used the fallen cross to shakily climb to the top of the crypt. She felt weirdly victorious up there and pumped her cane in the air. "Let's do this!"

Now for the harder bit, but she had Audrey and Zack by her side. She passed her cane to Zack and the hacksaw to Audrey and leaned forward, pressing herself against the cold iron of the statue. From this position, the bend of the Guardian's back allowed her to shimmy awkwardly, with Audrey and Zack pushing, until she made her way mostly up the statue. Then came the part she'd need to do herself, the bit that, without today's oxy, would've made her sob. She wrapped her hands around the throat of the Guardian and very slowly pulled herself up. Her muscles screamed at her, asking what the fuck she was doing. Ignoring them, ignoring the pain, she pulled harder. Hearing her friends below cheer her on, Osgood herself was astonished when she reached the point where she could throw her leg over the statue's right shoulder and sit upon it. From this vantage, she could see over almost the entire cemetery, lit by the nearly-full moon. She thought about all the years this thing had watched over the monuments, stones, mausoleums, and crypts. All at once, she doubted Remy's plan. Here she sat, ready to decapitate a monument above the graves of a young woman and her baby. Surely, that would stir up some feelings in the spirit realm. Wasn't this the type of desecration warned against in stories, that one might pay an awful price for?

"Os."

She looked down and saw Audrey looking back at her, holding her arm out, the hacksaw in hand, handle up. Would she be able to reach it? Osgood doubted it, but a jump by Audrey put the handle directly into Osgood's right hand. She sat for a moment, resting against the top of the Guardian's cowl. She felt the urge, the yearning, the seemingly unstoppable desire to lean down and look into the void that wasn't a face, but she resisted the lure and put the blade against what would be this thing's neck under its robes. She began to saw.

It seemed she was getting nowhere for the longest time, but then a *pop* told her she'd made it through the outer shell. The Guardian wasn't solid iron, so she only had to saw to this depth, all around its head, to take the fucking thing down. Saying it like that made her think she could do it, despite her arm already begging her to stop this nonsense. Osgood hadn't done anything close to manual labor in ages, and the sawing both exhausted and pained her. She knew, though, that this wasn't about her, her desire to not hurt herself, or even her greater desire to not hurt Audrey. Though all those were important, the most vital thing was to stop this incarnation of Graveyard Game.

Hours seemed to pass, with Osgood switching up hands and directions several times, feeling both of her arms grow numb. She began to take more and more frequent rests. Her cheerleaders had run out of things to say—telling someone *they can do it!* for an hour and a half eventually stopped feeling encouraging and began to feel sarcastic. She focused her entire attention on her task, looking at the back of its head as she sawed through its neck. She knew she was getting close, as the top of the hood had begun to wobble. Osgood thanked the gods, whichever were here with her tonight. She'd expected, what? That it might fight back somehow? The fact that it hadn't at all, only stood there and took what they'd brought, gave her pause. What if this wasn't it at all? What if she'd—

Osgood screeched! She heard it echo back to her off the other tombs, off the trees shedding their leaves, off the sky itself. Arms shaking, she looked down.

"What happened?" asked Audrey, jumping to her feet.

Osgood looked at her, then Zack. What *had* happened? Why had she— She saw it then, the hacksaw in her left hand, the blade a quarter inch into her right wrist. The blood flowing in rivulets. Dumbfounded, Osgood looked back to her friends. "I had an..." What, Osgood? Was the suicidal girl about to suggest she'd had an accident, when she'd blatantly held out her wrist and cut into it? Then they saw blood begin to hit the statue and fall down around it. Osgood felt herself growing woozy, but as she leaned against the Guardian's head, she felt it shift so dramatically that, in a flash, she knew this *was* it fighting back. And it wouldn't knock her out so quickly.

Osgood flung her arms backward and shook her way out of the leather coat, which billowed as it fell to the ground. Audrey and Zack were on the crypt, trying vainly to reach her. While still holding the saw in her left hand, Osgood yanked her shirt over her head, exposing her tits to the cemetery. She wished she'd worn a bra tonight, but that was the least of her worries. Her nipples popped out immediately, and goose pimples ran up her chest. She put the shirt down on her knee, pressing her right wrist against it, then yanked it tightly around and around and around. "Aud!"

Desperately trying to reach her, Audrey asked, "What?"

"Ponytail!"

Audrey looked up at her blankly before feeling back at the rubber band holding her hair in a ponytail. "Os, you need to get—"

"Gimme!" said Osgood.

Audrey did as demanded, flinging her ponytail rubber band up. Osgood thought it rather miraculous that she caught it, snagging it with the bloody teeth of the hacksaw blade. She looped it over her hand, then doubled it, and felt the surprising tightness of it around her wrist. That arm's throbbing subsided only a bit, but that was enough for her.

"I'm not that easy to kill," said Osgood.

"I'm getting the Jeep," said Zack, who gave her another look, then bolted toward the cemetery gates, surely locked and chained at this time of night.

"Os," shouted Audrey. "You need to—"

"Finish this," said Osgood.

"That's not—"

"Stand with Remy."

"What?"

Osgood pointed with the saw and watched as a perplexed Audrey walked over to Remy, who put both arms around her. Osgood wondered if Remy could take the pain from her, as it was so acute just now, but then refocused on the task at hand. She knew she needed to be precise; it may be challenging to kill Prudence Osgood, but she still had the same amount of blood as everybody else and needed a goodly amount to continue to function. "Let's end this thing," she told herself and resumed sawing on that last bit of neck. Quickly, she grew tired, then exhausted, and then her brain started to ask her what she was even doing. The old purple splotches came, obscuring and then filling her vision. She squeezed her eyes shut and shook her head to clear them, continuing to saw, continuing to saw.

Her head cleared momentarily as she looked up to see the headlights of Zack's Jeep speeding through the cemetery toward them. That moment was long enough, and she heard a *tink!* and then watched as the head of the Guardian tumbled forward off the statue.

Unfortunately, a moment later, Osgood did the same.

THIRTY-TWO

Opening her eyes in a hospital room, Osgood felt the startling sense of déjà vu collapsing in on itself. She was at once here today, whatever day today was, but also sometime in mid-December, after ejecting herself from a moving SUV. And also decades earlier, after the crash, with her legs and arms seemingly welded in place. In all three of those times was Audrey Frost, curled up in the chair at the end of her hospital bed, somehow managing to sleep.

"Hi, Aud," she rasped, then looked for the strange tan pitcher and cup. She went to reach for them but found her right arm held to her chest with bandages and a brace. Audrey blinked a few times, stretched her neck, and then made her way over to Osgood. As she grew closer, her face betrayed worry and tears, red and puffy.

"Hi, Os," she said, lightly kissing her forehead.

"Did I do it?" Osgood asked, though much of it came out as whispers.

"Did you cut the head off that statue before bleeding to death from trying to cut your own hand off?" She stood, then stared down at Osgood. "Yes, you did, you fucking psychopath."

"You once stabbed a demigod with a rebar spear," Osgood retorted.

"I did," she said. "Doesn't make what you did any saner."

Osgood shrugged, an excruciatingly painful gesture. "Are they at least giving me the good drugs?"

"Apparently, you have a doctor's note in your file that suspects you abuse OxyContin."

"Ah, fuck me," said Osgood. She remembered that doctor, too. Once he'd gotten a look at her scarred thighs, he'd become prudish and judgy. And had apparently made notes to that effect.

"I did convince them that you couldn't abuse something they put in your IV, though, so you've got the good drugs at the moment, just not for long."

"So what was the damage?" asked Osgood, flicking her head toward her disabled right arm. She saw her teal curls bounce.

And Audrey burst into tears.

Osgood watched for a moment, feeling as though she'd missed something. She reached out her left hand and took Audrey's limp fingers. "Shh, Aud," she said. "I'm okay. I—"

"You don't get it, Pru," she said.

Osgood admitted that she didn't.

"You hurl yourself headlong into things, without regard of what else could—"

"I always think of you, of Zack."

"You *don't!*" Audrey's face was defiant. Red. Angry, not sad. "You try to protect us physically, *maybe*, though I'm not convinced you even do that, really. But you give no thought to what would happen to us if you—" She turned away.

"If I what? Died?" Osgood feigned a laugh. "I'm starting to think I can't be killed."

"Yes, Os, I know you like to think that." She turned back, somewhat more composed. "But you can. And you know you can." Audrey pulled up her sleeve and showed her a bruise on her inner arm. "You have my blood in you now."

"Aud, I..." Osgood didn't know what to say. Something about that felt so intense and intimate that she couldn't even begin.

"Did you know we have the same blood type? AB Negative. The rarest type."

"See," said Osgood. "Made for each other."

"I don't know how many more times I can do this for you —be here, sleep here, watch you almost..." She caught her words. "I just need you to..."

"Look before I leap?" asked Osgood.

"Look, think, research!" Audrey squeezed her hand just a bit too hard. "If Zack says you can jump, then fucking go ahead. Until then..." She loosened her grip and sat in the chair by Osgood's bedside.

"Yeah," said Osgood. "Yeah, I can do that." She smiled at Audrey.

It took a moment, but Audrey returned the smile. "Do you remember, after your accident—"

"I don't remember much after my accident," said Osgood.

"Well, I'm not just asking you to conjure that time, I have something in mind."

Osgood smiled and asked Audrey to continue with her eyes.

"You were so broken."

"*That* I remember."

"They had your leg up in a cast, and one arm in a cast hanging above your head to keep it from rotating."

"Left one," said Osgood. "That's the one I rebroke, diving from that SUV."

"Seriously," said Audrey. "It's a miracle you can function at all."

"It's some kinda thing..."

"You were obsessed with me eating you out. And I kept telling you that I'd never be able to get my face between the casts."

"I'm *still* obsessed with you eating me out," Osgood confirmed.

Audrey just nodded. "So we compromised, and I fingered you until that nurse came in and asked what I was doing."

"If I recall, she did *not* believe you were a nursing student adjusting my catheter."

"No," said Audrey with a laugh. "That's when they decided I wasn't family and visiting hours were officially over."

The two women sat in silence, thinking about the moment, a surprising funny memory in the midst of one of the most horrible stretches of Osgood's painful life. Growing uncomfortable with the silence, Osgood broke it with, "You could eat me out now."

"You're... I don't even know."

"Just a suggestion. I feel like I might not be able to orgasm because I'm so mellow right now, but it'd be fun anyway."

Audrey's laugh was genuine, and Osgood returned it. They laughed hard together, in a way they hadn't in a long time. If only Audrey's phone hadn't *ping*ed, if only they didn't have to stop laughing.

"It's Zack."

"I assume he's been working while I've been here in my relaxing repose."

"He has," said Audrey, her face growing ashen. "But that relaxing repose has gone on for two days."

"Shit," said Osgood.

"And this thing is still going."

The smile vanished from Osgood's lips. "It what?"

Audrey took a breath and lifted a tablet from the side of the bed. She opened it to the Chicago Sun Times's website, where the horrifying headline screamed **North Side Ripper Kills Four.**

"Fuck," said Osgood.

"Fuck," agreed Audrey. "Now, if I convince them to discharge you, you won't get the good drugs any longer, but—"

"Fuck it," said Osgood. "We need to go."

"Yes," said Audrey. "Yes, we do."

THIRTY-THREE

Her homecoming was muted, amid a panicked scramble to cobble together something resembling a plan. She entered her apartment, surprised to find Sandy Hedges and Remy Yeagher with Zack in the living room. The screen above the fireplace showed a time-lapse heat vision, but Osgood was unsure of what. Leaning hard on her cane with her left arm, the right all but worthless for the moment, she announced to the room, "I'm alive!"

"I know," said Zack, before returning to Sandy with his tablet. She regarded Osgood with what almost looked like pity. But Osgood thought she ought to be charitable about the interpretation.

Remy approached and put her hand on Osgood's. "I'm... I'm so sorry, Os."

Osgood cocked her head at the woman. "You didn't do this."

"I wound you up and pointed you at something that was actively trying to kill you. I think I should bear the brunt of—"

"Absolved," said Osgood. "Forgiven." She shook her head. "Whatever, truly."

Remy nodded, still looking guilty, then embraced Audrey, holding her for a long while, a gesture that surprised Osgood both by its intimacy and how jealous it made her feel. Osgood darted her eyes between them. The women took a breath together, in, then out. Then they looked into each other's eyes, and Audrey gave her a little smile. When Remy turned back to her, Os knew the therapist had clocked whatever emotion was running rampant on her face.

Remy leaned in. "You don't have pain to give, Os. You have anger."

Osgood knew she was right. While the physical pain of her daily life was still present, the emotional pain had dramatically decreased. She thought there was still some, especially a recognition of her own responsibility for her friends' pain, but maybe that should wait. Or maybe she shouldn't lose that at all.

"Welcome back, Os," said Zack, as she sat in her Barca-Lounger. "I was... I was really fucking worried."

Osgood nodded. "I'm sorry I worried you."

"What?" Zack stood up, seemingly taken aback. "No, Os... You..."

Osgood waved it away. "So, where is it?"

"On the back porch," said Zack. "We didn't want it inside after... Well..." He handed a small remote to Sandy, who stood to address the group.

Osgood resisted the urge to smile; the young woman looked like she was about to present to a high school class. She remembered that Sandy had her own ghost-hunting group, the Southside Ghost Hunters, and had been an invited speaker at several conferences the Spectral Inspectors had attended over the years. Osgood crossed her cane over her knees and gave Sandy Hedges her full attention.

"After you left Lodge 9," began Sandy, switching to a heat vision image of Lodge 9, "Zack asked me to watch it. Our mobile command station captures heat vision by default..."

"Wow," said Osgood.

Sandy grinned. "It's pretty sweet." She cleared her throat and returned to serious mode. "So we have around twenty-three hours of this. Most of it shows nothing, but we got this at 1:33 a.m. yesterday morning." She hit play, and a long and drawn-out swath of pink slid through the sky's deep blue, disappearing, it seemed, into the second story of Lodge 9.

"What was it?" asked Osgood. She regretted the question quickly. It was the kind of thing that amateurs asked, noobs, normies. "Never mind."

"No," said Sandy. "Actually, we do have some idea what it was." She handed the remote to Zack, who popped another video onto the screen. This time, the heat vision showed the back of the Guardian's severed head.

"We filmed from the back, to be sure no one looked into it," he said.

"Smart," said Osgood.

"This is 1:29 a.m., the same morning, just before Sandy's video." He pressed play on his remote and, while the colors were different, as this view seemed to be inside, a brighter swath oozed into the frame, seemed to surround the head, then oozed back out over the course of a minute.

Osgood felt herself recoil. "Jesus, it's still working!"

"Notably," said Audrey, taking the remote herself. She brought up the newspaper headline she'd shown Osgood in the hospital. "The estimated time of death for the most recent victims of the North Side Ripper... Between 1:00 and 1:30 a.m."

"So, those kids die," said Osgood, "and then something comes to the head, and then it goes to the Lodge."

"That's pretty much what we've got," said Audrey. "Remy?"

"Wow," said Osgood. "When'd y'all get so good at presentations."

Remy came over, but rather than standing before the group, she sat on the edge of the coffee table in front of Osgood. She reached out and took Osgood's left hand, the good hand, and smiled.

"Boy," said Osgood. "If I never again feel an intervention coming on, it'll be—"

"Shh," said Remy. "Osgood."

"Yes?"

"After looking into the face—"

"—not a face."

"—of the Guardian, you first began to feel like killing yourself, and then like killing Audrey."

Osgood's eyes darted to Audrey's, and she felt the pain and embarrassment well up.

"Prudence!"

Remy's voice saying her first name, the cadence intense, snapped Osgood's eyes back.

"This is pain," said Remy. "Give it to me."

"I don't know what that—"

Remy shushed her again and squeezed her hand. Osgood felt the embarrassment begin to leave her.

"We think," said Remy, "after extensive discussions and theorizing, that looking into the ... hood, if you like ... of the Guardian dramatically increases a person's call of the void."

"Okay," said Osgood.

"To the point where they almost cannot help themselves." With the lightest of touches, Remy indicated Osgood's wrapped right wrist.

"And they kill themselves."

"Like Jackie Tomlinson," said Audrey.

"And the driver of that car," added Zack.

"But some people manage to hold out," continued Remy, who moved her hand to Osgood's shoulder. "So the Guardian goes to plan B."

"If you're not going to kill yourself," said Audrey, "maybe kill someone else instead."

"Jesus," said Osgood.

"It's why you wanted to kill me," said Audrey.

"I never *wanted* to—"

"It's why you felt compelled to," clarified Audrey, who then, hopefully, added, "Right?"

"Right? What? Of course I don't want to kill you."

"So, what're we left with?" asked Zack.

"If removing the head doesn't stop it completely...," said Audrey.

"Because there's outstanding debt," suggested Osgood.

"It *may* at least stop new ... participants," offered Sandy.

"Then the answer lies at Lodge 9, doesn't it?" asked Osgood.

Zack nodded, bringing the heat vision image of Lodge 9 back up. "Seems like it's the end of the line, anyway. Something is there."

"Something is definitely there," said Osgood.

THIRTY-FOUR

The Spectral Inspectors wove their way south to Willowbrook for the second time that week. Their entourage was slightly more extensive this time, with Remy Yeagher and Sandy Hedges in Remy's Trans Am behind the Jeep. When they arrived and pulled in across the street from the dark Lodge, they stared out the window at it. Osgood wondered what they were waiting for. To see some new spiritual energy slide in? To see if the front doors would open to welcome them? Osgood was sick of waiting and was first to climb from the cars. She slammed her cane down in the dust with her left hand, feeling her leather coat blowing in the breeze. She wondered if it'd fly away; after all, she only had one arm in it. But it held fast.

Zack looked to Sandy, who'd set up a heat vision camera atop the Jeep. A cable spiraled down to where she crouched behind the vehicles. She flicked him a thumbs up. "Just a reminder," he said, "when we go inside, we're officially breaking and entering. If any police stop by, we'll probably be going to jail."

"For a simple non-theft B-and-E?" asked Osgood.

"You know better than that," said Zack.

She did. She also knew that every piece of equipment they'd be using, from the electric key to get in the front door to whatever Zack had planned for that trophy case, was illegal, or at least hung out in the gray area where a police officer, already disinclined to like you (say because of your race, or sexuality), might decide to get you right the fuck off the street.

"Let's go," said Audrey. Zack nodded. Osgood nodded. Remy nodded. They went.

Zack looked up and down the street to confirm there were no cars before crouching at the front door and jamming his electric key into the lock. Within seconds, they heard the *click*, then *thunk*, of the metal lock opening within the door. Zack stood, looked at the street again, and then opened the door as he shoved the electric key back into his satchel.

The interior of the Lodge was lit by a single emergency floodlight, its duplicate partner seemingly burnt out, giving everything in the entryway long and moody shadows. Their whispers echoed off the decades-old linoleum. Once the four of them were inside, leaving Sandy Hedges to stand sentinel across the street, Zack re-locked the door.

"Anybody want a drink?" asked Osgood, quietly.

Zack shushed her.

Remy said, "Raincheck."

Before them was the trophy case. The harsh light from the emergency lamp showed that the glass hadn't been cleaned in a while. There were fingerprints, dust, smudges. All except for one spot, on the lower right. Zack pointed it out wordlessly, then mimed opening it. Osgood nodded, then mimed getting on with it. Zack tried, wrapping his fingers around the metal edging of the case, but it didn't budge. Audrey and Remy moved to help him, both women wedging themselves into the corner, backs against the wall, to shove. Still no movement.

Osgood leaned down, looking at the pictures within the

case, pictures that told a sad story of near extinction. As late as the '40s, there was a photo of the entire Lodge every few years. Boisterous men wearing suits and sashes, standing on an ornate stage before a throne. But after that, the gaps between pictures grew longer, and the number of people grew fewer. By the '90s, the Lodge was down to fewer than twenty men and one woman, whom Osgood was pretty sure she'd just met the other day. After the dawn of the new millennium, that number had fallen even further. The aughts didn't even have a photo, and this current era seemed an afterthought, an inkjet-printed picture of four people. Three of them she knew, one she didn't. She was struck by the oddest sense of sadness for a moment. This had been their space, where they'd felt cama-raderie and brotherhood. While she might find the very idea of a men's club or fraternal order as distasteful as she found the mini versions on college campuses, she knew what it was like to lose a group that you felt a part of. That you thought valued you.

After the scam episode, which Osgood had to constantly remind herself also included non-faked footage of possible ghosts, she'd grown steadily more ostracized from her commu-nity of fellow ghost hunters as it became an unspoken secret in their circles: "Didja hear Osgood and Frost *faked* their live show encounter?" With Audrey not around to defend herself, having immediately left the paranormal community, Osgood had tried to downplay the incident to save her own reputation, while simultaneously taking responsibility for it so that it didn't fall on Audrey. It was a tricky needle to thread, and Osgood wasn't equipped with the deftness to accomplish it.

But unlike this Brotherhood and this Lodge, the para-normal community had thrived without her. It had taken a decade for her to regain any semblance of respectability with her podcast, and even then, there'd been the threat of people reminding everyone what she'd done. A reminder Sam

Goddard had once shouted from the back of a lecture hall at a ghost-hunting conference halfway through her keynote speech..

Though, she thought, if the rest of the Luminous Brotherhood of the Eternal Flame were as dickish as their friend Leland had been, maybe it was for the best that this outdated, misogynistic, and probably racist group was dying. She wondered how they'd actually managed the last twenty years. If membership had fallen so far, how could they still be here? She remembered Leland's veiled reference to important people keeping them afloat, but even that felt ... off. Something was here. Whether Leland or Bev or Reggie knew it or participated in it was still a question, but regardless, something supernatural held sway over this place. Osgood could feel it.

"Jesus!" exclaimed Zack, full voice. After hearing nothing save the occasional whisper for several minutes, this full-volume exclamation surprised the hell out of Osgood. Frustrated, his hand covering his mouth, perhaps to prevent more loud words from tumbling out, Zack paced back and forth between the trophy case and the wall. He turned to Osgood, seeing her questioning expression, and explained, "There's no button. No latch. No hinges. Nothing."

"Maybe it's actually not a secret passage," offered Audrey.

Zack's withering glare caused her to recoil.

"It *is* a secret passage," he said. He punched his palm. Very, very occasionally, Osgood could see the *man* in Zack. Despite his gentle and helpful nature, there was still a bit of that testosterone beast within him, most evident when, as now, he allowed his frustration full expression. Seeing their growing skepticism, he pulled a Zippo lighter from his pocket and held it next to the case. The flame fluttered. "See?"

Trying to figure out what she was supposed to be seeing, Osgood leaned in.

"There's air coming from behind it." He flicked his lighter

closed and tapped the stainless steel against his lips, then, without warning, he walked out of the building.

"We could look for another way up, or…" suggested Remy.

Osgood stepped back, looking at the case, then the ground. It took her a moment, but she found the small arcing smudge that Zack had shown them. Just then, he stormed back in with a crowbar, lifted it above his head, and began to swing it toward the case. "Wait!" she exclaimed and pointed at the ground.

"What?" asked Zack.

"Something made the line. Like a clasp or—"

Zack caught up, eyes wide. "Or a locking pin." He almost leaped to the ground, pressing his cheek flat against the tiles as he looked beneath the case. "Fuck me, it's right here. I don't know how I missed it!"

He jammed the crowbar under the case and pulled. Then he climbed to a standing position and put all his weight on the bar. Finally, they heard an almost imperceptible click, and the trophy case leaned out ever so slightly. The three able-bodied trespassers pulled the case until its rotation gave them enough space to see the corridor beyond. The screeching as they did suggested it was not used often. Dark, covered in dust and cobwebs, the corridor itself also showed disuse. When Zack snapped his flashlight on, they saw why they'd come. "And there," he said, "are stairs." Sure enough, a flight of stairs, probably part of the original construction in wood, rose within the corridor and terminated at a wooden door.

"Well, I'd say we go up," said Osgood. She could feel a rush of nervousness move through her and assumed it hit the others as well, but they were too close now not to find their way to the end. After a moment, she took the lead.

"Os, wait," said Remy.

"Not if the answer's behind that door…" Osgood got to

the top, then shuffled with her cane, trying to reach out and turn the knob.

Zack made it up second and reached past her. Locked, of course. He crouched and looked at the keyhole of an old skeleton key. He looked up at Osgood. "Too old for the electric key!" He shuffled around in his satchel before pulling out a screwdriver. A bit of fiddling, and the door fell open. The space beyond was dimly lit and not what they expected at all.

"After you," said Osgood.

Zack laughed and turned toward the darkness as Audrey and Remy made it to the landing behind Osgood.

The space was large, seemingly too large for the building, and the flashlight wasn't powerful enough to illuminate everything. As Zack swung the beam across the walls, they saw mahogany bookshelves lining the room, filled with dusty and cracked leatherbound tomes. At the light a rat, or at least something that looked like a rat, skittered from behind one book to under another. Midway between the front of the room and the back, filled with what looked like piles of storage, sat an enormous wooden desk with a green-shaded banker's light on it.

"I... thought you might ... come..."

Osgood's attention snapped to the back of the room just as she heard the tinkle of a chain being pulled, followed by a *click*, and the dimmest bulb imaginable flickered on beneath the green shade. The shadows it threw were long and fuzzy and they didn't reach the walls. The light barely illuminated the thing behind the desk, a funnel-faced creature with enormous shiny eyes, clad in black.

"Welcome ... to the ... Luminous Brotherhood..."

THIRTY-FIVE

"I ... don't ... mean to frighten..."

The thing moved a limb of some sort, and Osgood heard the sound of a switch being flipped. One by one, small orb lamps situated on brass arms around the room snapped on, maybe twenty in total. Somehow, though, the creature remained in the shadows.

With a rhythmic creak it began to move its bulk out of the darkness until it finally was illuminated, revealing that it was not a beast. Osgood's mind was boggled nonetheless, taking in the apparent human before them, bit by bit. The funnel was an oxygen mask, the kind worn by jet pilots in flight, that looked cobbled together from World Wars I and II parts. It terminated in a tube that disappeared over the figure's shoulder. Above the mask, a pair of welding goggles obscured its eyes completely, the glass in them reflecting back the banker's lamp, the orbs, and Zack's flashlight. Atop its head was a broad-brimmed hat of wicker or straw, barely visible because, hanging over it and the person below, was a dense net, the type you'd hang over your bed in some countries to keep from getting malaria. The figure seemed to be propped up in an antique wheelchair, its high back the origin of the netting. Below the mask, its clothing appeared to be nothing more than taupe-colored draped linen. It hid its hands on either side on the arms of the wheelchair, a second layer below the netting. The linens terminated behind the desk, where the Investigators could see no more.

"What the *fuck?*" asked Zack.

Osgood was inclined to agree.

"You're Ambrose Ballard," said Remy, quietly, stepping forward.

The thing under the net reached a gauze-clad hand up and pulled its goggles to its forehead. The Spectral Inspectors took in the sunken eyes, dark purplish rings around them, milky cataracts swarming each iris. "That's ... preposterous," it said. "Ambrose Ballard ... would be ... What year ... is it?"

"2023."

The thing rattled with what Osgood supposed was a chuckle of sorts. "Nearly one ... hundred and se ... venty ... years old..."

"But you are," asked Remy. "Aren't you?"

They stared at each other for a moment. Long enough for Osgood to lean forward, squinting. The thing before her looked so much like that picture Zack had shown them, but at the same time different. Osgood wondered if she was just seeing what she wanted to, or if this actually was Ambrose Ballard. Regardless, the creature's eyes felt awful on her.

"Who ... beheaded ... my Guardian?" it asked, raising another gauze-covered hand to them.

"I did," said Osgood firmly.

Again, the rattle, though she also heard a definite titter this time. "And now will ... you behead ... me?"

"Just give me a reason," said Osgood.

"I take it ... you'd like ... my story ...?" offered the be-netted figure.

"No," said Audrey.

It reacted with surprise, as though it hadn't been surprised by a single thing in its preposterously long life. Its hands moved to the wheels of its chair, which slowly rotated in place, then slid forward around the side of the desk toward where Audrey stood beside Osgood and Remy. The ancient figure moved two or three feet before sighing and taking a moment to regroup. Then it looked up and moved an additional foot, rotating again to directly face Audrey, who opened her mouth but didn't seem to know what to say.

Its hand moved to its face, more like a marionette than a human, and unbuckled the oxygen mask. There was a slight sucking sound, then a hiss as it fell away. The nearly skeletal face beneath was hairless, with a wide lipless mouth that fell open, stringy saliva between its teeth. Osgood uncomfortably went back to a nightmare cartoon version of *A Christmas Carol* from her childhood, where doorknocker Marley had looked just like that.

"No?" it asked, much clearer but much throatier. As though the voice had skipped its mouth entirely and come out through a hole in its throat.

"No," Audrey repeated. Osgood stepped up next to her for emphasis.

"Then why have you come? To gloat?"

Osgood was startled by the newfound clarity of its speech without the mask, and realized that the oxygen flowing was probably what had given it such a strange cadence. But wait, without the mask, the voice tinged higher. Osgood squinted and stepped toward the thing in the wheelchair. "To stop what you're doing."

The ancient figure laughed wetly, seeming as though at any moment its throat might collapse in on itself.

Osgood looked to Audrey and Remy and ... "Zack?" The other two women also looked around, then turned back upon hearing Zack's footsteps rushing down the stairs.

"Maybe he found me repulsive," offered Ballard. "I wouldn't blame him. I do as well."

Remy stepped forward, moving all the way to the desk. She leaned down at Ballard, who looked up at her, head cocked like a dog's.

"What are you?" asked Osgood.

It laughed for real this time, a gasping chuckle that caused the necessity of another breath from the mask. When the mask was lowered again, the face had lost its humor. But now Osgood saw what she'd missed earlier. This thing before them, the ancient member of the Luminous Brotherhood of the Eternal Flame, wasn't what they'd thought at all. Wasn't even a brother. "You're Cora."

"What?" asked Audrey.

Remy leaned in, her eyes widening as the thing carefully tilted its head this way and that, examining Osgood's face as intensely as she had it.

"You are correct," it ... *she* said.

Now the ancient woman turned her gaze to Remy, leaning forward to meet her in intensity. If it made the psychologist uncomfortable, she hid it well. "What are *you*?" Cora asked, then swung her face toward Osgood, which made her jump. "What is *she?*"

"She's a person," said Audrey, in the tenor with which one might say "duh."

"Oh, no ... She's not," said Cora Ballard with a small wet chortle. "She ... shines."

Remy waved her hand back at them. Osgood thought she might be waving them off? Perhaps just asking to take over the conversation. Either way, Osgood waited.

"You're in pain," said Remy. "Excruciating pain."

Cora said nothing, but her mouth drew up, and oily tears ran down her papery cheeks. "For one hundred and twenty years, I've watched every soul that came to that statue. I've seen every one of them. Every death. Every suicide. Every murder."

"How?" asked Audrey.

Cora gave her a look that said she had no intention of stopping this story for questions. "They called themselves the Luminous Brotherhood, but I was the one who shone." She lifted a covered hand to gesture vaguely toward one of the bookshelves. Atop the middle shelf was a picture frame showcasing a group of men flanking the true Ambrose Ballard. She chuckled. "They would only let me *take* their picture. Heaven forbid I be in it."

"You died," said Osgood.

"Oh, yes," said Cora in a voice guttural and low that set Osgood's teeth on edge. "As did you."

Osgood could only nod.

"And you," she told Remy, but Remy's face betrayed nothing.

"It is quite amazing what you know, once you've seen beyond the veil." She turned back to Osgood and brought her hands down to the chair's wheels, moving toward her. "Did you know that is what the word apocalypse means? A 'lifting of the veil.'" Cora reached out a covered hand toward Osgood's, who yanked hers away, terrified that if she touched this thing, she'd get some sort of rotting disease. "We've all had our own little apocalypses, haven't we?"

"Can I ease your pain?" asked Remy. "Tell me."

Cora Ballard's voice lost its amusement and went small and hollow, like a waif in an empty room. "I thought you did not want my story."

"Tell me," repeated Remy.

"My husband Ambrose thought he was kind. He thought he was doing what was best."

"He resurrected you?" asked Audrey.

"I was not the same," said Cora, almost to herself, a hoarse and quiet whisper. "He could not look at me. Or our daughter." The side of her slit of a mouth twitched. "Though she was the first. And she was..." Cora's eyes rolled orgasmically, making Osgood want to wretch. "Magnificent."

"How did he do it?" asked Remy.

"There were those in the Brotherhood who had ideas that strayed from science. Those exploring alchemy. Witchcraft." Cora tapped at the arm of her chair with a finger so papery it almost appeared to be solely bone. "They were all quite convinced they knew what was best and had the means to achieve it. Are you familiar with Shelley?"

"Mary?" asked Audrey.

"Percy Bysshe. I was always partial to him. Ambrose told me that when I ... awoke from the darkness, I quoted Shelley. 'My name is Ozymandias, King of Kings; Look on my Works, ye Mighty, and despair!'" Cora laughed again, though her voice was becoming weaker. "He'd thought himself fearless and flawless. I ate him, you know. In the end." She waved her hand toward Remy. "Not physically. I haven't eaten a thing in a hundred and twenty years. Not since I wrapped that rope around my throat in February of 1903. But I ate his essence. Which I suppose you could call a soul. My time in the dirt disinclines me to believe in such a thing."

"You hung yourself?" asked Osgood.

"While looking out our picture window at Lake Michigan." Cora's voice turned woeful. "I never did see that lake again. But it sparkles in my memory." When she turned her face toward Remy it was no longer the face of a creature, a monster, but of an exhausted old woman. "My life has been extended so many times, for which I have that cursed statue and my knave of a husband to thank and blame. But I do believe that for every death the Guardian has called, I've been made to bear witness. So many have died, while I cannot. I hear them. I wonder if they're loud enough that you can hear them as well. There are so many. Of late, it's multiple times per day." She turned her face up to Remy, standing before her. "I am so exhausted. I no longer want this life. If you believe there's something you can do to make it stop. To make the pain stop. To release me from this horrid existence... Please." She looked down, sobbing, into her lap. "Please."

Remy knelt before her, the psychologist's face the very picture of empathy and understanding. She lifted the mosquito net like a groom might lift a bride's veil. Seeing Cora Ballard without the screen between them made her look even more artificial to Osgood. Her skin had the texture of mulberry bark, as though her entire head had been crafted of it. But there was no mistaking her eyes—they were human, if ancient. Remy reached up and put her hand on the side of Cora's face.

"Remy!" demanded Osgood. "Don't do it!"

Remy didn't look at Osgood, but Audrey did. She squeezed Osgood's hand as if to say, "Let it go."

But Osgood didn't want to let it go. "You could've stopped it. When you came back, when he didn't want you, you could've—"

"Yes?" asked Cora, turning her head. Remy's hand still rested on her cheek. "My husband put me here. Locked me away. If there's any person who holds guilt here, it's him. I served him, he served them, and all things serve the beam."

"You're saying you had *nothing whatsoever* to do with the deaths? The suicides? The murders."

"Prudence," said Remy quietly. Osgood turned to her.

"I was merely witness," said Cora.

"She has experienced a pain greater than any of us have ever known," said the psychologist.

Osgood looked at Remy and Cora, and they looked expectantly back at her, as though asking her permission to continue. She didn't know what to say; she only knew that Remy was modeling something she'd never quite been able to conjure in herself: forgiveness. Frustrated, and considering the scores of young people who'd recently contributed to this long life, Osgood turned away.

"Let it go, Cora," she heard Remy say. "Let it all go."

Cora Ballard opened her mouth, emitting a thin, high-pitched wail. More tears stained her cheeks, somehow black, trails rolling down. The wailing grew in intensity, drawing Osgood back. She turned around in time to see what looked like a tendril of light snake out of Cora into Remy's chest. But as she saw it and blinked, it was gone, leaving only a purple negative image behind. She watched in silence as their breathing synced, and then Remy began taking deeper and deeper breaths as Cora's grew more and more shallow. An incredible *pop* sounded, and the air rushed in, smelling of ozone. The lights flickered and then returned to their previous levels. Cora's head hung back as though her neck was broken, and Remy Yeagher fell backward to the floor.

"Remy!" Osgood exclaimed, rushing to her side. Audrey was right behind her. After the most prolonged, pregnant pause Osgood had ever experienced, Remy's chest began to rise and fall again. "Thank god!"

Remy's eyelids fluttered. "Are you okay?" Osgood asked desperately.

"Super-duper," said Remy, weakly throwing her a thumbs up.

Behind her, though, came a horror. A strong, deep voice. "Thank you for relieving me of that insipid guilt."

"Os!" exclaimed Audrey.

Osgood turned just in time to see Cora Ballard standing before her chair. The ancient woman reached out, the crumbling rags falling from her hands, and grabbed Osgood by her coat lapel. Audrey rushed forward, slamming into Cora's arm. Cora staggered but didn't fall, instead throwing the back of her hand into Audrey's face. Audrey did fall, crashing against a bookcase off to the side. Cora had lost ages in face and body, now seeming to be a sturdy woman in her early 40s, at most.

"The guilt weighed me down," said Cora. She leaned next to Osgood, whispering in her ear. "As I'm sure you know well. But without guilt, my longevity is glorious!" She grabbed Osgood's head in both hands and twisted, causing her to flop and roll onto her back. Stepping between her legs, Cora stood above her, grinning from ear to ear. But her smile wasn't the most horrible part, nor were her eyes; what Osgood saw then made her entire body shiver. Now that the netting and the linens had fallen away, she could see that, astride Cora Ballard's back, was a humanoid thing, bright translucent blue-white, with horrible eyes and a gaping purple maw. A long and smiling thing. That thing wasn't controlling the ancient woman, Osgood knew; that thing was what Cora had become. It'd been there at every death, hadn't it? In the periphery, off to the side, to take both the guilt—that Remy had unfortunately now relieved her of—but also the joy.

As Cora bent toward Osgood, the thing on her back pressed through her, reaching out for the ghosthunter. She felt the air almost freeze as it grew near, hearing a crackling sound. Its fingers neared her face, Cora Ballard grinning above them. "Do you know, the most joyous of deaths were the ones where an innocent killed another. I tasted those twice, like the finest ambrosia of the gods leeching into me. The little girl who killed her high school friends, well that may have been my masterpiece." Cora tilted her head. "I do lament that I never was able to taste you..."

"I make most people at least buy me a drink first," said Osgood.

"Hey, fuckhead!"

They all turned toward Zack, who stood in the doorway flanked by Sandy Hedges, holding the head of the Guardian between them. "Look here!" he said.

She watched as the thing atop Cora tried to shield her eyes, to stop her head from turning. But Cora Ballard looked, and she saw. She peered right into the abyss of the Guardian, and the abyss peered back into her.

"Wait, it's a woman?" Zack asked, utterly perplexed.

"Do it anyway, Zack!" exclaimed Osgood. "Don't look at it, Audrey! Remy!"

"I'm not," said Audrey. "I won't."

"I'm just going to lie here for a while," said Remy without raising her head.

Once again, the feeling of a vacuum was born in the room, connecting Cora's now gaping maw with the emptiness beneath that hood. The woman and the thing atop her began to contort, staggering toward the head as though tugged by some incredible force. Then Osgood could see that the force was Cora's essence, the twisted thing that represented the last of her soul. The white thing began to elongate, stretching toward the head of the Guardian. The grinning thing stretched like taffy, twirling, until it reached the hood. Like fire meeting different chemicals, the makeup of the thing changed, and it cycled from orange to green to the sickly purple of its mouth.

It wasn't smiling any longer, and Cora Ballard was shrieking.

Osgood saw Zack and Sandy beginning to shake, and she crawled across the floor to join them, to help hoist the head of the Guardian as Ballard was drawn closer and closer. But then, something odd happened. The thing atop Cora, now more like an umbilical cord between her and the head, a twisting tube of light that disappeared inside the front of the statue, appeared again out the backside, snaking its way up and over, a second tendril that blasted into Cora's forehead. The ancient woman's entire body spasmed, and she rose from the ground as the tendrils of the light cycled between the hood and the woman, faster and faster, like a bicycle chain.

Cora Ballard, now three feet off the ground, thrust her head backward, and this time, Osgood was sure she heard the woman's spine snap. Her mouth slackened and grew larger, her eyes began to roll up, and she shook as though in a seizure. The energy cycled faster and faster, tugging Cora closer, drawing her in. The whirring of it grew louder and louder, like a freight train blasting by. Bones creaked and broke as the ancient woman folded, arms and legs pointing straight toward the Guardian's head. The din's intensity grew, and the tether enveloped Cora until she was mere inches away.

When her body touched the head of the Guardian, the one Osgood had lopped off only days ago, a rush of air knocked Osgood, Zack, and Sandy backward. The head fell to the ground and rolled, dragging Cora's steadily more compact body with it, until it hit the side of the desk and stopped. A moment later, both Cora Ballard and the colorful energy were gone, snapping down to nothing inside the hood of the Guardian, as though inside it were a very tiny black hole.

Then, silence.

Osgood turned and saw Remy propped up on her elbows, red faced and looking like she could sleep for a year. She looked to Audrey, who stared at the head and laughed triumphantly. Zack and Sandy each ensured the other was alright before shakily standing and approaching the head. Audrey stood and then gently lifted Osgood from the floor, but even so, there was pain. She heard a *thunk!* and looked over in time to see

Zack kick the head a second time, sending it down the staircase.

"Zack," said Osgood, wanting to tell him to be careful. But Zack was always careful. Always considered.

"Let's go outside," he said after a while of kicking and prodding it. "I've got enough C4 to orbit this fucking thing."

Thirty-Six

While Zack's explosives may not have put the head into orbit, they were indeed powerful enough to blast it into dozens of tiny pieces, scattering them every which way in the field behind Lodge 9. They did it there, despite the risk, because as Audrey had said, "That thing is not coming home with us." Four of them watched as tech and (apparently) weapons expert Zack Nguyen wired up a make-shift bomb, cramming it into the hollow head of the Guardian and then, without warning, running, arms a-flail like a Muppet back toward them. The explosion, a shocking fireball that Osgood felt singe her arm hair, went up so suddenly and shortly after Zack ran, it was rather apparent he'd miscalculated the fuse.

Still, the wretched thing was no more than scattered pieces and a blasted crater.

Sandy rushed up to Zack, who was crouching and breathing heavily. When he stood, he had a swagger Osgood had rarely seen. Buoyed by Sandy's attention and affection, he grinned, playing it off as though the explosion had been no big deal, and kissed her like the hero at the film's end, which was how Sandy Hedges clearly saw him. Watching this moment, Osgood felt no jealousy that she'd lost his attention. It'd never been about romance with them, of course; from the moment they'd met, Zack had felt like the little brother her parents hadn't given her. She knew that irritated him at times, as he would much rather be seen as a peer, and he'd probably prefer fewer noogies on those rare occasions Osgood was in a playful mood. Watching him now, though, she knew that he was getting what he needed from Sandy. Not only a peer's respect, though she definitely had that for the vaunted Q of the Spectral Inspectors team, but also the intense affection and attraction that he'd never gotten (or wanted, for that matter) from Osgood. She smiled at them, resisting the urge to tell them to get a room. They had one, after all.

Osgood hobbled back to the open door of the Jeep Cherokee, finding Audrey standing behind it. The most sensible of the Spectral Inspectors, she was the only one who'd bothered to shield herself from the explosion.

"How do you feel?" Audrey asked.

"My wrist hurts," said Osgood.

"Well, you did try to saw off your hand," said Audrey.

Osgood nodded. No arguing with that.

"Otherwise?" Audrey pushed.

Osgood thought about it. When, on the second floor of Lodge 9, Cora Ballard had ... what? Phased out of existence? She'd felt immediately lighter. Coming down the stairs and out the front door into the crisp early-October evening air, she'd felt lighter still. And when the head had erupted and her arm hair burned, she'd felt a level of contentment she hadn't felt in ages. Couldn't remember, in fact. Perhaps that Christmas she and Audrey had spent together, just before COVID. But even that had been muted by the looming specter of Sam Goddard. It was as though she'd walked for decades with an emotional weight around her neck, dragging her head closer and closer to the ground, and suddenly so much of that weight had been lifted, first by Remy and then by the destruction of the Guardian. Enough that Osgood nearly felt she could stand up straight.

Metaphorically straight, of course-her knees and thighs and back still took issue with the notion of her walking erect. The cane would continue to be hers.

"I think I'm okay," she said finally, turning her face toward Audrey's with a smile.

Audrey mirrored the smile. "You'll tell me if you feel the urge to kill me?"

"Yeah," said Osgood, not quite as amused by her beloved Odd. "Love... I love you, Audrey."

"I know," said Audrey with a smirk, but then she added, "I love you, too." She poked a finger at Osgood's sternum. "And with my blood in you, you'll be even more difficult to kill."

"Ain't a force in the 'verse than can kill me," said Osgood, returning the smirk. They kissed lightly on the lips.

"Alright, alright," said Zack, blustering over. "Y'know, we should probably go lest we get arrested for ... well, take your pick. None of it's good."

Audrey and Osgood laughed in the hollow way of horror survivors. Audrey turned her attention to her shoes, rubbing the ball of one foot over the toe of another. "What about..." she began, seeming as though she didn't want to finish the thought.

Her reluctance, though, made Osgood understand. There was still a nit to pick here, wasn't there? One thread to pull. "The kind of thread that can unravel the whole sweater," said Osgood, more to herself than her companions.

"What are we talking about?" asked Zack.

"The North Side Ripper," said Audrey.

"The one that doesn't exist," added Osgood.

"What about..." he stopped himself, his eyes widening. "*Someone* did it."

Osgood nodded. "The Guardian didn't actually kill anybody. Neither did Cora Ballard, not really."

"It was kids," said Zack, his voice dropping, woeful.

"Do you think they know they did it?" Osgood asked. "Like, we would've heard someone's confession by now, wouldn't we?"

"Given the amount of death, I can't imagine everybody keeping quiet," said Audrey.

"Or being good at covering their tracks," said Zack.

"What's our responsibility here?" Osgood asked. She threw a glance over her shoulder to where the head once lay. They'd defeated it, the big bad. They'd stopped it in its tracks, hopefully for good. But there was fallout. There was always fallout.

Audrey took a deep breath and spoke carefully. "If they have no memory of doing these horrible things..."

Zack nodded. "Horrible things they were compelled—"

"Essentially forced," said Osgood.

"Right. Forced to do."

"Then can they even be considered responsible?" asked Audrey.

The Spectral Inspectors looked at each other, and in that moment knew they were all on the same page. None of them would say a word about who the murderers were. There might still be some fallout down the line, and their client, Vanessa Moreau would have to be told something. Something reassuring. A lie perhaps, but a good lie, a comforting lie. As comforting as anything could be about the murder of her young daughter.

Zack broke the silent concord. "I'm going to let Sandy know."

Audrey silently nodded.

Audrey nodded and went.

Osgood found Remy lying across the back seat of the Jeep. Door open, legs dangling out, hand over her face. "Everybody's asking if *I'm* okay," said Osgood.

Remy removed her hand from her eyes and tilted her head to see Osgood. "*Are* you okay?" Propped up on her elbows, Remy's face was ashen, her eyes sunken, their silvery irises faded to dull gray, and her sockets were rimmed with purplish red, as though she'd been punched.

"I'm..." Osgood shook her head, unable to hide her own concern. "Remy. You look beat up."

"I'll be fine. Tomorrow or the next day. Same old Dr. Remy." She nodded and smiled, though it was weary and sad. "Trust me."

"You took it all, didn't you?" asked Osgood.

Remy said nothing but looked away.

"Did she deserve it?"

"Deserve it?"

"To have her pain... Um...," Osgood didn't know how to refer to what she'd seen or what Remy could do. "Sucked?"

"Well put," said Remy with a weak laugh. "No one deserves pain. Even the worst of us usually hate ourselves more than anyone else ever could." She nodded to herself. "But I'll tell ya, I didn't expect everything that came out of her."

"She said you shine," said Osgood, not a question, but the prodding was apparent.

"I was once called a being of light, Prudence Osgood," said Remy Yeagher. "Can we leave it at that?"

Osgood nodded, putting her hand on Remy's knee. It took everything she had not to follow up on Remy's comment. "We should go."

Remy nodded back and pulled herself up.

"Need someone else to drive?"

She shook her head. "Nah. Feeling better already."

Osgood helped her from the Jeep's back seat, as much as someone with one working arm who needed a cane *could* help, and over to the Trans Am.

"You should see me in a few days," said Remy.

"Will you be doing cartwheels?"

"Doubtful," said Remy. "But I meant you should see me for you."

Osgood looked at her beautiful face, radiant, color beginning to return. Even her hair had started to look golden again. "I want to see you, Remy. But not for the reasons you're suggesting."

"How do you know what I'm suggesting?" asked the Doctor.

"I need the pain," said Osgood.

"No one needs—"

"I do," said Osgood, defiantly. "My body aches so loudly."

"I wish I could do something about—"

"No, I know," said Osgood. "And believe me, if you could make *that* pain disappear, I'd beg you to do it as soon as possible."

"But?"

"But the pain up here?" Osgood leaned on her cane, pointing to her head, then her heart. "And in here? I think it's why I'm me."

"We are all a product of our whole lives," said Remy, shaking her head. "I'm only suggesting that you don't have to endure quite so much trauma. You're not suddenly going to be Little Miss Happy-Go-Lucky. I just want to help."

"I know," said Osgood. "Thank you." She turned to walk back to the Jeep, then stopped and looked back at Remy. "The masturbation thing..."

Remy allowed a smirk to cross her lips.

"That was for you, wasn't it?"

"Well," said Remy, still smirking but showing a touch of embarrassment. "Didn't you enjoy it?"

"Of course, I enjoyed it," Osgood said. "But you got more out of it, didn't you?"

"Yes," admitted Remy. "I need to get topped off sometimes."

"Well, any time you need that again—"

"Are you offering?"

"Let's just do it in my bedroom."

"I can't have sex with you, Osgood." Remy leaned out of the Trans Am window and kissed Osgood gently. "Well... *Can't* is a big word. And life is long and weird." Dr. Ramona Yeagher drove from the field, and as soon as she hit the pavement, she gunned it.

Osgood heard the horses under the hood drive her away. When Osgood returned to the Jeep, she found the Spectral Inspectors waiting for her, plus Sandy. But Osgood supposed she deserved the title as much as anyone else. Climbing into the back seat, Osgood leaned forward and squeezed Zack's shoulder, then Audrey's.

"Let's go home."

THIRTY-SEVEN

"You're so quiet," said Nora.

"We're all basically dead already," said Osgood, too quiet for the girl, no the *woman* next to her to hear in the loud shuddering of the L car. That had been on her mind all this time. Since the first of the victims of what the police thought was the North Side Ripper had shown up, really. The line between living and dead feels significant to us when we're satisfied and happy. Death only happens to other people. But for Osgood, death had always been a trusted friend. And she'd died multiple times. Who's to say she *wasn't* already dead. Instead, she simply responded with, "What?" and affected a smile at the girl.

Nora's freckles said girl, her bob haircut said girl, and the bubble gum she chewed said girl, but she was a woman. *Need to get* girl *out of my vocabulary,* thought Osgood. She brushed back a lock of Nora's short, now-orange hair, which looked like the fire atop the matchstick of her body. Thankful to have regained full use of her right arm, Osgood put it around Nora in the seat next to her. The L rumbled, going from outside and elevated into the darkness of Chicago's subway, heading toward the Loop and the Christkindlmarket with Nora, who'd suggested the bustling winter night-market when asked what she'd most like to do on a date.

"We don't have to be so serious, you know." Nora said, leaning across the seat to kiss Osgood. Her lips were wet. Her mouth tasted of bubblegum and a youth Osgood knew she was far from. Nora put on a dour face and repeated the words that Osgood thought she hadn't heard in a deep and mocking tone, "We're all basically dead already."

Osgood nodded. She *had* heard. Shit. "When I say that..."

"It's not just you being an emo kid?"

"Kid?" asked Osgood.

"You know our age gap doesn't bother me," said Nora. "Only you."

Osgood turned away from Nora toward the glass. Before them was moving darkness, interrupted only by exposed bulbs in yellow, green, and red as they blasted their way under the city of Chicago. Their L was an express and should get them there faster. Was it true that the age gap was the issue here?

She didn't know. Not thinking about their age difference was likely a coping mechanism to ignore it, and one usually only wants to ignore things that would be bothersome if they came up. And the gap was nearly 20 years... She looked at Nora again. The girl was sweet, generous, giving, and desperate to please. Perhaps that was it, really, her desperation to show Osgood that she was *worthy* of this relationship, that she was *worthy* of her recently-claimed title of lesbian, which was something Osgood didn't quite understand. Osgood couldn't identify with either end of that particular spectrum and got by under the umbrella of "queer."

"Deep thoughts," said Nora. She looked down into her lap, where her hands seemed desperate to find something to do that wasn't touching Osgood's leg, as they'd been moments before.

Osgood sighed again, making it worse. "Could we just…" she began, hoping she'd have a way to follow it up. Instead, she just stopped.

"I don't know how to tell you this, Osgood, but you seem to want a relationship in its early twenties, while I'd like to be an adult."

"No, I—" Osgood began, then cut herself off. Was that true?

"I want romance. I want sappy gestures. I want anniversaries. *Love*making."

Osgood cringed, as she did every time she heard fucking described that way. After all, she'd only ever *made love* with one person.

"You can't hide your disdain for that," said Nora, her voice hardening and her playfulness waning. "You're awesome, Osgood, truly. And you're an incredible fuck. But you are a *terrible* girlfriend."

Taking a moment, Osgood knew she couldn't revel in being called an incredible fuck without reckoning with the second half of Nora's proclamation. She looked away, toward the full-panel front window of the L train. Before them, in the dark, a flash of sparks. Osgood bit her lower lip. She saw her reflection in the train's windows, nothing but a silhouette of herself, backlit by the sickly fluorescents of the train. Osgood could see the curls on half of her head, blown out from the shocking amount of wind they'd been blasted with while waiting on the elevated platform for the Red Line. She could see the edges of her glasses and the points of light where her eyes reflected back, if she looked closely enough. Otherwise, her face was darkness itself.

Without looking back at Nora, Osgood began the conversation she thought the woman beside her intended to have. "So, you're saying you want to break up?"

"Two dates does not equal a relationship, Os. I don't think we need to do anything as drastic as that."

"But what?" asked Osgood. But she knew. She knew that what she was suitable for was a booty call when Nora asked it of her. That wasn't such a bad position, was it? Nora's silence, though, spoke volumes. And she was right. After all, almost every one of Osgood's adult relationships had been short-term. Many no longer than the 24 hours it took to receive that text-message death. Where the conversation became ellipses, ellipses, ellipses ... then nothing. Another relationship born and died in the span of a single day.

Nora looked down.

Osgood could see the vague orange tinge of her head in the reflected silhouette. She was afraid to look to her right, to actually see. Was Nora crying? She didn't know. How was that fair? With Nora being the "adult" here, should Osgood be the sad one? For a moment, Osgood thought she saw a firefly before them. But that couldn't be. The train was moving ever forward, and for an insect to be looping its lazy loops before them was nonsense. "So, is this it?"

"Yeah." Nora's response was little more than a whisper. Osgood hadn't even seen Nora's lips move, though she was definitely trying to look anywhere but the girl's face.

When they'd gotten on the train, Osgood had made several assumptions about their day. Nora would thoroughly enjoy herself walking through the beginnings of Chicago's winter wonderland, as the first real snow had begun to stick. The day would grow dark early, letting them see the park lights, and they'd warm themselves with the mulled wine and glögg at the market. Then? Well, then she assumed they'd go back to her place and fuck. Or go to Nora's and fuck. They hadn't fucked on their last date, and Osgood had to be honest, she needed the release. If it didn't make her feel so weird, she would've called Dr. Remy for another masturbation session.

"I mean it, though, Os," whispered Nora. "You *are* an awesome human."

Osgood said nothing. But then she added an embittered, "Fine."

Nora sighed.

The firefly outside the window had a friend. But this conversation was more important, so Osgood resisted the urge to point it out to Nora.

"I didn't expect to have the relationship escalator talk today," Osgood said.

"Well, why didn't you?" asked Nora. "We've been on, like, eight dates over a surprising number of years. Most involved sex, sure. But I thought you actually liked *me*, too."

Osgood opened her mouth to protest but realized she had no genuine protestations. Somehow, she knew an insistence she *did* like Nora would be met with the implication that this was the extent of Osgood's ability regarding "adult relationships." Instead, she gave Nora a solemn nod.

"I wish it was different, Os," said Nora. "Really."

Osgood looked away again. The fireflies were ... dancing. Swooping and circling. Hitting eddies and spirals like Starry Night. It was increasingly challenging to rip her attention away from them.

"—for Audrey. Your *true* love."

"Wait, I—"

"It's always been Audrey," said Nora, fixing Osgood with a look of compassion. "She's the only person you've ever loved. Maybe the only one you've ever liked."

Osgood considered this, and Nora stood up next to their seat and folded her arms, only unfolding when the sway of the L car necessitated her grabbing the handle.

"I mean—" What could Osgood say? Audrey Frost had, yes, always been the true love of her life and likely always would be. "It's not Audrey," she said. "You're right, it's me.

Just not the relationship type, I guess." Osgood looked up at her, standing beside their seat. "You don't have to—"

"I'm sorry. I need to..." Nora laughed again and shook her head, choking back the tears at the end. She turned to look out the front window of the L car and stopped. "What is—"

The car crash at the crossroads in the sticks of Dekalb County, Illinois, the one that had literally ended Osgood's life for eight and a half minutes, had demonstrated to her the surreality of vision when it came to catastrophic events. She chalked it up to the brain trying desperately to record everything, every stimulus and input, slowing down the appearance of time. Nothing could actually slow down time, or stop it. But for a moment, as the fireflies' dance slowed, time seemed to as well. Their eddies were about six feet off the rails ahead. The dance pulsed with their rhythm and the synchronization of their lights. The light stayed on, and then Osgood saw what was before them, before the L car, on the tracks.

A burning orange eye. Staring right into her.

And when that eye ceased traveling at the speed of the subway train beneath the city of Chicago, the crash happened, and no matter how slow Osgood's brain tried to slow it, it happened fast. The front end of the L car crumpled in toward them, the brushed aluminum of the walls stopping just short of Osgood's knees. The glass of the windshield didn't shatter but split in a jagged slash from upper left to lower right, its two pieces now aimed toward them.

Slow slow slow, thought Osgood.

She watched as the glass on her side slid into her leg so easily that she couldn't believe the flesh was attached to her. Surely, this was some prop on a movie set. Some side of beef at a butcher's shop. Someone with exceptional knife skills was demonstrating how easily a professionally sharpened blade can slice right down to the ... bone. She could see it! Gleaming white! So bright it seemed to emanate its own light. But how on earth could she be taking the time to see her own bone. The hand falling into her lap distracted her, first with confusion and then revulsion. The hand of a man in his sixties or seventies. Liver-spotted and undoubtedly indicating early signs of melanoma. But that didn't matter, did it? It'd been excised. Edited out. Removed from the body and flung into the lap of this 44-year-old bitch having a relationship ender with her girlfriend on the L. Osgood thought she should throw the hand away but didn't. Apparently, only internal momentum had slowed. Externally, things still moved at speed. But wasn't that relativity? She almost laughed at that. Einstein would've laughed. Even sitting here, in the growing darkness, as the lights behind her snapped out one by one, an old man's hand in her lap, her once-girlfriend—

Nora.

Osgood couldn't turn quickly, but her eyes saw—peripheral vision is better than we think; we just never use it with intention. Somehow, Nora still stood beside her. Thank God she hadn't been thrown back into the throng of people sitting further behind them on the train. She'd held on; her grip on the backrest handle held true. Nora was looking at her. Side of the eye, again, because they were all moving through the river of time so very slowly. But her face didn't look ... right. She reminded Osgood of that painting that her aunt and uncle had, which had made her stay out of their basement when she was much younger. Portrait of Lunia ... something ... by Modigliani. The painting wasn't meant to be frightening, but it captured the unease of a lopsided face. A lopsided face like her grandfather's after the stroke, the left side seeming to slide down, as though disconnected from his skull. Nora's face wasn't lopsided, but a fine line traced from her chin to forehead.

Osgood's slow-stream reality needed to do some catching up. Because this here was an L crash, and she and her girlfriend had been sitting in the front seat. Then, the reflective motion came. Osgood could almost hear Mr. Budzich, her junior high science teacher, reminding her that every action has an equal and opposite reaction. And so, as the front of the car had crumpled to a stop, soon, very soon, everything would be thrown forward. As it happened, Osgood was lucky, and she had enough presence of mind to be thankful. The glass that had slid into her leg snapped, then shattered; had it not, it surely would've lopped the leg off just below the knee, giving Prudence Osgood one more reason to hobble about the world.

Nora was not so lucky.

The fine line down her face, the one that bisected it into lopsided Modigliani reflections, pushed through, sending the entire pane of glass backward. Osgood had to watch it because her brain was still desperate for more bits of information. This information was a doozy, as half of Nora, who now could genuinely be in two places at once, went backward with the pane of glass.

Osgood recalled a night when the Body Worlds exhibit had been at the Museum of Science and Industry, and she and some boyfriend she couldn't remember had gone to the final weekend's overnight. She'd seen the plate glass people there. The preserved bodies. The internals. But the thing that had bothered her most was one exhibit, featuring a flayed body holding its skin in its skull still had eyes. And as Osgood had stared into those eyes, she'd realized that at one time they'd stared outward. At one time they'd seen, too. At one time that thing was real, it was human, it was ... alive.

She'd had to sit down.

Nora's eyes had stared outward, too ... recently. Not once upon a time, but mere moments ago. Osgood hoped they saw no more as the plate glass traveled, with half of her stuck to it, showcasing a partial eye, and a brain, and surely that was a lung. Osgood wondered when the blood would flow. She wondered even more when reality would flow. All this was some netherworld of nothing, a dream state. But as much as she wanted it to be, this was no dream.

She felt herself leave her seat, not by choice but by the law of motion. Osgood was powerless to disobey as physics flung her into darkness, through what remained of the windshield, over and out of the car, into the echoing beyond. She heard the crash behind her, beginning to slowly catch up, and realized that not enough time had elapsed for everybody in the line of cars to even know they'd crashed yet.

But Nora knew. Nora had been standing. Because she didn't want to face Osgood anymore, she'd stood.

If she hadn't...

Time collapsed around Osgood as she tumbled through oiled and grimy gravel, between the rails in front of the L train, desperately hoping to avoid the electrified third rail. But hell, maybe it wouldn't be so bad if she hit it. At least it'd be a quick end to this all. At least she wouldn't have to—

We're all basically dead already, she thought.

And she could hear the echo of Remy's whisper from her dream. The pained intonation: "It's the end."

Then, like a clap of hands, black.

Real black.

Nothing.

***Dying to know what happens next?**￼*

There are as many stories in The Spectral Inspector 'verse as there are things that go bump in the night.

*Sign up at the address below and **Be a Specterino!** Then you won't miss a single thing, including exclusive shorts, early access to novels in progress, artwork reveals, conversations with the author, and more!*

SpectralInspector.com/news

*In the indie publishing world, reviews are more important than anything! If you enjoyed **Osgood Riddance** and are looking forward to future Osgood adventures, please post a review where you bought the book and on Goodreads! It's free and it helps a lot!*

About the Author

As a queer non-monogamous writer, Cooper S. Beckett loves to create characters that reflect the diverse lifestyles of his friends, his partners, and himself. If he can pit those characters against monsters and cosmic horrors he's all the happier. From a young age, his obsession with horror movies and books seriously concerned his mother. It probably still does. Given a choice, he would rather winter at the Overlook than the Waldorf. Like Lydia Deetz, he has always thought of himself strange and unusual, and is thrilled to be continuing that vibe in his Spectral Inspector series.

He lives in Chicago with his wife, constant, and binary star, Elle, their dog Egon, and their black cat Willow.

Want short stories, updates, and discounts in your email? Sign up today at CooperSBeckett.com/news

CooperSBeckett.com

Coop's Note

Alright folks ... Cooper here. I've never done this before, and perhaps it's ill advised, but I feel bad leaving y'all on that cliffhanger.

Because of that, I'm jumping the gun and including the first chapter of the VERY MUCH unfinished work in progress *Osgood as Dead*. I mean, y'all knew Os would survive, right? Unless the series ended there.

Wouldn't that have been mean? I'd never do that to you.

If you'd rather live in a world where Osgood's fate is VERY uncertain, don't read on. Otherwise, join me for a few more pages.

(Also, those who read this book within the month after it came out MAY have read a different first chapter. Oooh, such mystery.)

- Coop
February 5, 2024

ONE

What fresh hell..., thought Osgood before an entirely new level of pain coursed through every inch of her body; a knife cutting through her as through butter, its blade catching and ripping skin and tissue here and there, moving with indifference and alacrity. This knife could flay her to the bone. Maybe it was doing just that. She wanted to scream, she tried to scream, as her skin prickled everywhere as though each hair follicle and pore yawned open and swallowed battery acid. Her right leg, the "good" one, as far as that could be said of any part of Osgood's body, throbbed like it had its own circulatory system. Pain was such an abstract concept to most people; their ideas included that scraped knee, that hangover headache, a paper cut. But Osgood knew from pain. There was nothing like the pain of a compound fracture or a gaping wound that one could see bone through. There was the ache of pain, the throb of pain, the stab of pain, but something further atop it all. Pain at this level was heat, fire, an endless pulsing agony shooting through nerves right to the center of you.

She must be held in place because her view was only above

her. The world was a blur without her glasses, but she'd forgotten them enough in life that she could fill in the visual gaps. A repainted tiled drop ceiling, florescent tubes, a fire or carbon dioxide alarm, its LED blinking lazily. Sound emerged, the quiet murmuring of conversations a room over or outside her door. The endless droning *beep beep beep* that Osgood realized matched her heart, causing it to *beep* faster. A suction *shush* matched by a release that repeated and repeated.

It's breathing for me, realized Osgood.

"Good morning!"

The voice, a young man perhaps, cheerful, calm. He must not be surprised by the state she's in. He must have seen her before.

Osgood couldn't turn her head, and the breathing apparatus made speaking impossible, so she could only wait until the young man appeared above her. His hair was a delicate light brown, short, a little wild. He smiled, his baby face only betraying his adulthood with a scratchy bit of two to three-day-old beard. There was something in his eyes, though.

"Hi!" he said. "Oh, don't worry about saying it back." He moved away for a moment. "Your heart rate is elevated, Prudence." Then he came back and leaned down. "That's because you're with me, aren't you?"

Osgood wanted to respond, to ask him what the fuck was happening, to demand answers, to—

"Become belligerent? Pain in the ass Prudence Osgood?" The young man smiled and put his hand on her shoulder, a gesture that ignited a pain so searing she felt tears squeeze out and roll down her cheeks. "Oh my," he said, then leaned down and licked her right cheek. He stood again. "Salty!"

She felt a growing horror in her stomach as he smiled at her. She couldn't move, and this man above her was going to... what? Rape her? No, his face said something different. He wasn't here for that. He was here—

"You're never going to guess it," said the young man, and he moved away. She heard a sweep, and the conversation beyond the room went quiet. He'd closed the door.

Osgood wondered if she could muffle the pain in her head, to drift away, to disassociate. Could she go to the crossroads here and now? Let this… thing… have his way.

"Thing?" he asked with a laugh, reappearing above her face. Leaning down to get close. Even his breath on her skin seared her flesh. "You have no idea what I am!" This pleased him immensely. Osgood thought she heard a titter. His eyes were vivid brown and seemed like liquid. His irises moving, churning, an eddy swirling to the black drain of his pupils. "You're almost there." He leaned closer. "Oh! Wait!" He let out an expulsive laugh, nearly just saying "Haw!" then disappeared for a moment, fumbling next to him. A drawer opened and closed.

He slid something onto her face causing her temples to burn and catching and yanking hair out as he did so, but now the blurry vision above her was clear. She didn't know him at all. She didn't recognize his face or that strange smile. The smile seemed to strain him, the muscles in his jaw and cheeks throbbing. But now she saw his eyes weren't brown at all. They were orange. They were fire. Orange like—

"Your eye in the sky," he finished. "I thought it was about time we got acquainted."

New tears rolled down Osgood's face. The eye in the sky, present in her life and dreams since her car accident decades ago. The eye that was sometimes a quasar, sometimes a black hole. Sometimes an eddy of pure malace just somewhere out of sight, out of reach. But she always knew it was there. Watching. Waiting. Waiting for today perhaps.

"Obviously, I'm more than an eye," he said.

He can hear my thoughts, Osgood realized.

"That's a bingo," he said.

Well then, thought Osgood, *You should know I have very little patience for guys like you.*

"Oh, why," he laughed. "Because patriarchy? Believe women? Hashtag me too? Shall we pretend I'm an incel? MAGA? What do you prefer." He stared at her for a moment, not waiting for a response but seeming to consider his options. His smile drew in to pursed lips. "One sec." He called over his shoulder, "Alice, could you come in here?" He turned back to Osgood. "BRB." Then, his face was gone from her view.

Osgood felt relief, not from the agony as that was still very much present, but a relief from not seeing his face anymore. Her brain found it difficult to connect thoughts to each other, and though a nagging idea of what was happening here tried hard to take hold, she found herself pushing it away. *Can't ignore reality forever,* her mother's voice told her. She knew that, of course, but at this moment, she had to focus on the moment. Unfortunately, that moment brought the pain back to the forefront, and again, she wanted to scream until her voice gave out.

Just avoid it, she thought, *distract from it.*

A distraction came courtesy of a freckled-faced young woman with ironed straw-colored hair framing her face, which seemed to be mostly eyes. Her expression changed, first sincere and wanting to help, then, as she leaned in, Osgood saw that smile, those orange eyes again.

"How's this for your patriarchy?" asked Alice.

Osgood understood. And it annoyed her. *A shapeshifter.*

"Nothing so pedestrian," said Alice. "I wear them like clothing."

Straightforward, thought Osgood.

"Why beat around the fucking bush at this point?" asked Alice. Her grin became a leer. "Unless that's what you want."

You've reached me at a bad time, and I think my pussy is closed at the moment.

"Such defiance," Alice giggled. "Even through the pain."

Pain has been my companion longer than you have, thought Osgood. *So, fill me in. Who are you?*

"Ah, well..."

And none of that "I have so many names" bullshit.

"Fair enough," said alice, sounding almost impressed. "Call me Yoko."

Here to break up the Spectral Inspectors?

"Aww," said Yoko. "I thought that was your job."

You're the eye in the sky.

Yoko nodded.

And the quasar?

"One and the same."

Then I'll bite, thought Osgood. *The critical question isn't who you are but what you are.*

"Even that's pretty rote," said Yoko. "Thing is, *I am.*"

Oh, are we implying we're a God?

"We're some kinda thing," said Yoko. "Enough with all this, as it's not what I've come to talk with you about."

Oh good, thought Osgood. *Frankly, the conversation was becoming rather boring.*

"Ah, the perpetually petulant Prudence Osgood. You should be flattered, you know."

Should I?

"Of all the people in the world, of all the beings in the universe, in the outside..." Yoko trailed off, the grin leaving her face.

You picked me.

"No!" exclaimed Yoko. She reached up and drew her hand down Osgood's face. Her hand was soft but felt like coarse grit sandpaper. "You are!"

The fuck does that mean?

"Something happened when you died, there at the crossroads. That moment sent out an alert to the universe."

Bullshit.

"It's why he was there," said Yoko.

The Lord of the Hinterlands, thought Osgood. That thing made of shimmering light and smoke who'd consumed dozens upon dozens of young people, including Caroline Frost.

"'Lord,'" Yoko scoffed. "Nothing but a borrowed title playing at borrowed importance in a borrowed tower on borrowed land."

Alright, thought Osgood. Yoko was playing the power hierarchy game. "Remember that thing you thought was big and scary? I'm bigger and more horrifying."

Suddenly, Yoko coughed, then again and again. She disappeared from view. She came back looking ashen. She wiped her mouth. "Let me cut to the chase."

Please do.

"I want you," said Yoko, revealing more of a plea than Osgood expected.

Moving a little fast there, Yoko.

"Please, be serious."

Why? This is absurd! You're a figment of my imagination. Probably because of the drug cocktail I'm on as I lie here in the hospital after— Osgood remembered all at once. The dancing fireflies. The subway car stopping

(crashing)

abruptly. Nora, bisected by glass. Osgood, thrown from the car onto the gravel of the tracks.

"What was that you said about fireflies?" asked Yoko. The grin had ceased, and her face looked older and darker. Deadly serious.

I saw fireflies, a circle, a dance...

"An eye?" Yoko winked one of those flaming orange eyes at Osgood.

You caused the crash.

Yoko shrugged.

So you want me. I assume you're not here about sex.

"It can be a delightful distraction," said Yoko, "but no."

Then you want to wear me? Like poor Alice here.

At the question, Alice seemed to have an orgasm right there. Her eyes rolled back, her mouth hung open. A long line of saliva dripped from between her teeth. Then Yoko was back. "Intensely," she growled.

So why don't you?

Yoko's grin was gone, her eyes narrow, a fury growing. She stood tall above Osgood, almost seeming to touch the ceiling, at least from the bizarre perspective Osgood held at the moment. "Not going to make this easy, are you?"

Osgood wished she could laugh, but inside her head would have to do. *Sorry,* she thought.

"Alright," said Yoko through clenched teeth. She momentarily fumbled off to the side and brought up a long plastic tube.

And that is?

"Your life," said Yoko. She pinched the tube.

The result was nearly instantaneous. Osgood couldn't breathe. Her chest felt as though it had locked up. No oxygen would come, nothing. She tried to reach out and scramble to something but couldn't; she could only look into Yoko's flaming orange eyes. *Please!*

Yoko released the tube. Oxygen rushed back into Osgood, but it burned all the way, adding a whole new level of pain. "Listen, you stupid bitch..."

Wow, dropping all pretense now.

"You are in an awful position here."

Seems like.

Alice walked away. There was a clatter, a light crunch, then she returned holding a whiteboard that she must have yanked off the damned wall. "Yeah, I wanted you to see clearly."

She held the whiteboard over Osgood's head. On it was written a doctor's name, a nurse's name, a date,

(February?!)

and then words that made sense but horrified Osgood at the same time.

"Locked-in syndrome," said Yoko, tossing the whiteboard away. Her voice had become manic, a little feral. "You've been here for four fucking months and haven't moved a muscle."

No, no, no, no, pled Osgood.

Yoko took out Alice's cell phone. "I wish I knew her passcode, I'd—" a click. "Wow. Face unlock. It is frankly astonishing what amazing stuff is in this world now."

Osgood didn't acknowledge. She could only think about the words "locked-in syndrome." She'd only heard them in documentaries, maybe a made-for-TV movie. It was rare—rare and horrifying.

"Alright," said Yoko. "Looks like fewer than 1000 people in the US have or have had Locked In Syndrome. Mazel Tov! And there are something like 300 Million people in the US? That's fucking *rare*. Well, you always were special."

So why don't you just take me?

"Are you offering?"

Panic rose in Osgood, but she couldn't do anything about it. Her immobility, which she'd assumed was due to broken bones as it had been in the past.... (and maybe still was), meant she couldn't move at all. No fingertips, no mouth. All beholden to the breathing tube in—

"Prudence!" shouted Yoko, snapping her fingers above Osgood's face.

No. Osgood felt her defiance rising. *No, I'm not offering.*

Yoko sighed. "Well," she said. "My shift is almost up."

What does that mean?

"We're going to try plan B."

What does that mean?

"I want you to know we tried the easy way," said Yoko, leaning down until her lips nearly touched Osgood's eyes. "And that you shouldn't get too comfortable. All alerts stop if I disconnect the machines from the nursing station. I could do *anything* I wanted to you."

Ah, the rape threat.

"Is everything about your pussy, Pru?" asked Yoko. Her tone was playful, but her face didn't match it. "I mean: I could kill you. For real. Forever." Now, Yoko moved to Osgood's ear. "You know you've always kinda wanted that. That semicolon on your wrist isn't to call you a survivor but to remind you of the option, isn't it."

Again, tears ran down Osgood's cheeks. Yoko produced a syringe and stuck it into the hanging IV bag off to the side.

What's that?

But the world was already growing swimmy. The view above her narrowing, narrowing, narrowing, like the iris closing at the end of a Chaplin film. The world growing dark. *No, please...* Osgood begged. She knew what was in the dark.

"You may be hard to kill," said Yoko as Osgood drifted away. "But you can still fucking die, Prudence Osgood."

ALSO BY COOPER S. BECKETT

Fiction (Scary)

Osgood as Gone

Osgood Riddance

Fiction (Sexy)

A Life Less Monogamous

Approaching The Swingularity:

Tales of Swinging & Polyamory in Paradise

Non-Fiction

The Pegging Book

My Life on the Swingset:

Adventures in Swinging & Polyamory